Unlikely Traitors

An Ursula Marlow Mystery

Unlikely
Traitors

Clare Langley-Hawthorne

Copyright © 2014 by Clare Langley-Hawthorne

978-1-4976-5957-5

Distributed by Open Road Distribution
345 Hudson Street
New York, NY 10014
www.openroadmedia.com

For the laws of nature (as justice, equity, modesty, mercy, and, in sum, doing to others as we would be done to) of themselves, without the terror of some power, to cause them to be observed, are contrary to our natural passions, that carry us to partiality, pride, revenge and the like.

Thomas Hobbes, *Leviathan or The Matter, Forme and Power of A Commonwealth, Ecclesiastical and Civil*, 1651

Unlikely Traitors

PART ONE

ENGLAND

CHAPTER ONE

IT ALL STARTED WITH A REVOLVER. At least in Ursula's mind it did. Not the arrest. Not Chief Inspector Harrison's face or even Lord Wrotham's impassive response. No, it was the revolver that Harrison laid on the table that started it all, its blue tinged metal barrel glinting as it caught the electric light of the standard lamp that illuminated Ursula's front parlor. As the scene unfolded she felt as though she was watching herself on a Pathé newsreel—the horror of the situation creating an illusory distance between her body and her mind. But with her hand poised in mid air, like a half finished sentence, Ursula was close enough to read the inscription, Webley & Scott, Birmingham & London, stamped on the revolver's cylinder bridge. The diamond-checkered wooden grip was already worn from use and she shivered. Ursula could imagine the caption on the screen. Rather than risk dishonor, the Lord chose death.

"My Lord," Chief Inspector Harrison's voice cut through the close-held silence. Ursula's gaze shifted and searched Lord Oliver Wrotham's face for some kind of reaction, but his countenance refused to yield to scrutiny. He stood beside the mahogany side table, casting a long shadow across the Oriental rug. Amid the tangled vines and intricate scrolls of the pattern, his silhouette looked like a sleek black panther waiting in ambush.

The way Harrison had placed the revolver on the table as he announced he was making the arrest seemed an obsolete, chivalric gesture but one that appalled Ursula. There was no doubting the implication: Lord Wrotham had best turn the gun on himself rather than face public disgrace.

"You cannot seriously consider this an option!" Ursula exclaimed.

Lord Wrotham remained motionless. His blue-grey eyes fixed upon the gun, he gave no sign of having heard her.

"I can leave the room and let your lordship decide," Harrison said.

Lord Wrotham gave an almost imperceptible nod.

Ursula grabbed Lord Wrotham's arm. "What are you doing?!" she cried.

"Miss Marlow," Harrison said, stepping forward as if he were about to restrain a recalcitrant child. "You really should wait outside."

Ursula's grip tightened until Lord Wrotham, with slow deliberate movements, unfurled each of her fingers and moved her hand aside. Ursula rubbed her hand; his reaction had been like a slap in the face, only the sting was sharper. How could he fail to understand her anguish? Why did he not proclaim his innocence?

"I'm not going anywhere," she informed Harrison, "until you tell me the full details of the charges." Her head held high, hazel eyes ablaze, she tried to hold back her turmoil. She tried to replace it with outrage, but the distance the initial shock had brought, the sense that she was watching film footage, had gone. Lord Wrotham's reaction had ensured that. She felt battered by the weight, the full impact of that terrible word. *Treason.*

Harrison looked down at the floor and kicked one of the table legs with the toe of his polished black shoe.

"Chief Inspector?" Ursula pressed.

"If you insist . . ." he said slowly, "though you would think a lady would rather not hear such things."

Ursula felt the old flash of indignation and was thankful. Maybe if she could claw back her anger she would find the strength she so desperately needed. Yet she knew Chief Inspector Harrison well enough by now not to overreact. Despite Harrison's continued distrust of Ursula's various causes, especially female suffrage and socialism, he had begun to show a begrudging respect for a woman who now ran her father's textile empire, and who had, on at least two occasions, helped him solve a murder investigation.

Throughout both of these investigations, Lord Wrotham had been a constant presence, one from which she drew the strength as well as the will to stand on her own. Now she felt as though all that resolve was little more than chalk crumbling in her hands. Perhaps anger would provide its own measure of comfort, thought Ursula, and she drew herself up, summoning its force, before answering.

"You know me better than this Chief Inspector. I'm hardly the sort to take to my smelling salts or be left in ignorance like some weak-minded fool who prefers to bury her head in the sand. How can Lord Wrotham possibly be expected to defend himself when he has no idea what these charges are?" Ursula's voice shook but refused to break.

"Oh, I think it's safe to say that his Lordship is well aware of the circumstances leading to these charges—and what is at stake here," Harrison responded coldly. "You only have to see his countenance, Miss Marlow, to know that's the truth of it."

Ursula's throat tightened. Hot tears pricked her eyes. God, why did Lord Wrotham not speak? Why did he remain tight-lipped and silent? She knew from experience that he had the strength to maintain his self-composure in the face of great upheaval but, even for him, this impassivity and silence was chilling. Had she misjudged him so badly?

"Regardless," Ursula replied, steadying herself with one hand on the back of the Mackmurdo couch. "I need to know what this is all about."

Harrison drew out the arrest warrant from the inside pocket of his dark grey jacket. The normally creaseless three-piece suit looked crumpled and worn and Ursula noticed there were mud splashes across his shoes and trouser cuffs. She felt some satisfaction when she saw Harrison's hands shake as he unfolded the arrest warrant—he was no more immune to the horror of the situation than she.

Harrison began to read aloud.

"Lord Oliver Wrotham, Seventh Baron of Wrotham, King's Counsel and Member of the House of Lords, is hereby charged with high treason against His Majesty King George the Fifth and his government in that he did willfully and of his own volition conspire to assassinate members of His Majesty's government and family and sell vital information pertaining to British naval fortifications to representatives of Kaiser Wilhelm the Second, the Irish Republican Brotherhood and other foreign interests. In exchange for said information, Lord Wrotham is charged with seeking promises of military assistance from Germany for an armed uprising in Ireland, with aiding and abetting in the overthrow of the British administration in Ireland, and, by extension, the overthrow of His Majesty's government."

Harrison paused. Ursula waited but there came no defiant disavowals, no challenges from a man who spent his life as a barrister. Lord Wrotham remained rigid, his eyes like polished granite, saying nothing.

The allegations set out in the arrest warrant, at least, provided Ursula with some measure of relief.

"I've never heard anything so ridiculous in my life!" she exclaimed. "Lord Wrotham's views on the 'Irish Question' and Ulster are well known. As a Unionist he is hardly likely to seek aid for an Irish rebellion—and as for conspiring to assassinate members of the government or the Royal family—that's utterly preposterous!"

Ursula and Lord Wrotham held diametrically opposing views on the 'Irish Question' and she was sure Lord Wrotham would never change his pro-Unionist beliefs. He could no more be a supporter of an Irish Republic than she could be a supporter of the anti-suffrage Primrose League.

Harrison's jaw clenched. "Men are not always what they seem," he answered. "It is the mark of a traitor that he can so easily deceive those who are close to him." The bitterness in his voice was a reminder of how deeply felt Lord Wrotham's betrayal was for him. Although Ursula had never discovered the precise nature of the debt owed by Harrison to Lord Wrotham, she knew their friendship stretched back to the time when Harrison's family was tenant farmers on the Wrotham's Northamptonshire estate.

"You cannot honestly believe these charges," Ursula urged. "They are patently absurd. You, who have known him for years, cannot believe Lord Wrotham is a traitor to his country."

"Ursula, please." Lord Wrotham's voice cut through their exchange. "As much as I appreciate your stalwart defense, Harrison is just performing his duty."

"How can you remain so calm?!" she asked hotly, spinning round to face him once more. Lord Wrotham's physical presence, normally so unfaltering appeared to waver. In the fading afternoon light, as the recesses of the room grew increasingly dim and spectral, she was no longer sure she could distinguish the shadow from the man.

"Believe me Miss Marlow," Harrison intervened. "This is no easy task for me." His hands were still unsteady as he folded the arrest warrant and placed it back in his pocket. "I promise you, these charges are not without adequate foundation. We have both witnesses and documentary evidence that clearly implicates Lord Wrotham. If Admiral Smythe was here, he would, no doubt, reassure you that a man such as he would never bring such charges lightly."

Lord Wrotham watched Harrison's face closely. "You've spoken with Admiral Smythe?" he asked. Ursula frowned, there was a hidden implication beneath his words that she could not grasp.

Harrison's raised his eyebrows. "Admiral Smythe was reported missing by his housekeeper this morning."

Lord Wrotham inhaled sharply and for first time since Harrison's arrival, his composure slipped. "But I saw him just yesterday. He and I dined at the club together."

Ursula sensed his fear and dug her fingernails into palms of her hands. She had certainly heard of Admiral Smythe, but, apart from knowing that he and Lord Wrotham were old friends from Balliol College, Oxford, she knew little else about him. As far she was aware, Lord Wrotham and Admiral Smythe met exclusively at the Carlton Club and, despite her recent engagement to Lord Wrotham, she had never been introduced to the Admiral.

"You sound surprised," Harrison replied coolly. "And yet it was

Admiral Smythe's file that led us to you. Perhaps you know more about his fate than anyone else." There was a cold edge of suspicion in his voice. The two men regarded each other warily. A lock of dark hair fell across Lord Wrotham's face and he brushed it away roughly with his fingers.

"The file was found in his study," Harrison continued, watching Lord Wrotham's reaction closely.

Lord Wrotham gripped the edge of the chair. "And just what does this file purport to contain?"

Harrison frowned. "Surely you must know? Or at least had your suspicions? Why else would the Admiral now be missing?" Ursula noted that the East End accent Harrison tried so hard to suppress was creeping back, coloring his words with its rough nasal inflection.

"Lord Wrotham is hardly likely to arrange Admiral Smythe's 'disappearance' and then leave an incriminating file to be found, now is he?" Ursula interjected but neither man seemed to be listening.

"Have you any idea where Admiral Smythe might be?" Lord Wrotham asked Harrison.

"We have no information about his whereabouts"—Harrison hesitated—"No one has seen him since he left the Carlton Club yesterday. His housekeeper called Scotland Yard this morning when she discovered he had not come home last night. Given who he is, we started our investigations immediately."

Ursula opened her mouth to speak but Harrison silenced her with his hand.

"I think we have wasted enough time. My Lord"—Harrison directed himself to Lord Wrotham now—"I can take you down to the Yard directly or"—he paused—"if you would prefer?" Harrison motioned his head toward the revolver that still lay on the table.

"I appreciate that, Harrison," Lord Wrotham replied and even his voice seemed to have lost its resonance. "This won't take long."

"Very well," Harrison replied somberly. "Miss Marlow, if you will kindly come with me." He gestured for her to follow.

Ursula shook her head. This was not how it was going to end. She may feel like a terrified animal caught in a snare but, by God, she would not leave this room until she had the truth from Lord

Wrotham. She was not about to let the man she loved leave her. Not like this.

Harrison, white-faced and defeated, seemed unable to summon the strength to argue. His own inner struggle was etched on his face. The thought of leaving a man to his death, especially a man whom Harrison had known and trusted for the last ten years, had taken its toll.

"Could I prevail upon you to allow Miss Marlow a moment with me alone?" Lord Wrotham interceded. "You have my word I shall make no attempt to flee or in any way compromise your investigation, but Miss Marlow deserves at least an explanation before..." Lord Wrotham let the implication hang in the air. Harrison, his face contorted by emotions barely held in check, nodded quickly and exited the room.

Lord Wrotham picked up the revolver, holding it first in one hand and then the other.

"You aren't actually thinking of going through with it?" Ursula asked.

"I see no alternative," he said.

Despite his words, he placed the revolver back on the table.

"How can you say that?"

Lord Wrotham did not reply. There was no explanation. Only grim silence.

"You didn't even question the charges," Ursula said, lowering herself onto the sofa before her legs gave way altogether. The cool folds of the silken upholstery provided a welcome respite.

"No," Lord Wrotham eventually replied, and she noticed the slight tremble in his hands as he lit and raised a cigarette to his lips. "If it has come to this then it can mean only one thing."

Ursula closed her eyes. "And that is?"

"I shall hang."

Ursula's body started to shake uncontrollably. "How can you be so?—" she could speak no further.

Lord Wrotham sat down beside her on the Mackmurdo sofa. He closed his eyes for a moment and let the cigarette fall limp between his fingers. Ursula reached out and clasped his wrist. She closed her eyes and let the world, in all its senses and sounds, fade away. The rhythm of his pulse under her thumb seemed to be the only thing that stirred in the stagnant stillness of the room.

"This cannot be happening," Ursula whispered. Lord Wrotham sat motionless beside her. "I thought we had finally found happiness . . ."

With a flash of anguish across his grey-blue eyes, Lord Wrotham yanked his hand away from hers and the world, in all its cacophony, came crashing back into the room. The call of the newspaper boy on the street corner, the shriek of tires as a motor car drew up next door, the muffled voices of the policemen in the hallway—all seemed deafening to Ursula's heightened senses.

Lord Wrotham pressed the palm of his hands against his temple, the cigarette between his fingers still smoldering, unnoticed. "God, Ursula. If there was any other way . . . I would do anything to save you from this, but I have no choice. I will not risk exposing you to society's utter condemnation. I cannot face a trial knowing what it will do to you and my family."

"Even if you are innocent?" Ursula voice was hoarse. "For I cannot believe—"

The clock on the mantel struck the hour with four long, solemn chimes. Ursula stared blankly at the fireplace adorned with glazed green and blue tiles. Above the fireplace, framed against the eggshell blue walls, was a simple silver mirror, juxtaposed by two paintings by Kandinsky. Her eyes caught sight of the Liberty Tudric pewter bowl Lord Wrotham had given her, and their latest acquisition, the first piece of pottery they had ever bought together—A Ruskin high-fired, blue-vein vase.

She blinked back her tears once more.

Lord Wrotham tossed the cigarette into the fire. "What would you say if I told you the accusations were true?"

His face was inscrutable.

Ursula stared at him. "Then you may as well hand me the revolver and I will shoot you myself. Because if what Harrison said was actually true, then all that I know about you, all that I love about you, would be false."

They faced each other squarely. Lord Wrotham's eyelids flickered.

Ursula held her breath.

"I am no traitor," he said slowly, "but I am bound by an obligation of secrecy which I cannot break. All I can tell you is that Admiral Smythe's disappearance makes that obligation all the more confounding. Without him, I cannot defend myself against the charges made."

Ursula felt a surge of adrenaline accompanying his words. At least now there was something tangible, something solid, she could grasp. He had confirmed his innocence and, amid all the uncertainty and fear, maybe this was her opportunity to prove herself worthy of his confidence. There were many locked doors in Lord Wrotham's life. She was determined to open this one.

"Let me try and find the Admiral," she urged.

He shook his head. "I fear it is too late," he replied.

"I cannot believe that!" Ursula responded desperately, her sense of relief shattered. "I refuse to accept that you have no option but to shoot yourself or hang for a crime you did not commit!"

Lord Wrotham shuddered. "I've run through it over and over and I cannot . . . the alternative would be ruin for you. I will not subject you to that, no matter that I am innocent."

"Trust in me then!" she responded vehemently. "Trust that I will uncover the truth and clear your name."

He looked up with a faint, cynical smile. "Ursula, you cannot be expected to perform miracles."

"Damn it! I'm serious. I've a brain in my head haven't I? Need I remind you of the other cases I've helped with?"

"This is different," Lord Wrotham said.

"I'm not offering you a choice," Ursula retorted. "Why do you insist on being so utterly pig-headed?" She gathered up her breath to continue but something in the set of his jaw made her hopes sink. "Oh God, spare me from the Englishmen's sense of honor," she muttered, "and here I was thinking I was engaged to an intelligent"—She got no further before Lord Wrotham gathered her up in his arms and kissed her. For a moment she thought he was actually going to accept her offer, but then she felt him pull back and knew, with a stab of pain, that he was refusing her.

"I do this for you!" he said roughly. "I could not bear the pain this will inflict on you. I will not allow you to risk everything for me."

"So you still doubt me?" she whispered.

Chief Inspector Harrison pounded on the door to the parlor. "My Lord!" he shouted.

"It is not you that I doubt," Lord Wrotham said, ignoring Harrison. He scrutinized her with searching eyes. "I always knew there was a possibility that it would come to this."

"I will not let you take your own life—not like this, not now," Ursula replied, gripping his wrists once more.

"Ursula." Lord Wrotham extricated himself from her grasp. "Don't make this any harder than it already is. Say your goodbyes now and leave this room."

Her heart, which had been pounding so hard and furiously that her chest felt fit to burst, gave a sudden spasm. She moved quickly and was beside the table, the revolver in her hand, before Lord Wrotham could stop her. She held the gun unsteadily with the barrel pointing at her chest. She expected Lord Wrotham to be angry but instead her actions appeared to sap the last of his strength. He stood with his arms hanging by his sides, looking gaunt and pale, like one of the 'penitent proud' weighed down by heavy stones in Dante's *Purgatorio*.

"My Lord!" Chief Inspector Harrison pounded once more on the door.

"What is it to be then?" Ursula asked shakily. "Both our deaths or the possibility of reprieve if you let me try and help you?"

The parlor door burst open and Harrison entered accompanied by two uniformed policemen. "Miss Marlow," he stammered as he saw the revolver in her hand.

Ursula took a step back, and the cliff-edge to which she had forced them both, fell away.

"As you can see, Chief Inspector, we won't be needing this." Ursula handed over the revolver carefully. "In the future," she said. "You and Lord Wrotham should leave such dramatics to me."

Harrison stared at her in astonishment.

Lord Wrotham walked over to the fireplace, took his silver cigarette case out, and opened it with steadying hands. He lit another cigarette and inhaled deeply.

After a minute of silence, Lord Wrotham spoke, this time in the smooth, even tones he used as King's Counsel summing up a case before the High Court.

"Please advise Pemberton what has happened." Lord Wrotham's lips curled as he spoke. "See if he will deign to represent me. He's the best criminal barrister I know." The coldness of his tone was unbearable but, before she had time to respond, he started speaking again. "I'm afraid I must also rely on you to break the news to mother." Lord Wrotham was in full mastery of his self-control now, and his face had assumed the cold, angular aloofness that she remembered from their first meeting. "While you may not require smelling salts," he continued, "she most certainly will." He paused. "You'd also best let James drive you to Bromley Hall, he's more familiar with the roads."

Ursula looked at him blankly. She had visited Bromley Hall on numerous occasions and both she and Samuels, her own driver, knew the way there—but there was something subtle yet purposeful in his tone of voice and, though she did not think Harrison or the other police constables present detected it, she suspected there was a hidden significance to Lord Wrotham's choice of his own chauffeur.

Ursula nodded her head, her eyes never leaving his.

"Tomorrow," Lord Wrotham said, "you must also place a notice in *The Times*, calling off our engagement."

Ursula's head jerked back.

"No, Ursula, this is not a subject for negotiation," he said calmly. "By morning this will be in all the newspapers. It will no doubt cause some measure of public hysteria and you will be the object of intense scrutiny. You should profess utter disgust and horror at the charges and, if necessary, toward me. No"—Ursula opened her mouth to protest—"it is the only way. Anything else and you expose yourself to vilification."

Ursula shook her head. "But you are innocent! I will not abandon you. Not in private. Not in public. I will stand by you." Even as she spoke, however, the truth of the situation started to sink in. She knew better than anyone else the power of scandal; she had been exposed to it enough by now. The magnitude of this case could overrun her entirely. No one would do business with anyone associated with an alleged traitor—not with the ever-present threat of war with Germany.

"Ursula," Lord Wrotham said quietly. "There is no other way."

She scrubbed her eyes fiercely with the cuffs of her tailored silk blouse. Part of her wanted to launch into an indignant tirade, but the other part of her, a quiet and insistent voice within, knew he was right. Her only means of survival was to call off their engagement and distance herself from him.

"You must pass on my regards to Admiral Smythe's family," Lord Wrotham continued, less evenly. "And yours too. Express our deep concern for the Admiral's safe return. I've been a close friend of the family for many years and I would hate them to think"—Lord Wrotham stopped and Ursula, sensing his self control was finally faltering, automatically interjected.

"But of course."

Harrison shifted from one foot to the other. "My apologies, my Lord," he said. "But my orders were to bring you in immediately. I really cannot delay any further."

"I understand, Chief Inspector," Lord Wrotham answered as he threw the cigarette butt into the fireplace. He straightened his black cashmere frockcoat, flipped open his fob watch, checked the time with a quick glance, and tucked it into his waistcoat pocket once more. Then, presenting the very image of the composed urbane gentleman, he said, "I'm ready."

One of the uniformed policemen, head glistening with hair oil, walked forward, struggling to undo a pair of handcuffs.

"Jackson!" Harrison exclaimed. "Those will hardly be necessary. We are dealing with a gentleman here, not your common or garden criminal!"

The young police constable turned beet red, halted, and stood in the middle of the room. "Oh, sorry . . . I mean, pardon . . . pardon me, my Lord . . ." he stumbled over his words.

Lord Wrotham regarded him impassively. "Please," he replied with a shrug. "No need to apologize."

That night, Ursula sat in her study, staring at the fire. Her feet were curled up in the chair and a plate of supper lay discarded and uneaten on the floor beside her. Chief Inspector Harrison had refused to allow her to accompany Lord Wrotham to Scotland Yard, where he was to be formally charged and placed in protective custody. Instead, she had been forced to remain at home, like some domestic pet, caged and abandoned. Ursula, never one to tolerate captivity easily, had spent the next two hours restlessly pacing the room and making telephone calls.

The first call she made was to Sir Robert Pemberton KC, who sounded as though he had just returned to his Mayfair home from a long, late lunch at White's. His response was one of bewilderment, but in slightly halting tones (he had obviously indulged in some fine wine over the course of the afternoon), he assured her he would go directly to Scotland Yard and apply for Lord Wrotham's release on bail. Ursula knew there was little likelihood of bail being granted but regardless she clung to that hope and waited anxiously by the front parlor window. By nine o'clock it was clear Lord Wrotham was not returning and she stalked back into the study. Since making this first telephone call, Ursula had spoken to no one else except Biggs, her butler, who, upon hearing the news of Lord Wrotham's arrest, paled but otherwise gave no outward indications of alarm. The fact that he promptly returned with a strong cup of coffee was comfortingly predictable, although Ursula had been surprised to find it was liberally laced with whiskey.

By ten o'clock Ursula was frantic. How she wished her good friend Winifred ('Freddie') Stanford-Jones was here rather than on an extended lecture tour of the United States. Freddie had long been missed, having left for New York almost six weeks ago, but now Ursula felt entirely bereft.

Not knowing what else to do, Ursula contemplated calling Hugh Carmichael, her business partner and friend, but knew he would only insist on rushing to London to try and help and she feared that would only fuel further rumors. London society already viewed her as an improper and unsuitable match for Lord Wrotham and she wanted to avoid any additional speculation that she was turning to another man in her 'hour of need'. Having been the subject of many a lurid story, she knew all too well how the newspapers could manipulate the truth.

Ursula collapsed on the chair next to her father's desk and buried her head in her hands. She felt she had to speak to someone or she would go mad. She picked up the telephone receiver, hesitated, replaced it again, and then finally placed a call to Gerard Anderson, her father's old business colleague and her financial advisor. Ursula regretted her decision as soon as she heard his voice. Anderson, would, of course, focus on the potential business losses a scandal of this magnitude was likely to inflict. He was incapable of providing her the comfort she yearned for. *What was she thinking?*

After fifteen minutes of expressing his disbelief and outlining all the worst case scenarios possible for Marlow Industries, Anderson finally said, "I'm proud of you, Ursula. Your telephoning me shows you've finally learned to think with your head rather than your heart." His words left her feeling cold and empty. *Was this the woman she had really become? The sort of woman who called her business colleagues ahead of her friends?*

This dreadful thought depressed her still further until she found, to her astonishment, she was lifting the receiver once more to call Mrs. Eudora Pomfrey-Smith. Mrs. Pomfrey-Smith had been her father's paramour and, ever since his death, she had attempted to act as Ursula's guide through the intricacies of London society. For the past three years Ursula had rebuffed most of her offers for 'societal assistance', but tonight she felt she had no one else to turn to.

"My dear!" Mrs. Pomfrey-Smith cried as Ursula broke the news. "You shall be ruined!" Ursula nearly hung up the receiver then and there, but Mrs. Pomfrey-Smith, with what Ursula could only imagine was an ingrained sense of loyalty to her father, immediately offered her unbridled support. Motherless since she was a child, Ursula had always spurned Mrs. Pomfrey-Smith's kindness in the past, feeling somehow that it would be an affront to her mother's memory. The lone voice of maternal kindness now reduced her to sobs. Ursula agreed to let Mrs. Pomfrey-Smith place the notice in *The Times* calling off her engagement. It was a task too terrible for her to bear.

After the drama of the afternoon, the restless pacing and the telephone calls, the mantel clock finally struck eleven and the house fell eerily quiet. Ursula dismissed Biggs and ignored her maid Julia's entreaties to come upstairs and get some sleep. Instead, she sat, alone and weary, amid the books and papers that once belonged to her father. Inside her head a thousand questions screamed, but she had exhausted her tears. She wasn't the same woman she was three years ago when her father had been taken from her. She had defied society's dire predictions and proven herself to be a successful businesswoman. She had built a life of her own, in which she remained true to her principles as best she could. Yet without Lord Wrotham it felt as if a piece of her soul had already been carved away and she was bleeding internally. The lack of him, the absence of him, was palpable in the room.

Ursula was in danger of sinking into a deep depression when she reminded herself that Lord Wrotham was innocent. He had assured her of that. And despite all his protestations and stiff upper lip, he needed her help. It was this need that revived her. It helped her focus the questions in her mind. She got up and walked across the room to the window, clearing her head with each step and reaffirming her determination to remain undaunted. Courage, she told herself, courage and conscience. That was all she needed to defy them all.

LONDON SOCIETY COLUMN OF THE DAILY TATTLER
FRIDAY JANUARY 17ᵗʰ 1913

The fortunes of Miss Ursula Marlow took another ominous turn last night with the shocking arrest of her fiancé, Lord Oliver Wrotham, Seventh Baron of Wrotham, of Bromley Hall, Northamptonshire, on charges of high treason. While lurid details of Lord Wrotham's arrest are no doubt being plastered across the daily newspapers, we at the Society Column, feel obliged to express our strong suspicion that Lord Wrotham's current predicament arises directly out of his unfortunate association with Miss Marlow.

As readers will no doubt recall Miss Marlow's own father was murdered two years ago as part of a ghastly spree of killings that included two children of Robert Marlow's long-time business associates, Misses Laura Radcliffe and Cecilia Abbott. Miss Marlow's own involvement in the investigation raised a number of eyebrows not least because of her foolhardy defense of the woman initially accused of Miss Radcliffe's murder—Miss Winifred-Stanford Jones (who is currently on a lecture tour of the United States speaking on the merits of radical action to achieve universal suffrage). Dear readers we need hardly remind you of last year's

*calumny in which Miss Marlow was a witness to yet another death—
Mrs. Katya Vilensky, while on an excursion to Cairo, Egypt. The death
of Mrs. Vilensky's sister in one of Miss Marlow's factories merely served
to compound the whole sorry state of affairs at Marlow industries (and
which was no mere coincidence, no matter what Scotland Yard would
lead us to believe). After the events of recent years we must surely start to
wonder whether Miss Marlow's own radical political views at the heart
of all her troubles. Is she really fit to be handling the large inheritance
and business interests left to her by her father?*

CHAPTER TWO

BROMLEY HALL, NORTHAMPTONSHIRE

"NONSENSE!" The Dowager Lady Adela Wrotham got to her feet with a sniff of disdain. "I just need to make two calls and I'll get this whole situation sorted out once and for all. I have a cousin at the Admiralty and another with the Foreign Office, not to mention that I know the Prime Minister personally. Scotland Yard indeed. Pack of imbeciles if you ask me. Wait here Miss Marlow and let me handle this—and when I return we can talk all about my plans for renovating the East Wing."

Ursula looked at the dowager, unsure whether she should be amazed at her powers of self-delusion or shocked at her blithe assumption that this little 'misunderstanding' could be sorted out by a couple of telephone calls. Uncertain of what to say, Ursula lay back on the pale green chaise longue and absently stroked the ears of one of Wrotham's two collies sprawled out next to her. The dowager had already redecorated the Green Room at Bromley Hall in anticipation of access to Ursula's substantial wealth and Ursula feared she was about to endure yet another recital of Lady Wrotham's 'splendid' renovation plans for the estate. Lady Wrotham's recent redecorating stint had converted what was once the epitome of late Victorian opulence into a Japanese inspired drawing room. Although the dowager had professed to seek Ursula's opinion, in reality she had gone off and chosen the silkscreened wallpaper, Japanese inspired imitation-bamboo chairs and ebonized table by herself. Ursula suspected Lady Wrotham needed the reassurance that she was still the preeminent 'lady' of Bromley Hall and left well alone. She had learned, by now, to choose her battles.

Now she wasn't sure how to approach the upcoming skirmish at all. She had expected Lady Wrotham to dissolve into hysterics, but instead she had surprised Ursula with an initial resilience, even if it was coated in self-delusion. Surely Lady Wrotham had to be aware of the seriousness of the situation. The police constables and motorcars lined up outside could hardly have gone unnoticed, yet Lady Wrotham seemed to be in total denial. Ursula dreaded what was likely to happen when the truth finally sank in.

Ursula had driven up to Lord Wrotham's estate in Northamptonshire that morning in the new two-seater Bugatti (or the 'deathtrap' as her housekeeper, Mrs. Stewart called it) she had bought herself for Christmas. Having seen the newspaper headlines in the early morning editions, Ursula knew she would have to resort to clandestine methods if she was to have any hope of reaching Northamptonshire without attracting undue attention. Accordingly she instructed her own chauffeur, Samuels, to play decoy in 'Bertie', the silver ghost Rolls Royce Ursula had inherited from her father. He was probably still driving about London with Julia, Ursula's lady's maid, in the back seat, attempting to confuse 'the enemy' as Ursula now called the press.

Despite Lord Wrotham's request that she ask James to drive her, all her telephone calls and letters to him (directed to Lord Wrotham's Mayfair home) had, so far, gone unanswered. Lord Wrotham's part-time the housekeeper could only advise that James had left the morning of Lord Wrotham's arrest. No one, it seemed, had seen James since.

Ursula nervously chewed her lip as she waited for Lady Wrotham. Originally she had planned to visit Lord Wrotham before driving up to Bromley Hall, but a messenger had delivered a note from him (via Pemberton) first thing that morning. The note was characteristically brief: *On no account visit me.* There were no endearments or protestations of innocence. No information that could be useful to her at all. He was too aware of the risk of interception by either the police or the press to risk that, but the note had still left Ursula feeling disconsolate.

She had been hoping that Lord Wrotham would have reconsidered his silence. Nevertheless, she maintained her vow that, once she returned from Bromley Hall, she would initiate her own investigation.

Lady Wrotham was taking so long that Ursula began to wonder if she was going to make it back to London at all that day. She didn't fancy her chances driving the Bugatti in the dark. Eventually, however, Lady Wrotham did return, ashen faced and trembling. She stumbled unevenly through the door to the Green Room and headed straight for the whiskey decanter sitting on the sideboard. She poured a large glass and sat down heavily on one of the inlaid chairs opposite Ursula. Fearing an attack was imminent, Ursula reached down and rummaged in her skirt pocket for the bottle of smelling salts she had the forethought to bring in case of just this situation.

"Don't bother my gal," Lady Wrotham said sharply, downing the whiskey in one long gulp. "Salts are useless. All I need is a good stiff drink."

"Lady Wrotham, I'm so terribly sorry," Ursula stammered, unsure of what else to say.

The dowager snorted in disgust. "Don't you apologize! You're not the idiot who got himself into this mess. Really, I can hardly believe Oliver. As if poor Gerard didn't cause me enough grief! Now I have to contend with another son who brings me nothing but shame and disgrace." The folds of skin around her mouth started to crumple. "What am I expected to say at the Empress Club? How can I ever show my face at royal functions after this?!"

Ursula hastily got to her feet and caught the empty glass as it dropped from Lady Wrotham's hands. The collie, irritated by her fidgeting, got off the chaise lounge, shook his sable and white coat, and padded off in disgust.

"I'm not sure my nerves can take it!" Lady Wrotham collapsed back in the chair and Ursula thought it best if she poured her another glass of whiskey.

"But you know Oliver is innocent." Ursula said walking over to the sideboard. "He would never do what they have accused him of."

Lady Wrotham closed her eyes. "I don't know what to think. Oliver was always a complete mystery to me. Gerard, I understood. He

23

had his foibles, yes. But he lived life to the full. Oliver was like a closed book. He could have been the right hand man of the Kaiser himself for all I knew. What with his comings and goings ever since Oxford. Oh, I knew it was some sort of government nonsense—but little did I guess . . ."

Ursula hastily poured Lady Wrotham the glass of whiskey and handed it to her.

"It's not even the principle of the thing. My mother was German. For God's sake half our family is German or Russian—but how could Oliver have been stupid enough to get caught?! What a fiasco." Lady Wrotham took a swig from the glass and licked her lips. "Once of a day, a gentleman would go outside and shoot himself in the head rather than dishonor his family."

Ursula opened her mouth to speak, but the dowager refused to broach any interruption. She merely glared at her and continued apace. "Nowadays they just don't have the courage for it! Nor for that matter do they have the decency to warn a gentleman ahead of time. I know Admiral Smythe and his family—he was one of Oliver's tutors at Balliol—and yet I hear Smythe actually had the gall to implicate Oliver in this mess. A fine state of affairs!"

"Admiral Smythe is missing," Ursula reminded her as she sat back down, smoothing out her navy serge wool skirt, "and Oliver is very concerned about what may have happened to him."

"Poppycock!" Lady Wrotham insisted. "Smythe was the traitor—he just left his mess behind so Oliver would take the blame. He's probably swanning around on the French Riviera by now. I can't say I'm surprised. I never did approve of their friendship. The Smythes are of common stock don't you know. Naval men as may be—but still, good breeding always wins out!"

Ursula curbed her tongue. She need not remind Lady Wrotham that, as the daughter of a Northern mill owner and granddaughter of a coal miner, she too was of 'common stock'.

"Of course, you know who's really to blame don't you?" Lady Wrotham's eyes bore down on Ursula and she steeled herself for the expected tirade, but Lady Wrotham did not rail against her, instead the main target of her vitriol was a man called Fergus McTiernay, a friend of Lord Wrotham's from his days at Balliol College. Ursula regarded Lady Wrotham blankly. She had never heard Lord Wrotham mention anyone by that name.

"He was a friend of Oliver's at university. The 'inseparables' they called them," Lady Wrotham finally explained. "A 'radical thinker' Oliver used to say—a Fenian rabble-rouser more like—but when did my opinion ever make the slightest difference to Oliver?"

"So this man McTiernay . . . you think he may have something to do with Oliver's arrest?" Ursula asked, doubtfully.

"How should I know?!" Lady Wrotham exclaimed in ill-humor. "It just stands to reason that Oliver's ill-advised friendships would land him in trouble one day. I thought he was done with him and Friedrich, that damnable cousin of ours, but no—Oliver would insist on reviving old friendships that were better left dead and buried."

"I'm sorry, but Oliver has never mentioned Fergus McTiernay or his cousin, Friedrich, was it?"

"Count Friedrich von Bernstorff-Hollweg," the dowager responded imperiously, "Oliver's second cousin, on my mother's side. Although," she admitted, "there are many on that side of the family who would rather disown him. I, for one, was never fooled by his charms, and I never approved of him latching on to Oliver like he did." Lady Wrotham gave a dramatic shudder.

"I still don't see . . ."

"You wouldn't would you?" came Lady Wrotham's caustic reply. "Given the friendships you seem to insist on cultivating . . ."

Ursula flushed at the insinuation but she knew better than to inflame the situation by getting into an argument with Lady Wrotham. Instead she got to her feet and murmured a hasty excuse that she had "best see how the police are progressing in the library." She had seen the police vehicles lined up in the driveway the moment she arrived and was in no doubt as to their mission. She was also sure that observing their investigations was more likely to yield useful information than any long-winded (and no doubt offensive) discussion with Lady Wrotham over Lord Wrotham's 'imprudent' choice of university chums.

Ursula exited the room as quickly as she could.

She encountered Ayres, the Wrotham family's butler, as he approached along the narrow corridor leading from the East Wing of the house. "Ah, Ayres," Ursula exclaimed. "I was just wondering whether the police had finished."

Ayres sniffed. "No, my Lady. They have not."

"I'm concerned about the damage they might cause to the collection," Ursula said, "and please, Ayres, no need to address me as 'my Lady.' Unfortunately my engagement to Lord Wrotham has had to be called off while all this is going on. So until such time as I do marry him—and I pray that that day will come soon—you should address me as Miss. I'm sure the dowager will pick up the *faux pas* readily enough, if you don't."

Ayres stared down at the floor boards for a moment before meeting her gaze.

"You know it was not my choice to call off the engagement," Ursula looked at Ayres earnestly. "I plan to do everything in my power to clear his lordship of these terrible charges."

For the first time since she met him, Ayres looked her candidly in the eye. "You know, my Lady," he said (deliberately ignoring her request), "I believe you will."

Ursula lips parted, and her mouth would have dropped totally open at his unexpected frankness, had she not tempered her surprise almost as quickly as it had registered. Ayres' face assumed its usual passive, world weary façade. "I shall show you to the library," he said. Although she knew her way by now, Ursula understood his need to cling to whatever sense of normalcy he could in the circumstances, so she merely nodded her head and accompanied him back along the hallway.

They continued along the passageway together, entering the long picture gallery that connected the East Wing to the main section of the house. They passed an imposing portrait by Joshua Reynolds of the Sixth Baron of Wrotham, Lord Wrotham's father. As the light from the window opposite struck the painting, the red of his hunting jacket seemed to leap out from the cracked varnish.

"How are the rest of the servants taking the news?" Ursula prodded, trying to ignore the ominous blood red reflection of the painting spilling onto the floor.

"We've already lost Mary," Ayres said. "She resigned as soon as she heard of Lord Wrotham's arrest."

"I am sorry to hear that. Should I suggest to the dowager that she gather the rest of the staff together and explain the news? Perhaps that might mitigate against . . .?" Ursula's voice trailed off as she saw Ayres stiffen. She frowned uncertainly, but Ayres merely said, stiff-jawed: "There is no need. The rest of us have vowed to stay and serve."

"Thank you Ayres," Ursula responded gratefully. "I know your loyalty will mean a great deal to Lord Wrotham."

"I am too old, that is all," Ayres said but Ursula was not deceived.

The clang of the servant's bell being rung from the Green Room echoed along the picture gallery.

"Ayres?! Ayres?! Where the devil are you?!" Lady Wrotham's voice boomed down the corridor and Ayres braced himself.

"Go," Ursula said gently. "I know my way to the library well enough. I will speak to the police and see if I can't get them to finish up as soon as possible."

"Yes, my lady," Ayres replied with a bow.

"Ayres?!" Lady Wrotham shouted again. She appeared to be wandering disorientated towards the entrance hall.

"You best see to Lady Wrotham. I suspect as long as you keep the whiskey decanter replenished she will be fine."

Ayres didn't miss a beat. "But of course," he said before turning and heading back in search of Lady Wrotham.

Ursula hurried to the library. The packing cases full of books and straw out in the hallway were reason enough to cause consternation. Once inside she was horrified to see uniformed policemen thumbing and tossing books with as little thought as if they were discarding fruit at the Blackburn market. Ursula had grown up in Lancashire, surrounded by the poor cotton mill workers her father employed, but she had never seen men treat books with such patent disregard as she witnessed now.

The library had been in the Wrotham family for generations and Ursula knew that Lord Wrotham, in honor of his father, had spent many years restoring and adding to the collection. Just last week he and Ursula had spent an afternoon browsing the books at Foyle's bookstore in Cecil Court, searching for a rare first edition of Sir Walter Scott's novel *Waverly*. It horrified her to see all their efforts, all their love of literature, being treated with such contempt.

"Chief Inspector?!" Ursula exclaimed upon seeing Chief Inspector Harrison. "What on earth is going on here?!"

Harrison tugged his mustache. "I'm sorry, Miss Marlow, but I really must ask you to leave. We are undertaking official police business. I have a warrant to search the entire estate for evidence."

"Surely Lord Wrotham's chambers would be a more appropriate place to search? What do you expect to find in his personal library, apart from books, obviously?"

"Books may well turn out to be a critical source of evidence," a well-bred voice called out from behind. Ursula whirled round and came face to face with a man of ample girth, fashionably coiffed hair, and florid countenance.

"And who, sir, are you?!" she snapped. The man drew himself up, but as he was hardly taller than Ursula herself, it had little discernible effect.

He was dressed formally in a large black frockcoat, wingtip-collared shirt and blue striped Windsor knot tie. He unbuttoned his coat, releasing his belly, to reveal a scarlet silk waistcoat with mother of pearl buttons. Ursula arched one eyebrow. This man was definitely not a member of the Metropolitan Police Force.

Harrison coughed. "Miss Marlow, this is Sir Reginald Buckley of the War Office. He and I are conducting a joint investigation." This time both her eyebrows lifted. The War Office had been established the previous year but she was surprised that they would be involved in what was, she assumed, essentially a matter for Scotland Yard.

Sir Reginald Buckley regarded her with pale blue eyes that provided a startling contrast to the abundant dark waves of his hair, black beetle-brows and the corpulent layers of his neck and chin. Although Ursula guessed he was much the same age as Lord Wrotham, in his middle thirties, he looked as though he had already settled in to a body more suited to the idleness and excesses of late-middle age.

"Miss Marlow hardly needs to be kept informed of the progress of our investigation," Sir Buckley replied smoothly. "Indeed, I'm sure her time would be much better spent riding horses or playing golf, whatever it is 'modern women' now claim as pastimes, or perhaps"—he paused, a glint in his eyes—"Miss Marlow prefers breaking windows and harassing cabinet ministers like her fellow suffragettes?"

Ursula's involvement in the Women's Social and Political Union had long been a source of tension between her and Chief Inspector Harrison, and it was obvious that Sir Reginald Buckley held her political views in similarly low regard.

"Oh, you are out of date Sir Buckley," Ursula replied smoothly. "Don't you know we've moved on to planting bombs?" Ursula immediately regretted her indiscretion. It was hardly in her or Lord Wrotham's interests to sound like an extremist.

"No doubt you'll be wantin' to get back to Lady Wrotham, Miss Marlow," Harrison intervened hastily. "I'm sure she appreciates having you here."

"Lady Wrotham appreciates my presence as much as she ever did," Ursula responded dryly and made no move to leave the Library. One of the young constables in uniform called for Sir Buckley, who, with a pale-eyed last glance, sauntered off leaving Harrison and Ursula standing beneath the arched entrance to the library.

"Be careful of that one," Harrison said in low tones. "He's a right nasty man to cross. Went to Oxford with Lord Wrotham and believe me, there's been no love lost between them. He's baying for blood now—so I'd just watch myself if I was you."

Ursula was startled by his candor.

"Thanks," she replied. "Consider me duly warned, but," she lowered her voice, "you know this is excessive—what can they possibly hope to find here?"

All the police constables were gathered in the far corner of the library, beneath the stained glass window depicting the Wrotham family's royal blue and silver family crest. Under the coat of arms the family motto—*Sequere iustiam et invenias vitem*—follow justice and find life—was written in gothic black letters. The policemen and Sir Buckley were out of earshot. "Oh come now," Ursula pressed. "You don't really believe Lord Wrotham would betray his country?"

"After all that has happened over the last few days, I don't know what to believe," Harrison replied. He tugged at a strand of his short dark hair, pensive and distracted.

"Then trust your instinct," Ursula urged. "Help me. Lord Wrotham told me he was innocent and my instinct is to believe him."

Harrison sighed and the lines around his eyes tightened as he watched Sir Buckley talking with his constables. "I dare not," he said, struggling to hide his frustration. "Even if I believe him. My entire livelihood is at stake. And, much as I hate to admit it, this is a significant investigation for me. Likely as not it'll lead to promotion. A promotion which I need if I'm ever going to be able to afford to marry and have a family"—He paused before continuing—"Unlike you, Miss Marlow, I didn't inherit money. My parents, God rest their souls, were poor tenants on this very estate. I can't fight the system like you lot can."

Bitterness crept into his voice and Ursula felt the stirrings of compassion. In that moment Harrison revealed more about himself that he had in all the three years Ursula had known him. His ambitions, his background, and his motivations—none of that had ever been fully bared—until now.

"All you need to do," Ursula said quietly, hoping to appeal to his conscience, "is tell me what they hope to find here. Give me that and I will trust that, deep down, you believe Lord Wrotham is innocent, even if you cannot overtly say it." She kept a close eye on Sir Buckley across the room. He had his back to them as he pored over a large portfolio of drawings.

Harrison shoved his hands into his trouser pockets and stared at the floor.

"Sir!" A young tow-headed policeman hurriedly entered the library. "The first load of boxes is ready to be transported. The driver said 'e needs your signature to authorize 'em to take 'em back to Scotland Yard."

Sir Buckley looked up and his chest puffed out with self-importance. "I will be back momentarily," he advised the police constables before crossing the room with short, swift strides. He passed Harrison and Ursula brimming with self-importance.

"Make sure she's out of here by the time I get back," he said as he walked by.

Harrison gazed directly ahead, avoiding looking at Ursula. The remaining police constables were still trying to replace the papers back in the leather-bound portfolio. Ursula winced when she thought of the damage they were undoubtedly inflicting. She knew the drawings, they were a series of controversial ink drawings of *Salome* by Aubrey Beardsley. They were unlikely to be relevant to the investigation, but no doubt Sir Buckley was convinced they demonstrated some prurient side of Lord Wrotham's character.

"Sir Buckley believes that a notebook we found in Admiral Smythe's wall safe was encrypted using a book as the key." Harrison murmured under his breath. "He's pretty sure some kind of numeric cipher is involved"—Ursula frowned—"where a number is substituted for the first letter of a word from a book or document," Harrison explained. "The difficulty is that without knowing the text used it's almost impossible to decipher."

Ursula leaned in closer. She had some limited experience with codes and ciphers, having assisted the WSPU with Lady Catherine Winterton the previous year. The WSPU had long been concerned about the police intercepting messages related to protests or other militant action and Ursula's good friend, Winifred Stanford-Jones, had enlisted her help in devising a new secure system for communication. Ursula had studied for a brief time the use of codes by Mary Queen of Scots while she was at Somerville College. Her knowledge remained, however, rudimentary and incomplete.

"That's why we're here," Harrison continued. "Sir Buckley has been scouring all of Admiral Smythe's and Lord Wrotham's files about other operations, looking for further clues as to the code used. He's convinced that he can work out the cipher that Wrotham and Smythe have been using over the past two years. I don't really understand this cryptography stuff, but Sir Buckley figures if he can find the book used, he'll be able to decode Admiral Smythe's notebook."

"So Sir Buckley is an expert on ciphers and codes, is he?" Ursula asked acidly.

Harrison's moustache twitched. "He certainly fancies himself as an expert, but no, he'll probably hand it over to the boys at Naval Intelligence."

"Naval Intelligence?" Ursula queried.

"Where Admiral Smythe worked," Harrison replied quickly. "Did you not know that? Smythe's one of the leading lights in the Naval Intelligence Department of the Admiralty. Wrotham's worked with him for years, as a kind of amateur gentleman agent, using his legal work with shipping companies and industrialists as a cover for gathering information and helping government negotiations where needed."

"I had no idea," Ursula confessed. Harrison eyed her closely and Ursula suspected he thought her remark disingenuous, but in reality, she had a million and one questions. Although she had long been aware that Lord Wrotham served as some kind of clandestine liaison for the Foreign Office, he had never divulged the nature of this aspect of his work. The fact that Lord Wrotham could have kept a whole part of his life hidden from her was not just disturbing—it smacked of a deeply held distrust.

"I think this search is a wild goose chase myself," Harrison said. "Wrotham's clever—he's not likely to leave the cipher key lying around anywhere obvious."

"Though a library is one of the best places to hide a book," Ursula mused.

Before Ursula could pursue any further questions, Sir Buckley returned, red-faced and breathless. No doubt he had hurried for fear that Ursula would interfere with his search, but she was equally determined to make her position clear.

"I'm here," she said, "because Lady Wrotham wants me to make sure that the valuable books are being properly handled." Ursula ignored Harrison, who would know she was lying (the last thing Lady Wrotham would ever concern herself with was the state of Lord Wrotham's books).

Buckley's eyes narrowed. "Not one of those bookish women are you?"

"'Fraid so!" Ursula replied. "Went to Oxford and everything."

"Well, I can assure you"—Sir Buckley thrust out his chest, but rather than impress his point upon her, it merely added to the ridiculousness of his pomposity—"that all necessary precautions are being taken to ensure the books are properly dealt with!"

"Then you won't mind if I reassure myself by double-checking," Ursula said. "Don't worry, Sir Buckley, you can watch over me as I do so."

Sir Reginald Buckley heaved a phlegmatic harrumph and shot Harrison a malevolent look for not having got rid of Ursula sooner. Eventually, however, he seemed to deflate, realizing, perhaps, that there was no way Ursula was leaving the library unless he agreed to her demands. Ursula set off to investigate some of the boxes and Sir Buckley reluctantly followed.

The first packing crate contained the complete series of *Clarendon's History of the Rebellion and Civil Wars in England*. Ursula bent over and rearranged them so that the spines would not be damaged. She made more of a show of it than was necessary and Buckley's face darkened with irritation.

"I believe you knew Lord Wrotham at Balliol," Ursula asked with feigned innocence. She stood up and dusted off her tweed skirt. Sir Buckley could barely hide his contempt. "Yes, His Lordship and I had the same tutor for moral philosophy, Professor Prendergast."

"I studied political history at Somerville," Ursula said with one of what she called her 'helpful' smiles. "I believe that was Admiral Smythe's subject, or so Lord Wrotham once told me." She picked a book from the top of one of the piles. It was a slightly moldy copy of Sir Robert Herman Schomburgk's *Twelve Views of the Interior of Guyana*. The inscription inside was dated 1903 and signed by Aubrey St John Smythe.

"Yes," Buckley's face grew blacker still as he tried to restrain his exasperation. Ursula opened the book and idly flipped through the first few pages. "I only ask as I wondered if you were not all friends at college," she said. She noticed with interest that the next book in the stack was an early version of Alfred lord Tennyson's *Idylls of the King*. She opened it, saw a dedication on the front piece in German by Count Friedrich von Bernstorff-Hollweg, and closed the book quickly.

"No," Buckley answered, spittle forming on his lower lip. "His Lordship and I were not close friends. He was too busy consorting with the college rabble, upstarts like Smythe and Fenians like McTiernay."

Ursula took note of Buckley's resentment towards Lord Wrotham behind the flicker of her eyelashes.

"Oh, I'm sorry," she replied. "I didn't realize I was speaking to a man with such high scruples. You must feel quite put out conversing with the daughter of a Lancashire mill owner"—Ursula was losing self-control now—"My apologies if I have offended your sensibilities, but now, if you please, I had better go and console Lady Wrotham. This whole matter has been a terrible shock. I will return later this afternoon and ensure the remaining books are in order. I confess my time at Oxford spoiled me somewhat—the one thing I cannot abide is a narrow mind!"

Ursula walked away, inwardly cursing her impetuous tongue. She knew that, despite Harrison's warning, she had just made an enemy out of Sir Reginald Buckley.

Ursula returned to Chester Square just before nightfall, having endured an arduous road journey that required her to change a tire that blew out near Dunstable and refill the gas tank on the outskirts of London. Luckily Ursula was familiar enough with the vagaries of road travel to carry both spare rubber tire rings and petrol cans but still she arrived, grimy and oil-streaked, vowing that next time, press or no press, she would take the ever reliable 'Bertie' instead.

Outside the front of her home, a bevy of journalists and news boys had already massed, laughing and talking with an easy camaraderie that no doubt came with the shared anticipation of exposing an ongoing scandal. Cigarettes were being tossed and lit, vacuum flasks of hot tea and coffee unscrewed and poured, and an enterprising young barrow boy was even selling hot pies and pastries. As Ursula applied the car brakes, the throng turned and spotted her in an instant. There was no use even attempting to drive around to the back of the row of houses that lined this part of Chester Square. Instead, Ursula merely pulled up to the pavement, ducked her head under the brim of her hat and drew a length of scarf around her face. Buttoning up her duster, she climbed out of the Bugatti, ignored all calls for comment, and hastened to the front door. Biggs, ever vigilant, opened it as soon as she reached the top step, and she hurried inside. He closed the front door behind her with a resounding bang.

Ursula threw off her long coat and hat and ran upstairs. Julia was waiting in the bedroom and a fresh set of clothes was already laid out on the four poster bed. The headache that had begun during the long drive home was now making Ursula feel nauseous. She was thankful that Julia had the foresight to have started running a hot bath for her.

When she had been forced off the road by the blown tire, Ursula had vented her anger by shrieking at the motor car. In the narrow, deserted country lane, there had been no one to hear her screams. Now, surrounded by journalists outside and servants inside, she knew she could not make a sound. She had to keep it all bottled up inside and that only made her feel all the worse. At this moment she hated Lord Wrotham. Hated him for letting her be lured by the illusion of having somebody she could rely on. Over the last two years she had found the independence she had sought and then, just as she had begun to believe in herself, feel comfortable in her own skin, he had torn up the foundations she had struggled so hard to build.

CHAPTER THREE

BRIXTON PRISON, LONDON

THE FOLLOWING MORNING Ursula visited Lord Wrotham in Brixton prison on the south west outskirts of London. Infamous for having some of the worst prison conditions in England, Brixton was the place where untried prisoners were sent while they awaited trial. Ursula's vision of Lord Wrotham's cell was of a dank, dark, rat-infested place and, as she entered the foreboding prison entrance, she saw nothing to assuage her fears. Samuels stopped the motorcar and, as she stepped out, Ursula shuddered. If she failed and Lord Wrotham was found guilty of treason, he would be taken from here to Pentonville prison and hanged, his life as expendable and deplorable as all the other murderers and traitors. The idea sickened her for a moment and, holding on to the car door to steady herself, she tried to banish her morbid thoughts. With a deep breath she lifted the narrow woolen skirt beneath her pannier and ascended the wide stone staircase that led to the main prison door. Her sturdy Oxford shoes echoed as she walked across the entrance hall to the visitors' desk.

Deep in her thoughts, she almost walked into Sir Robert Pemberton KC, who was striding forth from one of the corridors, top-coat flapping behind him. He pulled up once he saw her and regarded her intently with his shrewd brown eyes.

"I see you decided to ignore Lord Wrotham's advice and visit after all," he said.

"Yes," Ursula replied, refusing to be intimidated.

"Well, while you're here you may as well try and drive some sense into the man!"

Pemberton's mood darkened.

"Pardon?"

"Get him to tell you something, anything, that I can use by way of a defense! At the moment he refuses to disclose anything. At this rate, he may just as well plead guilty. Bloody fool!"

Ursula looked startled.

"Pardon my language," Pemberton apologized, misinterpreting her reaction. "But he is really being most infuriating. I've practiced law alongside him at Temple Chambers for nigh on ten years now and I've never known him be like this."

"Not being a lawyer," Ursula said. "I really don't know all the issues that have to be addressed in a treason case . . ." She looked at him expectantly. Perhaps he could tell her something to steer her way to finding the evidence she needed to clear Lord Wrotham's name.

"It is most unusual, I admit, for a charge of high treason to be made during peacetime. I fear Lord Wrotham must have many enemies in Whitehall, if this is the path that they have chosen. Though planning an assassination of a member of the Royal family—I hardly feel that even merits a response, it is so plainly ludicrous! No, it is the question of Ireland . . . and the Germans . . . that worries me the most. I only wish he would tell me what else I am to make of his meeting with McTiernay and Count von Bernstorff-Hollweg—if not to foment rebellion then for what?"

"Are you saying the charges against Lord Wrotham relate to some meeting he had with Fergus McTiernay and Friedrich von Bernstorff-Hollweg?!" Ursula was surprised to hear the names of the two men Lady Wrotham had mentioned repeated here.

"Yes, most of the crown's evidence hinges on details related to a meeting held at the Count's castle in December 1911. Indeed, the Count, himself, is the main witness in this case."

"He is?"

"Yes, though I have only just received the preliminary papers in the case. That much, at least, is clear."

"And what of Mr. McTiernay's role in the case?" Ursula asked.

Pemberton shrugged. "Your guess is as good as mine. Only information I have is that he is an Irish Nationalist hell-bent on the idea of an Irish Free State. He's listed as a co-conspirator but, as far as I'm aware, he has not been found or arrested, as yet."

Ursula had to bite her tongue—the corridors of Brixton were hardly the place to interrogate Pemberton on the intricacies of Lord Wrotham's case but, nonetheless, she needed both his assistance and his advice to know what further investigations needed to be undertaken.

"If I am going to help 'drive some sense' into Lord Wrotham," Ursula started, "I should know what you think is required. Would you be able to write me up a summary of the law pertaining to treason, perhaps?"

Pemberton's eyebrows disappeared into hair. "Good Lord," he exclaimed. "I've never had the future wife of a defendant ask for that. I'd be happy to provide a summary of the law as it pertains to treason but, my dear, who is going to read and explain it to you?"

"Well," Ursula replied, failing to restrain her sarcasm. "I was rather hoping I'd be able to do that all by myself."

Pemberton looked at her incredulously but, before he could make any further comment, he caught sight of the clock mounted on the wall. "Is it really quarter to ten?! Good Lord!" He pulled his fob watch from his waistcoat pocket and confirmed the time. "I'm going to be late for court, if I don't leave now." Pemberton fussed with pulling on his leather gloves. "You should also know," he said, "that I've had no luck getting bail issued, I'm afraid. Judge won't budge. I'm filing a motion this afternoon though, trying to suppress the newspapers from printing anything prejudicial Lord Wrotham's trial— Although after reading the scare-mongering in the *Daily Mail* this morning, I'm not holding out much hope. Now if you will excuse me"—Pemberton tipped his top hat—"I'll telephone you tonight if I hear anything further. Good luck with Wrotham. Tell him to stop being an idiot."

He turned and walked swiftly away. Ursula walked down the bleak central corridor and gave her name at the visitors' desk. After being subjected to a rough search by one of the female prison wardens, she was escorted to one of the small, airless, visiting rooms. She sat down on one of the wooden chairs provided and, after nearly fifteen minutes, Lord Wrotham was finally brought in to see her. He was still wearing the same suit he was arrested in and, unable to shave, already had a dark shadow of stubble. There were circles beneath his eyes, and haggard lines had begun to form at the corners of his mouth.

"What the hell are you doing here?!" he demanded.

"Lovely to see you too," Ursula responded, placing her hands demurely in her lap.

"Didn't you get my note? I asked Pemberton to make sure you got it as soon as possible."

"I got your note," she confirmed.

"Then why did you come?! It will be in every newspaper by this evening." Lord Wrotham's tone was sharp and Ursula flushed.

"You think I don't know that?" she snapped. "But I had to see you all the same."

Lord Wrotham sat back in his chair and crossed his arms. Ursula felt the old tension rise between them—the way it had been during Freddie's incarceration—when she would rail against his admonitions. Had so little changed? She clenched her fists, reminding herself that things were different now. She was different now.

"Don't worry," Ursula said, in measured tones. "I plan to issue a statement from the prison steps as I leave here today. I'm sure a swarm of reporters is already gathering outside. I thought if I told them I felt it was my Christian duty to visit you, they might look favorably upon me. It may appeal to their readers' nobler instincts."

"I doubt the readers of the *Daily Mail* have much in the way of noble instincts," Lord Wrotham retorted.

"That may be, but I cannot simply let you rot in here without trying to help."

"There's nothing you can do, Ursula, so please don't interfere."

Ursula rolled her eyes. Were they going to argue about this once again? Surely he knew her better than that by now.

"Can they hear us in here?" Ursula asked, ignoring his reply. She tilted her head enquiringly towards the prison guard who was waiting outside.

"No," Lord Wrotham looked around him. "I don't believe so."

"Then I need to tell you that there's a chap from the War Office, Sir Reginald Buckley, who appears to be heading up the investigation. I met him yesterday—the police were turning the library at Bromley Hall inside out. Buckley thinks he's going to stumble upon the key to unlocking some kind of book code."

Lord Wrotham eyes glinted for a moment. "Go on . . ." he said.

"As I said, he's turning the library upside down. Chief Inspector Harrison was present at the time but, apart from a little run down on your activities with Admiral Smythe of Naval Intelligence, he didn't give me much to go on." Ursula paused but Lord Wrotham said nothing. "Pemberton tells me that Count Frederich von Bernstorff-Hollweg is one of the Crown witnesses against you."

"Yes," he replied, his face impassive. "The Count is my second cousin."

"So I hear, and from your mother of all people," Ursula replied. "It's amazing what I'm finding out about you. Who knew you were friends with the likes of Friedrich von Bernstorff-Hollweg and Fergus McTiernay? . . . I certainly did not."

Lord Wrotham watched her closely but she was not about to give him the satisfaction of an outburst. For his part, it was clear, he was not about to give her the satisfaction of an explanation either.

"I received word this morning that Harrison and Sir Buckley want to interview me about your alleged activities," Ursula finally said, after the silence between them became too painful to bear.

"They must be desperate if they think you know anything," Lord Wrotham responded.

"Thank you very much," Ursula replied drily. "Though as it happens I don't really know anything do I?"

Lord Wrotham visibly flinched and she was pleased that her retort had finally hit home. She was startled by the extent of her anger that he had never confided the truth in her. Only now did she realize, as the bitterness rose acrid inside her, how humiliated she really felt.

"I cannot help you unless you tell me what this is all about," she said.

"I've already told you I cannot."

Ursula reached out her hand and clasped his. "I know, because of some obligation of secrecy. But surely in the circumstances?" Ursula paused, but her plea, however, went unheeded. Lord Wrotham remained silent. "I won't let it stop me," she said. "You may as well accept that."

He looked away for a moment, but his hand remained in hers.

"Has the notice of our cancelled engagement gone in?" he asked, gruffly, eyes downcast.

"Yes," Ursula replied, clearing her throat. "It's in *The Times* today. Mrs. Pomfrey-Smith placed the notice for me. I haven't yet had the courage to read it."

His hand gripped hers.

"Are they treating you fairly?" Ursula asked in little more than a whisper. She no longer trusted herself to rein in her emotions.

"Yes, I suppose they are," Lord Wrotham replied and, if his appearance lacked his usually fastidious formality, his voice did not. "Pemberton is seeking to allow me to have a change of clothes and the possibility that I might bathe and shave."

There was a knock at the door signaling that their time together was at an end.

"Can I kiss you?" she asked.

The door opened and the prison warden walked in.

"Best not," he replied.

Ursula bit her lip. She wanted him, just once, to throw caution to the wind. Say damn it all and kiss her, but the moment passed. He made no motion to approach her. He would not even look her straight in the eye. She knew it was his way of keeping his emotions in check, but still, it pained her.

"Goodbye for now, Lord Wrotham," she said, all cold formality.

"Good bye, Miss Marlow," he answered hollowly.

On her way back from Islington into central London, Ursula, seated in the backseat of 'Bertie' began to feel light-headed. Making the press statement on the steps of Brixton prison was a spectacle she would rather forget. The jostling of the reporters, each vying to ask her questions, and the photographers, their tripods already set up, blinding her with their flashes. It had been a humiliating debacle, as each journalist pursued the most salacious angle of the story. *Your ideas on Ireland and female suffrage are well known Miss Marlow*, one man had shouted, *don't you think you are the one to blame?* Another called out. *Tell us, did he do it for you? Was he corrupted by your extremist views?*

By the time Samuels turned into Oxford Street, the strain she had felt over last few days was near to breaking her. Ursula leaned forward and unbuttoned the top of her blouse and said to Samuels, "I need some air."

Samuels looked around with concern. "Do you want me to pull over, Miss?" he asked.

Ursula nodded. "Anywhere along here is fine . . ."

Samuels navigated his way along the busy thoroughfare that was Oxford Street on a Monday afternoon. He pulled up at the corner of South Moulton Street, just outside the Bond Street underground station, and turned to her from the driver's seat.

"Are you sure you're all right, Miss?" he asked.

"I just need to walk for a while to try and clear my head," Ursula replied.

Samuels jumped out of the motor car, walked round and opened the rear passenger door. The cool brisk air embraced her as she stepped out onto the pavement.

"It's a long way to walk to Chester Square, Miss," Samuels said doubtfully. Ursula drew in a deep breath and steadied herself. The smells of the city, the acrid smoke, petrol and oil, horse manure and hot street food, assaulted her senses. But already, the bustle and chaos was helping distract her from her thoughts. She needed to be anonymous for a while, just another person hurrying along Oxford Street, without destination or purpose.

"Wait for me at Marble Arch," she instructed Samuels. In truth she did not feel capable of walking all the way home. Samuels still looked concerned and she patted him on the arm. "I'll be fine. The walk will do me good."

"Very well, Miss," Samuels conceded. "I'll be waiting for you on this side of Park Lane."

Ursula nodded, turned, and started to walk down Oxford Street towards the imposing Selfridges' Department Store. Given the fair weather, the street was packed with pedestrians, motor cars and the ubiquitous omnibuses with their placard advertisements. Ursula lost herself in the swell of the crowd, finding herself going in and out of stores, turning down side streets, returning and crisscrossing Oxford street, all the while letting herself be blindly drawn along by the pedestrians' currents and streams. Outside one of the glass and brass doorways to Selfridges she saw Baroness Dalrymple-Guiney, society hostess and patron of the local Belgravian debating society. She was pulling on her long gloves and wrapping her long mink stole around her. Thankful to see a friendly face, Ursula approached with a weary smile. She was only steps away when Baroness Dalrymple-Guiney shot her a look of such disgust that it stopped Ursula in mid-stride.

"Hesta," Baroness Dalrymple-Guiney addressed her lady's maid who was a couple of paces behind her. "Pray come help me. I'm afraid my stole is dragging along in the mud. Really Oxford Street is a nightmare. You never know what filth you might encounter."

Ursula could feel no more humiliated than if Lady Dalrymple-Guiney had ground her into the pavement with the heel of her elegant boots. Three women who were about to enter Selfridges turned round at her words and stared at Ursula.

Ursula backed away, only to collide with Lady Catherine Winterton, exiting with a pile of packages in her arms.

"Ursula!" Lady Winterton cried. "I hardly expected to see you here!"

Ursula knew Lady Winterton from the local branch meetings of the Women's Social and Political Union and always envied her ability to move seamlessly between her political work and her role in London society. Today she looked as unruffled as always in an elegant navy blue day suit that complemented both her chestnut hair and her deep blue eyes.

Ursula was shaking too much to reply. She watched Baroness Dalrymple-Guiney's Rolls Royce drive up and her chauffeur help her into the rear passenger seat.

"Ursula? Are you feeling ill?" Lady Winterton exclaimed.

"No," Ursula responded unsteadily. "Just give me a minute. I will be fine."

Lady Winterton looked over Ursula's shoulder and cried. "Oh! No wonder you're looking peaky. I've just seen that horrid little man Hackett from the *Daily Mail* across the way. He's probably been following you."

"Oh God." In all the turmoil, Ursula had forgotten about the press. No doubt Hackett had witnessed the entire episode with Lady Dalrymple-Guiney.

"Here," Lady Winterton asked with a brief glance at her own Lady's maid who was hovering a few feet away. "Do you fancy a cup of tea? Grace can take everything home for me, and I'm sure it will make you feel better. You must be in a dreadful way, my dear. Obviously, I've read all about it in the newspapers by now. But I didn't like to call—didn't feel you would want visitors just yet."

"No," Ursula admitted, color slowly returning to her cheeks.

"How is Lord Wrotham holding up?" Lady Winterton queried. Although her tone was neutral, Ursula noticed the way her teeth chewed at her lower lip, as she waited for Ursula to respond. She suspected that, despite her words, Lady Winterton was a little uneasy about being seen in Ursula's presence. Although she and Ursula knew each other from the WSPU and from their work on encoding messages within the organization, their friendship had cooled slightly since Ursula's engagement to Lord Wrotham.

Lady Winterton's husband died five years ago and, since he had been an old university acquaintance of Lord Wrotham's from Balliol, there was a long history of friendship between them. While Ursula suspected Lady Winterton's feelings for Lord Wrotham may have deepened over the years, causing a measure of friction, this seemed unimportant now. At least Lady Winterton was still speaking to her.

"I've just come from seeing him," Ursula answered. "In Brixton, I mean. I think I was trying to lose myself, quite literally, in the crowd when I bumped into you."

"Understandable," Lady Winterton said and Ursula was grateful for her compassion.

"Will you at least join us on Monday?" Lady Winterton continued. She was referring to the regular WSPU meeting held each Monday evening. Ursula shook her head.

"I know that seems like such an irrelevancy right now. But you could probably do with the support," Lady Winterton continued, ignoring Ursula's obvious skepticism, as she nimbly stepped out of the way of a man delivering wicker hampers. "Believe it or not, there are those among our set who view him as an Irish patriot. Strange world we live in, is it not?!"

Ursula blinked rapidly, unsure what to say.

"You wouldn't have had the chance to read some of the more radical editorials, I'm sure, but I believe Lord Wrotham has garnered quite a following in Irish republican and anarchist circles," Lady Winterton commented with a wry smile. Though she was a supporter of female suffrage, Lady Winterton remained true to her class. She did not subscribe to any of the more radical, socialist ideals that Ursula was renowned for.

"The world is a very strange place indeed . . ." Ursula murmured. She noticed that Lady Winterton had not said anything about whether she believed Lord Wrotham was guilty of the charges laid against him.

There was an awkward pause followed by an exchange of pleasantries about the weather that struck Ursula as both stilted and mundane—but then no one quite knew what to say. The etiquette books did not cover 'charges of treason' in their pages and, after bidding each other farewell, Lady Winterton and Ursula separated. After only a few steps however Ursula felt compelled to turn back.

"Lady Winterton!" she called out. "Just out of interest, did you ever meet a man by the name of McTiernay? He was at Balliol with Lord Wrotham and your husband I believe."

Lady Winterton scrunched up her delicate nose as she thought for a moment, before answering. "I suppose I must have at one time or other," she replied. "Though Nigel had been sent down from university by the time I met him. McTiernay had a reputation for being a firebrand though—I certainly remember that—but why do you ask? Is he involved in some way?"

"I don't know exactly how," Ursula admitted. "But then, I'm not sure I know anything anymore."

Ursula kept a close eye on the reporter, Hackett, as he shadowed her along Oxford Street. She also began to notice, to her further embarrassment, that she was attracting ever increasing attention from passersby. There were whispers behind cupped hands, pointed stares and, as she hastened toward Marble Arch, an occasional insult muttered as she walked past.

A man stood on a soap box on the corner of Park Lane, set apart from the usual eccentrics that populated the Speaker's Corner of Hyde Park. He wore a placard pronouncing the 'end is nigh' with a caricature of an English lord bowing to the Kaiser. It seemed strangely ominous and Ursula bent her head to avoid looking at him, as she hurried toward the sleek silver Rolls Royce waiting for her on the corner.

Mindful of what had happened with the staff at Bromley Hall and with today's humiliations still raw, Ursula was determined to speak with her servants as soon as possible. None of them could fail to be aware of the seriousness of the accusations leveled against Lord Wrotham, they had been trumpeted by the news boys all across London since the newspapers announced the arrest. Nor could they fail to understand the implications for Ursula. A household's servants were, after all, only as reputable as the master or mistress and Ursula's position in society was now more tenuous than ever.

Once back at her Chester Square home, Ursula summoned Biggs into the study. She stood beside one of the long bookshelves that lined the study walls, and ran a nervous hand across the row of leather and gilt-edged spines.

"I need to gather everyone together to explain the current circumstances, but before I do, Biggs, I wanted to ask you whether anyone has spoken to you about leaving"—Ursula hesitated, unsure how to continue.

Biggs straightened his grey waistcoat and cleared his throat. "I regret to say that two members of staff have already spoken to me about tendering their resignations."

Ursula gripped the edge of the book shelf.

"Who?" she whispered.

"Mrs. Stewart and Bridget, I'm afraid."

Ursula closed her eyes, her head throbbing. She could scarcely believe it. She had spent her whole life with Mrs. Stewart. She was the one who had comforted her the day her mother died, the one whose kindness and loyalty she had never questioned. Ursula knew, however, that Mrs. Stewart had long been concerned over the implications of Ursula's behavior—from her defense of Winifred Stanford-Jones to the impropriety of her relationship with Lord Wrotham prior to their engagement. Ursula had even overheard her voicing her qualms to Biggs, but she had never thought, never even considered, that it would come to this. She could not have predicted that a threat to Lord Wrotham's reputation, rather than her own, would have finally tipped the scales.

"She thinks it's because of my influence, doesn't she?" Ursula said hoarsely. Biggs was in no doubt who she was talking about. He nodded as Ursula stumbled to take a seat in the armchair behind the large mahogany desk.

"Where are they?" Ursula asked,

"Mrs. Stewart and Bridget are both in their quarters upstairs. I told them they'd best pack and be ready to leave."

"Yes, I see," Ursula replied, but truth be told she felt as though she was only beginning to comprehend the full ramifications of Lord Wrotham's arrest.

"Before you send them down," Ursula said slowly, dreading what she must now ask. "Tell me what of Cook? What about Samuels? Or Julia?"

"Cook informed me she is too set in her ways to seek another position. She will stay."

"Hardly a ringing endorsement," Ursula murmured. "But I thank her for it."

"Samuels also intends to stay, for now at least. Although, he confided in me that he has received an offer to take up an apprenticeship as a garage mechanic. I fear he may not be long in domestic service."

"And Julia?" Ursula swallowed quickly. "What has she said?"

"As you are no doubt aware, Julia has become increasingly drawn to missionary work, but she appears content to minister to you, for the time-being." Ursula detected a note of censure in his voice as if she had been naive to expect anything more.

Mechanically, Ursula reached over and lifted the lid of the silver cigarette box that her father had always kept on his desk. With shaking fingers she lit a cigarette and tried to restore some semblance of equanimity. Ursula leaned back in her chair and drew on the cigarette. Was she really little more than an object of their pity?

"Now, I must ask about you," she hesitated. "You who have always shown my family such loyalty, must I see you leave as well?"

"You need never ask the question," Biggs answered and his gaze never wavered. "I remain, as I have always been. I hope I need say no more."

"No," Ursula replied with a weak smile, "and, please, forgive me for asking. I should have known better than to doubt you."

Biggs bowed stiffly. A slight flush behind his ears the only sign of his discomfiture.

"Shall I send in Bridget and Mrs. Stewart?" he asked.

"No," Ursula replied. "Summon the others. I want to speak to them first."

Biggs looked uncertain.

"It is all right, Biggs," Ursula reassured him. "I will not take long, and I trust you know me well enough to know that I won't throw Mrs. Stewart or Bridget out on the streets after dark. Samuels can either drive them or they can stay tonight and leave first thing in the morning. I have no intention of doing anything that may provoke undue attention or comment."

Biggs simply nodded and then exited the room to fetch the other servants.

Ursula closed her eyes and prepared herself.

Biggs was the first to enter, followed by Samuels, who, in his chauffeur's uniform and boots, still reeked of grease and petrol. Ursula was sure he had been hard at work checking that she hadn't caused any damage to the Bugatti during her trip to Bromley Hall. Samuels was very protective of her motor cars and, despite successfully teaching Ursula to drive, remained skeptical that women should be allowed on the road at all. Cook arrived next, wiping her hands on her white apron and straightening her cap. She rarely left the kitchen and looked ill at ease in the unfamiliar surroundings of Ursula's study. Catching sight of one of Ursula's latest acquisitions, a lithograph by Paul Klee, she gave a sniff of disapproval. Finally Julia walked in the room, clutching the bible that was now her constant companion. She looked around anxiously, noting Mrs. Stewart and Bridget's absence.

Ursula cleared her throat and began: "I know these are difficult times, but I want to reassure you all that I am grateful for your continued loyalty and support." She looked around, trying to gauge their reaction. "Your loyalty will, however, be sorely tested in the coming weeks. This morning a notice appeared in *The Times* announcing that I have called off my engagement to Lord Wrotham."

Julia went pale and swayed dangerously. Samuels reached over and steadied her before escorting her to a chair. Cook responded with a snort of disgust. She was never one to countenance Julia's 'overwrought' emotions, as she called them.

"I must, for all our sakes, distance myself from what has happened," Ursula continued. "I warn you that *we*—and I do mean *all* of us—will be subject to a great deal of unwanted publicity, not to say distress, over the coming weeks. Already there are two amongst us, Mrs. Stewart and Bridget, who have decided to leave rather than face such scrutiny."

Ursula waited for the full import of her words to sink in. It was hard to say such things to a group of people she had known and trusted most her life, but she knew it had to be done. She took a deep breath, dreading what had to come next. "I do not wish anyone who feels at all compromised by what has happened to Lord Wrotham, to feel that they have to remain in my employment. So if anyone else considers that it would be improper to stay"—Ursula's words caught in her throat—"You have the opportunity to hand in your resignation to me this evening without fear of censure. I promise you that I will respect your decision, and provide you with a full and glowing reference."

Everyone remained silent, except Cook who, with eyes half-closed had begun muttering under her breath. Julia remained in her seat, a stricken expression on her normally rosy-cheeked face.

"There will be people, reporters and the like, who will offer you money for your story," Ursula reminded them. "They may offer you money to say almost anything about me, or, indeed, about Lord Wrotham. I must tell you now that I cannot tolerate any disloyalty. If you should tell the press anything at all, I will prosecute for slander, and ensure that all of London society are aware of the reason for your dismissal."

Biggs straightened his coat tails. "Miss Marlow," he said solemnly. "I hope I speak on behalf of all of us here when I say that we are committed to preserving the good name of both the Marlow and Wrotham households."

"Thank you Biggs," Ursula replied. "So am I."

CHAPTER FOUR

CHESTER SQUARE

IT WAS CLOSE TO MIDNIGHT when Ursula, sitting in her study reading a book of Christina Rossetti's poetry that Lord Wrotham had given her, heard the bell ring at the servants' entrance below. In truth she had not been reading, but rather turning the events of the last few days over and over in her mind. Images from her interview with Mrs. Stewart, barely two hours ago, were still raw. She could see Mrs. Stewart sitting before her, her gaze teary but defiant. Unable to face another emotional confrontation, Ursula had cut off Mrs. Stewart's lengthy explanation in mid-sentence saying coldly: "I have no desire to hear your reasons, no doubt you are satisfied with them. I simply wish to know whether you require a reference from me." Mrs. Stewart's face, as she heard Ursula's words, haunted her still. This was not how either of them had wanted things to end.

It seemed a long time till morning and, with her head still aching despite the Bayer Aspirin powder she took earlier, Ursula was nowhere near being able to sleep.

The servants' doorbell rang once more. Ursula put down the soft, leather-bound book, marking her place with the pink ribbon and checked the mantel clock. She rubbed her eyes, murmured, and decided she had better go investigate on her own.

She met Biggs on the staircase leading up from the kitchen.

"Who is it?" she asked.

"Chief Inspector Harrison, Miss. He wishes to come upstairs and meet with you but wants to make sure all the curtains and blinds are drawn."

Ursula raised an eyebrow. "All this cloak and dagger seems a bit unnecessary—the press are hardly likely to be skulking about near midnight—but you can reassure him everything is closed and he can come on up."

She stretched her neck and rolled her shoulders, trying to clear her head.

"May I offer you and the Chief Inspector some refreshment?" Biggs asked.

"Tea would be lovely," she replied. "Thank you."

Biggs padded off down the stairs, soft-shoed as always.

Ursula walked back into the study and turned off the geometric glass and bronze lamp on her desk. The room dimmed, illuminated now only by the electric standard lamp in the far corner of the room. Ursula moved a chair next to the fretwork screen in front of the fireplace for Harrison and eased down in the deep leather armchair opposite.

Chief Inspector Harrison entered, closing the study door behind him carefully.

"Miss Marlow," he said and paused beside the chair. He looked uncomfortable at being alone in her presence.

"Sit down, please," Ursula urged. "You look tired," she said. "I've asked Biggs to bring us some tea. It's late. Have you had dinner? Supper?"

Harrison shook his head as he sat down.

"Then I'll get Biggs to see what he can rustle up," Ursula replied. She leaned forward resting her chin on her hands and gazed at him expectantly.

Harrison's face was inscrutable. "I came because"—he chewed on his lip—"I think I might need your help."

"Really?" Ursula answered, leaning back as she crossed her arms.

"Look," Harrison replied. "I know it didn't appear so at first, but I've had time to mull over things a bit more and I've started to have . . ."

"Doubts?" Ursula prompted.

"More than doubts," Harrison answered. "I'm starting to be concerned about where this investigation is heading. Sir Buckley's convinced Lord Wrotham's guilty, but I'm worried no one has taken a step back and thought about Admiral Smythe's files or the circumstances in which we found them." Harrison traced the outline of his mustache with his index finger. "When I first moved to Scotland Yard I was assigned to the forgery section. Most of the cases involved obvious document forgeries—mortgages, wills and the like but one thing my experience taught me was to use my instinct. More often than not, if it looked too good to be true, it probably was."

"You think the files could be forgeries?" Ursula queried.

Harrison licked his lips; he still looked uneasy. "I'm just saying, it seems a little too convenient that we found incriminating files in Admiral Smythe's study—like they were deliberately left or even staged for us to find as soon as Admiral Smythe was reported missing. We only found Admiral Smythe's notebook, however, after an extensive search that uncovered his secret wall safe. All the entries in the notebook were encrypted—but the files we found—"

"Were not?" Ursula supplied.

Harrison nodded.

"Do you think someone deliberately planted those files to implicate Lord Wrotham?" she asked.

There was a tap at the door and Biggs, entered carrying a tea tray and, preempting Ursula's request, a plate piled high with Lancashire cheese, bread, and pickled onions for Harrison's supper. Biggs placed the tray down on the sideboard behind Harrison's chair, passed him the plate and poured them each a cup of Darjeeling tea. Harrison looked strangely embarrassed, as if he had not expected to be treated with such hospitality.

"Thank you Biggs," Ursula said absently, her mind still processing what Harrison said. Biggs exited the room in silence. "Has Sir Buckley sent the files off for handwriting or fingerprint analysis?" she asked Harrison.

53

Harrison's brow lifted in surprise, but he answered. "Yes, or rather I arranged for that to be undertaken. It will take some time of course. Fingerprint analysis is a relatively new science after all and I'm not sure what they will be able to find."

Ursula pursed her lips, deep in thought. "So tell me," she said, trying to ignore the pounding in her head. "What did these files purport to say?"

Harrison hastily took a bite of bread and cheese and a quick swig of tea before answering. "One of the files provides details of an alleged meeting in December 1911 at the castle of Lord Wrotham's cousin, Count Frederich von Bernstorff-Hollweg."

"Second cousin," Ursula reminded him.

"Yes, well . . ." Harrison continued awkwardly. "As you, no doubt, know by now, the Count is one the main witnesses in the case against Lord Wrotham. But at this meeting there was also a man called Fergus McTiernay—another old friend of Lord Wrotham's from Balliol."

"Yes," Ursula prompted him.

"McTiernay is a known Irish Republican sympathizer even though he's a gentleman. Special Branch has been watching him for years but, up till now, we always believed he was an advocate of political rather than military action. But at this meeting it seems as though plans to sell information regarding the naval defenses on the South-West coast of England were discussed—a plan that ultimately led to a conspiracy to assassinate and overthrow the British government in Ireland."

Harrison took some more bread and cheese and Ursula noticed how much his manners reminded her of her father. It was in way he hesitated as he decided how to hold the knife and his deliberations on how best to tear the bread. It was always the first thing that revealed your class, she thought ruefully. Harrison, like her father, never could escape his origins.

Ursula got to her feet, crossed the room and picked up her notepad and pencil. She returned to her seat and starting taking notes.

"Tell me more about McTiernay and Lord Wrotham's cousin," Ursula said.

"The Count is a well-known philanderer with a reputation for dabbling in whatever get rich scheme he can get his hands on. Hardly a stellar witness, yet, given his title, he moves easily among both German and British high society."

"Are he and Lord Wrotham estranged, is that why he is testifying against him?" Ursula asked.

"I was rather hoping you might be able to tell us that—for as far as we know the two men were good friends as well as relations. The Count is also said to be favored by the Kaiser himself—possibly because of his military aspirations, but, most likely, because of his business associations."

Ursula watched Harrison, her expression becoming steadily more guarded. "As I've already told you," she said. "Lord Wrotham has never spoken to me about the Count or his dealings with him . . ."

"The Count spends most of the year on the continent, but in the past we've had no reason to suspect he was a German agent. Perhaps Lord Wrotham mentioned meeting with the Count whilst he was been in Europe?"

"No, as I said Lord Wrotham has never mentioned the Count at all."

"Supposedly the Count was Lord Wrotham and McTiernay's contact in Germany," Harrison continued. "The deal was made to sell the information on the basis that Germany would supply arms to the Irish Republican Brotherhood and provide further military support should there be an uprising in Ireland or a war with Germany."

"That part still doesn't make any sense to me, given Lord Wrotham's politics."

Harrison exhaled loudly. "I know, but Admiral Smythe seemed to think—at least in the files we found—that Lord Wrotham had been drawn to the nationalist cause in his youth and, since working with the Admiral on a number of missions, had become disillusioned with the British government. Given his family ties with Germany, financial problems with his estate, and conflicted loyalties from his days at Balliol, Lord Wrotham apparently chose to ally himself with McTiernay. Lord Wrotham's business ties and influence made him a valuable asset in securing contacts in Germany."

"I don't really see Wrotham being the disillusioned diplomat turned German spy, do you?" Ursula said. "Even if, which I entirely doubt, he was involved in any kind of radicalism in his youth"—she leaned forward once more in her chair—"he would hardly need the money after becoming engaged to me."

"You forget," Harrison reminded her. "The meeting was at the end of 1911. I believe at that time you had rejected his Lordship's offer of marriage."

Ursula flushed.

"But I admit," Harrison conceded. "The picture that Admiral Smythe paints in his files is not one that entirely fits with the Lord Wrotham that I know."

"And what of McTiernay then—what has he got to say? Does he corroborate the Count's story?"

"McTiernay has disappeared," Harrison said bitterly. "Special Branch no longer has the network of informers or friends within the Nationalists that we used to have, so he's going to be hard to find. We suspect he's gone to ground somewhere in Ireland."

"Is McTiernay married? Does he have family that you can contact?" Ursula asked.

"McTiernay's wife's Fenian political views are well known—she is also a member of the Irish Women's Franchise League." Ursula was well aware of the Irish women's group dedicated to securing votes for women and of Harrison's animosity towards the suffrage issue.

Ursula felt her hackles rise. "I suppose you think because of that I am somehow in league with her?"

It was Harrison's turn to flush. "We're more concerned about finding Lord Wrotham's chauffeur, Archibald James," he said, changing the topic. "As I recall, his Lordship told you to ask James to drive you to Bromley Hall."

"I have been unable to contact Lord Wrotham's chauffeur," Ursula replied. "And I'm not sure what he's got to do with any of this, anyway." Her right foot tapped the upholstered skirt of her chair.

"You haven't seen or heard from him then?" Harrison asked.

"No, of course I haven't," Ursula replied.

Ursula's cup of tea went untouched beside her.

"Surely Lord Wrotham must have mentioned his meeting in Germany in December 1911 . . ." Harrison probed. "Or perhaps he discussed McTiernay with you? He's more likely to have been candid with you about his dealings with the Count and McTiernay given your well-known political support for Irish Home Rule."

"Lord Wrotham never saw fit to tell me anything about this meeting," Ursula answered, stiffly. "Or about his friendships from Balliol."

"What about any of his other visits abroad? Perhaps he confided in you about these, but you never understood the implications—until now? Maybe if you think hard you'll recall something—it may be trivial—but it might be enough to help Lord Wrotham . . ."

By now Ursula was sure his presence here was a ruse and nothing more. It was clear Harrison had only given her information to make her believe that he thought Lord Wrotham was innocent—when, all along, he was only trying to draw her out and discover what information Wrotham may have shared with her.

"I never realized," Ursula said, leaning forward and pinning him with an icy stare. "How stupid you really thought I was."

After Chief Inspector Harrison left, Ursula tried desperately to sleep but she found herself tossing and turning in agitation. Harrison's duplicity sickened her. Her thoughts awhirl she kept coming back to the names of the men: Smythe. McTiernay. Wrotham. Count von Bernstorff-Hollweg. All four of them Balliol men. All four of them now somehow involved in a plot to sell Britain's military secrets. Sleep eventually gained a foothold and, as she slipped off the precipice into the dark, deep chasm, her final thought was of Oxford. It was the first door to Lord Wrotham's past that she needed to unlock.

CHAPTER FIVE

BALLIOL COLLEGE, OXFORD

URSULA DECIDED TO LET SAMUELS drive her up to Oxford in 'Bertie' rather than risk breaking-down en-route in the Bugatti. Although she managed to leave via the servants' entrance to her Chester Square home without undue harassment, the journey took longer than anticipated after Samuels spotted a reporter following them just as they approached High Wycombe. It took a lengthy detour and some ingenuity on Samuels' part to evade their follower and resume their course towards Abingdon and Oxford.

It was with some trepidation that Ursula left for the journey to Oxford. She felt tainted by the scandals that had dogged her since she left Somerville College and unworthy of returning. Although the main aim of her visit was to investigate the relationship between Wrotham, Smythe, McTiernay and Balliol college, she could not help but be wistful on her own account—for what might have been. She had taken her finals in the end of Trinity Term in 1908. Back then the world held such promise. Her father was alive and she still believed she could convince him to let her make her own way in the world as a political journalist. Sitting in the back seat of Bertie she heaved a sigh as she remembered cramming one night for her finals, a cup of hot cocoa steaming in one hand, a torch in the other and a copy of Homer's *Iliad* propped up on her knees. Seated on the narrow bed in the airless room that had been her home for the past three years, she had been was content to switch off her torch and watch the moonlight inch its way across the page as the night drew on. She had felt so restful at that moment, held in the eternal spell of stone and mortar, that she had felt as if, were she to close her eyes for even a moment, she would drift into an infinite, book-filled sleep, never to awaken.

Now, as they drove up Headington Hill and caught the first glimpses of Oxford's shimmering spires, those memories seemed little more than a cruel illusion, sent to taunt her with images of all that the world could have been. A vision of innocence, in which she had all the promise of a future career and love, untouched by scandal, untouched by death.

Samuels with a quick glance round, slowed the motor car. "Would you like me to stop, Miss?" he asked.

"No," Ursula replied, falling back against the leather seat. "Not this time."

For the first two years, Ursula had arrived in Oxford by train, lugging her trunk along the platform and joining the chattering hordes of other young men and women calling for porters and embracing their fellow students who were also returning. In her final year, however, Samuels would drive her to Somerville, and pull over, just about now, so Ursula could jump out, climb the stile on the fence by an old farmhouse and take in her first glimpse of Oxford.

Now she contented herself with the view from the car window, slumped in her seat, feeling the cool winter air seeping in through her shoes and stockings. There were still traces of frost on the hedgerows after a cold night but the recent spell of milder weather had beckoned a few hardy spring flowers to venture forth, pushing up through the hard ground along the edge of the rutted road. They passed St. Stephen's House and headed over Magdalen Bridge before turning down Longwall Street. Ursula noticed that nothing seemed to have changed since her last day at Somerville; the students still weaved their way along Holywell Street on their bicycles, and the gates of Balliol were as graceful and imposing as ever.

She asked the porter at the lodge if she could to be shown to Professor Prendergast's rooms at the college. As a Senior Fellow of the college he had rooms at the back of the old quadrangle looking out over the Fellows' garden. The head porter escorted her as they passed beneath the two archways that led through the small front quadrangle to the large quadrangle behind it, where they stopped at a door marked VI, leading to one of the wooden staircases to the rooms above.

"Up the stairs and first room on your left, Miss. He's expecting you."

"Thank you."

"Would you like me to provide your chauffeur with some refreshment?"

"Oh, I'm sure a cup of tea would go down a treat. Samuels has been driving for hours."

The head porter tipped his cap and walked back across the quadrangle. Ursula opened the wooden door and sniffed the familiar musty smell she had come to love at Somerville: the smell of centuries of dust on wood and stone, and the permeation of damp rainwater from winters past. She closed her eyes for a moment before ascending the narrow winding wood staircase.

She came upon the door marked with a white card in a metal nameplate on the door, Professor Evan Prendergast, M.Phil, Professor of Moral Philosophy and Law, Senior Fellow of Jurisprudence. She took in a deep breath and knocked.

The door opened almost immediately and Ursula was startled to find herself face to face with the antithesis of the professor she had been expecting. On the telephone, he had sounded like a frail and doddering old academic, full of stutters and hesitations. But now, as she viewed the sprightly looking man with wild white hair and bushy white eyebrows, she was taken aback. He was clearly well into his seventies but despite this his eyes were full of remarkable clarity and intelligence. He held out an eager hand, crying: "Come on in, my dear! I hope the journey down was suitably uncomfortable . . . I always find that any journey worth taking is always uncomfortable!"

Ursula stammered out an incoherent response as she entered the room. She took off her brown velvet hat and leather gloves and placed them gingerly on the top of a stack of books piled up next to what must have once been a coat stand, but which now teetered in the corner, looking as though it could no longer sustain either coat or hat.

"Take a seat, take a seat. I have tea if you wish, or perhaps a drop of sherry?"

"Tea, please. That would be lovely."

Ursula sat down and as Professor Prendergast hummed around pouring the tea, took the opportunity to take in the room. Again, everything was different from what she had expected. She had anticipated a room that looked like ones the tutors and fellows at Somerville maintained—muddled and cluttered with the feel of a prefect's study like those she grown up with at the Skipton Ladies Academy. This room looked like hurricane strength winds had torn the place apart, scattering papers and books over every conceivable surface. There was a narrow pathway leading from the door to the large desk and two filing cabinets in the corner, one armchair for visitors of well scuffed and fading brown leather, and a series of massive bookcases lining the walls, jammed with books. Beside the armchair was a tall stack of books—all new leather and crisp cut paper. Ursula glanced down and picked up a copy. It was a book by Professor Prendergast on *Moral Thinking and Rationality*.

"Er, thank you for agreeing to see me, Professor Prendergast." Ursula began, picking a stack of pamphlets off the chair. The top one was entitled *Hobbes' Leviathan and the Justification of Regicide*.

"But of course, though I suspect that you are not here to seek philosophical guidance with respect to Lord Wrotham," he smiled and took the pamphlets from Ursula. "Especially not this sort of guidance"—he said with a grin.

"Hardly," Ursula responded. "The last thing I want right now is an affirmation of a Hobbesian view of the world!"

Professor Prendergast looked at her curiously. "You've read the *Leviathan*?"

"Not all of it, I must confess. We touched upon it in a class I took on political philosophy."

"Where did you study?"

"Somerville," she replied with a smile.

"An Oxford educated fiancée?! Excellent!!" Professor Prendergast clapped his hands together. "Of course, I should have expected nothing less of Lord Wrotham."

Ursula blinked. "You're the first person ever to make that comment. Most people seem to think I'm the very last sort of person he would marry."

"Ah, yes. But they did not know Lord Wrotham when he was young," he replied, clasping his fingers together as he rocked forward on his chair.

"Well, Professor Prendergast, I can see I'm going to have to work hard to find out more after that tantalizing glimpse," she admitted. "To be honest, my wish in coming here was to discover more about Lord Wrotham and Admiral Smythe's time here at Balliol. I'm trying to understand how they both came to be mixed up in this unfortunate state of affairs and whether that has any connection to Oxford."

"I can't imagine that it does—but you seem a sensible woman and you certainly impressed upon me the urgency of your enquiries on the telephone yesterday," Prendergast responded. "Even though I doubt I can shed any light on recent events, I'm happy to oblige and answer your questions. Lord Wrotham was one of my most promising students. He was a natural leader and a keen scholar with a strong sense of loyalty to the college. I cannot think of anyone less likely to betray their country." Once he got going Prendergast had a beautiful Welsh lilt to his voice.

"Can you imagine any reason Admiral Smythe might have had in betraying Lord Wrotham?"

"None whatsoever. Admiral Smythe was another of Lord Wrotham's tutors and as far as I could tell they had a close and cordial relationship. I've seen both men reasonably regularly even after they left here, at college dinners in London and the like. I know they remained friends and I've never heard of any rift between them."

"What about Lord Wrotham's friend, Mr. McTiernay?"

"What about him my dear? He and Wrotham were terrific chums. We called them 'the inseparables' even though they spent most of their time in heated political debates."

"McTiernay is supposed to be quite the Irish firebrand," Ursula said.

Professor Prendergast smiled indulgently. "He made no attempt to hide his radical politics but he was charming with it—and he was the only man I ever saw, apart from myself of course, who managed to best Lord Wrotham in a debate. He was also one of the finest batsmen on the Balliol cricket team."

Ursula rubbed her nose. She hoped this interview was going to yield a little more than misty-eyed reminiscences.

"It seems strange to me," Ursula said, "that Lord Wrotham and McTiernay should have been friends at all given Lord Wrotham's pro-unionist views."

Prendergast broke into another wide smile. "My dear, there are many gentlemen to whom politics are no bar to friendship. Why the two of them even formed their own private debating society. I think it was something rather like 'The Other Club' in London."

Ursula had heard of 'The Other Club,' co-founded by liberal politician and First Lord of the Admiralty, Winston Churchill, and conservative 'Tory' parliamentarian, Frederick Edwin Smith. The purpose of this club was ostensibly to offer a venue in which personal friendships could form (over wine and dinner), despite the rancor of political divisions.

"They encouraged," Prendergast continued, "fierce debate between members across the political spectrum. At the end of the debate however they all had dinner, drank copious amounts of wine and spirits, and toasted the ability of high minded men to put their differences aside and enjoy each other's company."

"May I ask for the names of those in this private debating society?" Ursula asked, digging out her pencil and notebook.

Prendergast raised a white bushy eyebrow. "My dear, the whole point was that it was *private*. Names were not bandied about and, as far as I was aware, it was an invitation only affair."

"Were you or Admiral Smythe members?"

"At an undergraduate society meeting?!" Prendergast replied in mock horror, refusing to answer her question directly.

"But Lord Wrotham and McTiernay were definitely members."

"Yes. Along with Lord Wrotham's cousin—Count Hollweg something or other. Oh, and young Winterton too, I expect, though he was a hopeless debater. I think he was in it for a while before he was sent down."

Ursula knew from Lady Winterton that her now-deceased husband had spent two terms at Balliol before being sent down for lack of academic progress. As if reading her thoughts Prendergast said, "Winterton never was much of a scholar. Terrific fun of course. He and McTiernay could drink most men under the table, but Winterton was the sort who could never knuckle down. I think it was at the end of his second year that he was sent down. Didn't seem to bother him though—enjoyed the London and Dublin society scene much more than these moldy old halls."

Ursula had a sudden vision of a young Lord Winterton, charming and roguish. She could well imagine Lady Winterton's attraction. She was then reminded of another Balliol man—one certainly far less appealing.

"Was Sir Reginald Buckley a member of this debating society by any chance?" Ursula asked, trying unsuccessfully to maintain an air of impartiality.

"Who?" Prendergast asked blankly.

"Sir Reginald Buckley—I believe you were also his tutor—He's with the War Office now . . ." Ursula racked her brains to try and think of any other distinguishing trait that was not insulting to Sir Reginald Buckley.

"Buckley . . . hmmn . . . name's not ringing a bell," Prendergast rocked back in his chair. "Oh," he said after a moment. "You mean old 'Buckles'!"

Ursula raised an eyebrow.

"Oh yes, 'Buckles' or should I say Sir Buckley now. Son of some minor cousin of the royal family. Totally undistinguished academic record if I recall. Probably left with a third class degree." Prendergast screwed up his eyes as if remembering something particularly distasteful. "I do recall he wrote dreadful essays! Nothing more than rehashed, unverified facts, muddled up with other people's opinions." The professor finished with a sniff.

"Can you remember anything else about him?" Ursula prompted.

"Apart from his inordinate love of fine food and wine? . . . No."

"Do you know why there may be animosity between him and Lord Wrotham?"

"Good Lord, no! Wrotham wouldn't have given him the time of day. Probably just professional jealousy. You know the sort of thing—Wrotham, the precocious younger son, full of ambition and intelligence, and there was old 'Buckles', the eminently forgettable son of sir nobody in particular."

Ursula wasn't sure how to respond so she moved on to the question of Count Friedrich von Bernstorff-Hollweg. When asked, Professor Prendergast had nothing to say, only that he had not been the Count's tutor and had therefore very little occasion to know him. Ursula stifled a sigh. This interview wasn't being as helpful as she had hoped.

Ursula took the opportunity to look about the room and her gaze took in the jumble of photographs perched on top of the tall wooden filing cabinet behind Prendergast's desk.

"I like to keep a memento of all my top students over the years," Prendergast said. Sure enough, each photograph included the professor standing beside two or three young men in academic caps and gowns. Her eyes lighted upon one particular photograph in an ornate silver frame. She squinted, not quite ready to believe the image.

"Yes, it is him." Professor Prendergast got to his feet and pulled down the photo frame, wiping the dust off the glass with the sleeve of his tweed jacket.

He handed it to Ursula. "That's young Wrotham on the right there with McTiernay and I do believe that's Admiral Smythe walking across the quadrangle behind them. It must have been taken at the end of their final term. Before they all headed off to Guyana."

Ursula looked inquiringly.

"McTiernay and Lord Wrotham's cousin were headed there on some fool scheme to discover gold or diamonds and Lord Wrotham joined them. Apparently he and Admiral Smythe were to assist with the dispute over the border between Guyana and Venezuela. Sounded terribly dull to me, but I always suspected it was the first of many special ... er ... diplomatic trips the two of them undertook—I mean a naval man is hardly interested in a boundary dispute now is he?"

"Did they ever speak of these "missions"?" Ursula asked with barely restrained eagerness.

"Of course not," Professor Prendergast looked at her intently. "You're barking up the wrong tree if you think I know anything about that sort of thing, my dear!"

Ursula shoulders sagged.

"I haven't been much help have I?" Professor Prendergast's voice was suddenly gentle. "I think you were hoping that there was some sordid underbelly to their time here at Balliol, am I right?"

Ursula sighed. "I was hoping for more," she admitted. "But I'm really only just beginning my investigations. All I have at the moment are unanswered questions."

"Ah—well, it could be worse." Prendergast replied, pulling his pipe from the pocket of his tweed jacket. "They could be unanswerable questions!"

Professor Prendergast lit his pipe and started coughing as soon as he started drawing on it. Ursula waited for the coughing fit to finish before carefully placing the photograph back on the desk.

"Keep it," he urged. "Something to remind you of the bright summer of youth in these troubling times."

Ursula stammered out her thanks and then couldn't resist asking, "what was Lord Wrotham like while he was here?"

Professor Prendergast laughed. "Do you think he has changed that much?!"

"I don't know."

"Well, things were different I must admit before that terrible accident"—he paused—"Now what was her name?"

"Lizzie Wexcombe," Ursula replied softly. Lizzie Wexcombe was Lord Wrotham's first love who died in a riding accident when he was only nineteen. The real tragedy for him, however, was the discovery, after her death, that she never really loved him but had been 'spreading her favors' among many men. Ursula was not convinced he had ever recovered from that shock.

"Yes. Before that all happened he was like many other young men of Oxford—all bluster and ambition. Though he had more brains than most. But the accident knocked the stuffing out of him. Happened at the end of his second year I think. Anyway, that final year he was different. More secretive. Closed off from the world."

"And McTiernay?" Ursula asked.

"Oh, a charming lad!" Professor Prendergast exclaimed. "One of the few Catholic students we had.[1] I still remember his paper on Thomas Aquinas. Inspired."

Ursula opened her mouth but Professor Prendergast answered before she even got the question out.

"Admiral Smythe—or rather Captain Smythe, as he then was, came from a long line of naval men so it was obvious where he was going to end up. But he was forcibly retired on the grounds of ill-health. That's when he decided to come and teach here. I think he became quite the mentor to young Lord Wrotham, especially after the incident with Miss Wexcombe—you see Admiral Smythe never married, but I always wondered if there wasn't some tragedy in his past too—but he never spoke of it. I just felt there must have been something and that was what drew the two men together"—He exhaled loudly–"It's awful to think he is now missing."

"Yes," Ursula agreed. "Unfortunately, no one seems to have any clues as to his possible whereabouts either. If he was—I don't know—in difficulties, who do you think he'd turn to?"

"Aside from Lord Wrotham you mean? No idea."

"There's never been any hint of a possible marriage for him?"

"Good Lord, no!"

"But there's never been any insinuation of . . ." Ursula let her question languish.

"No, no . . . Nothing of that sort either! And believe me, we knew that when we saw it. No, as I said, I just suspected there'd been some heartbreak of some sort when he was a lad from which he'd never quite recovered. Wary of women don't you know—but then so was Wrotham."

---

1 Until 1854, attendees at Oxford had to accept the doctrines of the Church of England in order to take a degree. Even after this was changed, the Catholic Church issued a decree in 1867 forbidding Catholics to attend Oxford University. This was relaxed in 1895, although some Catholics did attend the university before this decree was lifted.

"Sounds like you knew them both pretty well," Ursula said. *More than you're admitting to me*, she thought.

"Oh not really," Professor Prendergast responded. He fiddled with the fountain pen on his desk absentmindedly.

"But both Admiral Smythe and Lord Wrotham would come to you if they were in any sort of difficulty, wouldn't they?" Ursula surprised herself with this question. Some instinct had taken hold of her and demanded she pay attention.

Professor Prendergast looked at her with a queer sort of smile. "Oh my dear, whatever makes you think that?"

And although she laughed lightly in return as he expected, she sensed that for the first time in their interview, Professor Prendergast was lying.

Ursula and Samuels returned from Oxford well after nightfall. As Samuels pulled up in 'Bertie', Ursula peered out the window and relaxed in the reassurance that came from being home at last. After her mother's death when she was young, Ursula and her father had grown up together, insulated in their own world. Though his textile empire stretched across the country, he had always made her feel that she was the center of that world. Now that he was gone, Ursula had endeavored to create her own cocoon, here in Chester Square. She drew upon the strength that it brought her now. She walked up the familiar stone steps, pass the place where her father had died in her arms, to the front door. Biggs greeted her with a solemn nod as he opened the door, and Julia took her coat, gloves and hat in silence.

Ursula proceeded down the hallway to what had once been her father's study. The house, however, seemed quiet without Mrs. Stewart bustling about as usual. Ursula even missed hearing Bridget singing as she polished the banister upstairs. She wandered into the study with growing despondency, her hopes for reassuring home comforts rapidly fading. With a sigh she sank down onto the leather chair, warming her legs in front of the fire. Biggs entered bearing a steaming mug of cocoa. There was comfort in that at least.

Biggs returned with a tray bearing this afternoon's post and placed it on the mahogany desk. Ursula put down her cocoa and walked over.

"Thank-you Biggs, is that all for today?" She asked, glancing at the paltry pile that awaited her.

"Yes Miss, the last post was delivered an hour ago. But this came by messenger boy. I thought you would want to see this first."

"Oh yes," Ursula looked up and took the letter from the tray quickly.

It was from Chief Inspector Harrison. She slid open the envelope with an ivory-handled letter opener.

Admiral Smythe's body washed up on the banks of the Thames a couple of hours ago. Coroner investigating cause of death. Looks like murder. Perhaps now you will be willing to talk.

CHAPTER SIX

LONDON

CHIEF INSPECTOR HARRISON WAS WAITING for her at the Northern end of Blackfriars Bridge—a place all too familiar given its proximity to the Inns of Court and Lord Wrotham's chambers at Inner Temple. Ursula had Samuels drop her a block away from the bridge but she knew that would not deter members of the press who continued to monitor her every movement. She could only hope that, in a few more weeks, interest in her story would diminish. Although, given the constant level of German paranoia, she was knew that this particular 'spy scandal' would continue to provide fodder for the alarmists in Parliament.

As Ursula approached Harrison she tried to put aside the unpleasantness of her telephone call with Admiral Smythe's sister that morning. She had been attempting to pass on her and Lord Wrotham's condolences, but when faced with the sister's vituperative and accusatory response she had almost dropped the ear-piece, certain the police were convinced that Lord Wrotham was both a murderer as well as a traitor.

Harrison was leaning over at the wrought iron arch looking down at the dirty, brackish water slapping against the pylon below.

"Well, I'm here," Ursula said refusing to hide the challenge in her tone.

"Admiral Smythe's body was found just under the second arch of the bridge. It was spotted by one of the paddle-steamers going to Greenwich," Harrison said, bypassing all preliminaries, as he continued to gaze at the water below. "the initial report from the coroner suggests the body had been in the water for probably a week or so. Given the tides and currents, the body likely entered the water upstream from here—perhaps near Westminster. Although the coroner ruled the official cause of death was drowning, Admiral Smythe was already in the throes of cyanide poisoning when he fell, or was pushed, into the water. The man had enough cyanide in his body to have killed three men."

"Cyanide?" Ursula responded.

Harrison turned from the river to face her. "The Coroner obviously cannot determine whether Smythe deliberately took it himself or if he was an unwitting recipient, but cyanide acts fast—it can't have more than ten or fifteen minutes from when he ingested it to when he fell, otherwise he would have already been dead before he hit the water."

"And you said the estimated time of death was about a week ago?" Ursula asked.

"Yes, although the coroner cannot be sure, not after this long in the water, but he estimates around seven days, perhaps more. Death probably occurred the night before Admiral Smythe's housekeeper reported him missing."

"It's possible he came down to the river after dining with Lord Wrotham and took his own life by drinking cyanide," Ursula said.

"Anything is possible," Harrison responded dryly, "but we found nothing on the body or in Smythe's office to support a suicide theory."

"You're sure he was murdered?" Ursula posed her question as a statement of fact.

"A person committing suicide is hardly likely to take cyanide if he plans on drowning himself in the river," Harrison replied. "Besides, I hear cyanide poisoning is a painful way to die."

"No doubt Sir Buckley is convinced that Lord Wrotham murdered Admiral Smythe," Ursula began hotly.

"But of course," Harrison interjected. "Lord Wrotham was, after all, the last man to see Admiral Smythe alive—and they did dine together at the Carlton Club."

"I can just see Lord Wrotham whipping out his trusty hip flask of cyanide and lacing Admiral's Smythe wine while no one was looking—"

"Then you understand Buckley's sense of imagination," Harrison replied, deadpan.

"I'm sure Sir Buckley will outline all his fanciful theories in my interview with him tomorrow, so tell me . . . why did you really summon me here?" Ursula asked, folding her arms in tight. She was tired of this game of evasion.

"I wanted you to look at something."

Ursula's skepticism did not diminish.

"It's one of the Naval Intelligence files on Lord Wrotham which I thought you should see. We've only just started sifting through all of the files in Admiral Smythe's office cabinets but I think it's only fair that you read this—so you know the kind of man Lord Wrotham really is. Part of it comprises an old case report about an incident in Guyana. Lord Wrotham and Admiral Smythe were both there from '02 to '04, ostensibly to report on the boundary issue between British Guyana and Venezuela—but as you will see, there was more involved than first appears."

"And you are giving me this because?"

"Because I think you deserve to know the truth."

Ursula's eyes narrowed. "Why should I trust you after the other night?"

"That was Sir Buckley's idea, to see if I could draw you out before we formally interviewed you. I told him it was stupid and that it would only serve to make you more determined than ever to clear Lord Wrotham's name—and I was right. But you must also know that I am the very last person who would ever want to think badly of a man like Lord Wrotham. I owe him a debt which can never be repaid"—Harrison held up his hand to silence her—"No, Miss Marlow, I am not about to let you into my confidence regarding that. But I would hate to see you throw away everything you have fought so hard to attain to defend a man that is not worthy of your defense."

For once Ursula held her tongue.

"Just look at the file," Harrison said. "And make your own judgment."

He pointed to a lone reporter waiting on Victoria embankment. "Obviously, given the number of eyes watching this case, I cannot hand you the file in public but I'll make arrangements for it to be at your house this afternoon."

"All right," Ursula said. "I'll look at it. I'm not promising, however, that it will change anything."

"I can only spare the file for tonight or they'll get suspicious," Harrison said. "If you leave it in an envelope with Biggs, I'll retrieve it in the morning."

Ursula nodded, but as Harrison stepped back, preparing to turn and leave, she caught hold of his sleeve. "Chief Inspector," she said by way of warning. "If I discover that you are playing me false or what you are giving me is merely a ruse to discredit Lord Wrotham, then I will do whatever it takes to ruin your career." She took a deep breath. "I may be friendless at the moment but I am still wealthy."

"Don't worry, Miss Marlow, the one thing no one ever lets me forget," Harrison replied, "is your wealth."

By the time Ursula returned to Chester Square, the file Harrison spoke of was already waiting for her on her father's old desk in the study. While she sat and stared at it, Biggs brought in some much needed tea and a slice of Cook's lemon cake.

"Biggs," Ursula asked slowly. "Do you think it is possible to be totally misled about the true nature of someone's character?"

"I'm not sure I understand the question, Miss . . ."

"Do you think I have been mistaken about Lord Wrotham's character?" Ursula continued. "I was wrong about Tom Bates wasn't I? I was even wrong about my father . . . do you think"—Ursula stopped, the memory of her former fiancée, the man who had hanged for the murder of her father, was still raw.

"I'm hardly the person to ask," Biggs replied with an embarrassed cough.

"I know, but, Biggs, who else can I ask? Who else will tell me the truth?"

"Miss, I'm not sure anyone can ever know or judge the true nature of another unless he has walked in his shoes."

"How can I ever possibly hope to do that?" Ursula demanded.

"Quite simply you can't, Miss. I suppose you'll just have to have faith."

"In him?" she asked.

"In yourself."

Ursula opened the file to discover it comprised only five typewritten sheets. The first few pages were a case report prepared by Admiral Smythe, while the remaining pages appeared to be extracts from a police report along with a series of photographs adhered to paper. The photographs were faded and the paper foxed along on the edges. As she spread out the file contents in front of her, Ursula remembered that evening in Venezuela when she and Lord Wrotham had stood on a verandah on the shores of the Orinoco, listening as a thunderstorm approached. *It reminds me of nights in Guyana*, he had said and she had known in that instant that there was a part of him, a part of his past that would be forever hidden from her view. Now, perhaps, Harrison had given her the opportunity to take a glimpse into this secret world, but in so doing Ursula feared he had also given her the instrument by which all her faith in Lord Wrotham would be shattered.

July 23$\underline{^{rd}}$, 1904: Unexpurgated Case Report
submitted by Admiral Smythe. Re: Action Taken
with Respect to Death of Bernice Balder

For Internal distribution only

As per my report dated September 3rd 1903, W. and I have become increasingly concerned about the risks to British colonial interests posed by the wide-spread dissatisfaction with wages and standards of living by Indian indentured labourers working on sugar plantations in Guyana. The death of six Indians in an incident on Plantation Friends in May of 1903 only served to compound our concerns and raise questions about the possible implications of the death of the wife of a leading agitator, Bernice Baldeo. Mrs. Baldeo had come to the gold fields in early '04, ostensibly to meet with representatives of the Imperial Diamond and Gold Mining Company (IDGM Co.) regarding employment opportunities for free emigrant Indian labour. W. and I long suspected, however, that Mrs. Baldeo's presence reflected a wider interest by local agitators in understanding the nature and extent of IDGM Co.'s holdings in the area.

After her body was discovered in the waters of the Mazaruni river below the Aruwai falls, W. and I took swift action to suppress all information in relation to Mrs. Baldeo's death to ensure local sensitivities were not aroused. In particular, any possible connection to IDGM Co. or its activities were strenuously denied.

A coronial inquiry was, nevertheless, undertaken by the local authorities and the cause of death determined to be cyanide poisoning, the source of which was never identified. While some of the preliminary operations undertaken by IDGM Co. experimented with using gold cyanidation, no link has been established between the victim's death, this company's mining endeavors, or the actions of any of IDGM Co.'s officers or representatives.

Given sensitivity over colonial relations with emigrant Indian labour as well as the native populace, I authorized W. to persuade the local authorities that there was insufficient evidence upon which any arrests (or further inquiries) could be made. All further investigations were therefore halted and any link to our operations (or those of IDGM Co.) in Guyana expunged from the files. W. is

75

to be commended for both his discretion and his
attention to detail.

Three typed postscripts were added at the bottom of the report, dated
December 1905.

*A strike at the Plantation Ruimveldt has spread
to sugar estates on the Eastern Bank of the Demer-
ara river.
**A stevedore strike in Georgetown prompted
rioting and looting, the death of at least eight
strikers, and the arrival of two British warships
carrying troops.
***To date no mention of the Baldeo investiga-
tion has surfaced despite continued worker unrest.

On the final page was a postscript dated October 1st 1907, in the same
detached official tone.

W. is once again to be commended for his handling
of the legal case, El Dorado Investments v. The
Imperial Gold and Diamond Mining Company, and has
given all necessary assurances regarding the ongoing need for secrecy. Following W.'s successful
defense of the plaintiff's appeal, The Imperial
Gold and Diamond Mining Company filed for bank-
ruptcy and ceased all operations in Guyana in 1907.

W. confirms that all company records have been
destroyed.

Ursula set the case report aside and started reading extracts from
the police report on Bernice Baldeo's death. She could not determine
whether these were pages from the original report or whether they had
been transcribed; she suspected the latter as the pages included photographs that had been adhered using some kind of brittle brown glue.

She read the report with a growing sense of dismay. Had Lord Wrotham really been privy to the suppression of a murder investigation in Guyana?

> Interviews with witnesses revealed that Mr. F McTiernay was last seen with the deceased on the evening of July 6th, 1904. Witnesses report hearing an argument around 10:00pm and Mr. McTiernay was seen leaving Mrs. Baldeo's campsite at around quarter past that hour. Witnesses also report heated discussions between Messrs. McTiernay, Wrotham and Smythe in the early hours of July 7th.
>
> At the request of British authorities no further witness statements were obtained in relation to the events of the evening of July 6th. Assurances were given regarding Mr. McTiernay's whereabouts between midnight and four in the morning—the time period corresponding to the time that the coroner estimated death to have occurred.
>
> Assurances were also provided by a representative from The Imperial Gold and Diamond Mining Company, Count von Bernstorff-Hollweg, that cyanide was not utilized in the gold extraction process used by the company.
>
> All matters relating to this case now referred to the Governor's office under the direction of Lord Wrotham, Esq.

The photographs were grainy and misty age but Ursula could make out a waterfall and the dark outline of the jungle beyond. At the top of the first photograph she recognized Lord Wrotham's handwriting in ink: *Site where body of Bernice Baldeo discovered.* Similarly on the next photograph he had written: *Body in situ.* All Ursula could make out in this photograph was the half submerged body of a woman. The final photograph showed native bearers carrying the body to shore. Four men were looking on. One she recognized as Fergus McTiernay from the photograph in Professor Prendergast's office and the other was Admiral Smythe (although she needed to pull out the photograph she had brought back from Oxford to be sure). He certainly had the bearing of a naval officer despite the fact that he wore no uniform. The man standing next to him was possibly Count von Bernstorff-Hollweg for Ursula could detect a slight similarity in his features to that of the young Lord Wrotham standing beside him. It was the expression— or rather the lack thereof—on each of the men's faces that struck Ursula. Admiral Smythe had a stoic grimness about him reminiscent of a stern preacher one might encounter at a nonconformist church. It had a haunted quality that disturbed her. Lord Wrotham's face was as inscrutable as ever, shrouded in the shadow of the dark hair that fell across his temple. The Count, in contrast, seemed only mildly curious about the whole affair. He looked like the epitome of the continental gentleman abroad—from his neatly trimmed moustache and beard, to the monocle swinging from the fob chain on his waistcoat. Only Fergus McTiernay's face betrayed any real depth of emotion. He was staring down with the stunned, hollowed eyed expression of one both horrified and stricken by what had occurred.

So this was the four men of Balliol, Ursula thought. The four men inextricably linked to a past Lord Wrotham had denied her access to. Although she was yet to understand the full implications of the file, she was determined to record a copy of all that she had read before returning it to Harrison. As she transcribed the file into her exercise book, she reached the words "W. is to be commended for both his discretion and his attention to detail," and took pause. Were these just euphemisms for what really occurred in Guyana?

Ursula looked down and realized that where she had paused, where she had let the fountain pen rest, a pool of black ink had formed, seeping slowly as it was absorbed by the paper, until its slippery, glossy form had been entirely sucked dry. Ursula turned the page quickly, fearful she might start believing in omens if she looked too closely.

CHAPTER SEVEN

URSULA FOUND IT HARD to shake off the dread she had felt while reading the file that Harrison had provided her. Although Harrison was clearly unwilling to provide her with any material relevant to Lord Wrotham's current case (and really, Ursula chided herself, that should have come as no surprise) he had also felt compelled to reveal this aspect of Lord Wrotham's past—but to what end? To show her that he was a man willing to cover up murder for his country? To seed doubt in her mind because of the use of cyanide poison in both cases?

The obituary for Admiral Smythe appeared in the *Times* that morning ("*Distinguished Naval Officer Drowns in the Thames*") but made no mention of cyanide. The cause of death listed was drowning. When Ursula saw that a date for a private memorial had been set, she hesitated. After yesterday's accusatory telephone conversation with Admiral Smythe's sister, it was probably unwise to even consider attending, but she felt, as a result, that she had failed Lord Wrotham somehow. The obituary listed a number of charities that Admiral Smythe was associated with and Ursula decided that a donation to one of these was probably the most prudent cause of action.

She was still unsure what to make of Harrison's behavior but she had no opportunity to question him further before her interview with Sir Buckley that morning. As Samuels drove her to Whitehall she reflected that most of what she had read, should she admit it, was entirely in keeping with the man she knew to be Lord Wrotham. When he was her father's barrister and trusted advisor, hadn't he kept her father's secrets from the world? Hadn't he always acted with an enigmatic 'discretion' ideally suited to government work? But that hardly supported the notion that he would turn traitor—indeed it merely reinforced Ursula's belief that there was much more to this situation than anyone—Lord Wrotham, Sir Buckley or Chief Inspector Harrison was telling her.

Ursula was shown into Sir Reginald Buckley's office by a dour man in a grey pin-striped suit, whose military bearing and pinched disdain for her, as he looked her modern, mannish day suit up and down, left Ursula under no illusion as to his opinion of her. Where was her respectable marriage, her respectable home life and her respectable, well-behaved children? To the secretary, Ursula suspected, she was little more than a tainted specimen of 'independent womanhood'.

"Please take a seat, Miss Marlow," Sir Buckley said as she entered and his tone was surprisingly felicitous compared to their last meeting. "May I offer you a cup of tea, perhaps?"

Ursula could tell, from the cut and cloth of his Saville Row suit (probably made by Gieves & Hawkes who outfitted many in the Royal Navy) and his foulard-print Ascot necktie, just how much Sir Buckley venerated his status amongst 'the establishment'. Perhaps someone in the War Office had reminded him of the size and wealth of the textile empire Ursula's father had left her? If so, Sir Buckley was astute enough to recognize that with money came influence, even for an outsider and a woman like Ursula.

Hmm, though Ursula, *perhaps Pemberton was right, they are just trying to 'soften me up' in the hopes that I might turn Crown witness.* That was what Pemberton had told her he suspected when she had telephoned him earlier that morning. No doubt Sir Buckley was hoping that she would see the error of her ways and provide assistance in his case against Lord Wrotham. If that was indeed true, Ursula thought, as she handed the secretary her hat and gloves, he was sorely mistaken.

"No tea, thank you," Ursula answered Sir Buckley, all politeness. "I'm not here for a social chat."

As she took her seat, she shot Chief inspector Harrison a quick glance. He was perched on a wooden chair beneath a small window, a notepad and pencil in his lap. He acknowledged her presence with nothing more than a nod.

"I take it your lawyer won't be joining us, then?' Sir Buckley said.

"No, should I have asked him to?" Ursula replied. "I was led to believe that I am not a suspect in this case."

"No, no, of course not," Sir Buckley assured her as he sat down hastily. As he was arranging his papers on the desk and adjusting his shirt cuffs (revealing ostentatious gold and diamond cuff links), Ursula noticed the display of framed photographs on the nearest set of bookshelves: Sir Buckley with Winston Churchill, First Lord of the Admiralty; Sir Buckley with Sir Edward Grey, the Foreign Secretary; and, of course, Ursula murmured, Sir Buckley with Andrew Bonar Law, leader of the Conservative Party and staunch supporter of the Unionist cause in Ireland.

Sir Buckley cleared his throat and began to speak. "I regret Miss Marlow that we last met under very trying circumstances. I hope you understand that we were engaged in the delicate task of identifying and collecting evidence, but I promise you that every effort was made to protect the books in Lord Wrotham's library." Sir Buckley fiddled with his gold tie pin. "Now, I'm afraid, I do have to ask you a number of questions regarding the charges laid against Lord Wrotham . . ."

"You would have hardly ordered me here, otherwise," Ursula responded. She regarded him grimly, unmoved by his apology.

"Yes, well . . ." Sir Buckley cleared his throat once more.

"Before you start your questions," Ursula said, leaning forward in her chair and pinning him beneath her gaze. "I must formally protest the insinuation that I was in any way involved or had any knowledge of Lord Wrotham's activities. Lord Wrotham has never discussed his governmental duties with me. I was never aware of his movements or meetings abroad and I have never, ever, been privy to discussions with him regarding the activities that led to these charges. As far as I was aware, Lord Wrotham's politics were clear and unambiguous. He did not support home rule for Ireland. He had no love for the German imperialist cause and he was, and always maintained himself to be, a patriotic Englishman."

Ursula's statement seemed to momentarily take the wind out of Sir Buckley's proverbial sails but, all too soon, he recovered and asked, as the air blew out his cheeks. "But what of your politics, Miss Marlow? What influence did they have on his Lordship?"

"None whatsoever," Ursula answered. "It was one area we tried best to avoid. We held opposing views on the question of female suffrage, Irish nationalism and trade unionism . . . and, believe me, the list could go on. In short, there was very little in terms of politics that we did agree on."

"So you had no idea of his support for the Irish nationalist cause?"

"What support?" Ursula replied. "I have already told you, he was a Unionist."

"So you are not aware of these, then?" Sir Buckley drew out a file from the pile on his desk and opened it. He spread three papers in front of her. The first appeared to be a broadsheet entitled *Freedom of Thought, Freedom of Expression: The Radical Undergraduate* co-authored by Lord Wrotham and Fergus McTiernay. The second were typed minutes of a debate at the Oxford Union on *Ireland for the Irish?* featuring Lord Wrotham as the one of the speaker for the affirmative. The third was a copy of an invitation dated October 1911 for the Hanover Club—an Oxford University society that had been formed to promote Anglo-German relations during this time of crisis. It listed Lord Wrotham as one of its prominent after dinner speakers.

"No," Ursula said, looking up at Sir Buckley. "I have not seen these before."

Her finger nails dug into the palms of her hands as she hid both her shock and her bewilderment behind a mask of feigned self-possession.

"But you knew about Lord Wrotham's strong business and family ties to Germany," Sir Buckley said.

"Yes."

"And you knew about Lord Wrotham's frequent visits to the continent?"

"I was aware of them," Ursula admitted.

"And were you aware of the nature of his visits to Germany?" he asked.

Despite his initial solicitousness, there was no mistaking that Sir Buckley was now relishing Ursula's discomfiture.

Ursula shook her head.

"What about something like this?" Sir Buckley held up a small black notebook. "This is Admiral Smythe's, but our witnesses report seeing Lord Wrotham possessing a similar notebook."

"As far as I'm aware Lord Wrotham carries no notebook, only a slim volume of poetry by Alfred Lord Tennyson on occasion."

"Do you know which volume that might be?" Sir Buckley asked sharply. He was clearly eager for information that might help identify the cipher key Harrison had spoken of, but Ursula was in no mood to satisfy his curiosity.

"No," she lied. "I do not."

She saw Harrison raise his eyebrows but he did not interject.

Sir Buckley handed her the notebook. "Please take a look Miss Marlow and tell me if you recognize anything."

Ursula took the notebook and opened it. Inside, the lined pages were filled with strings of numbers, all of which appeared to be in no particular order or sequence. *So this was what the cipher looked like*, Ursula thought. No wonder Sir Buckley was anxious. Mindful of her brief experience with codes the previous year, Ursula tried to focus on anything in the pages that might reveal some kind of pattern—but she could discern nothing. Inwardly she vowed to dig out her notes from the research she and Lady Winterton had conducted for the WPSU as well as her history books from Somerville College, where she had first become interested in the use of ciphers by Mary Queen of Scots.

"No," Ursula repeated, as she perused the notebook. "I've not seen anything like this before . . . Tell me, are you any closer to knowing what these numbers refer to?"

"No," Sir Buckley replied stiffly. "We are not."

The questions continued to go back and forth for the remainder of the hour but as much as Sir Buckley tried to draw her out, Ursula was determined to reveal as little as possible. Lord Wrotham may well have kept many secrets from her but she would not abandon him now, and she was certainly not about to trust the likes of Sir Buckley.

After Sir Buckley had finished, Chief Inspector Harrison drilled her for a further hour about Lord Wrotham's business relations with her father, his role as her guardian, and his involvement in the management of Marlow Industries. Throughout the interrogation, Harrison remained aloof and unemotional, though Ursula sensed unsettled currents beneath the smooth exterior of his countenance.

"Are you aware that Bromley Hall may have to be closed due to unpaid debts stemming from Lord Wrotham's brother's mismanagement of the estate?" Harrison asked.

Ursula knew Lord Wrotham's brother, Gerard, had almost bankrupted the estate before his death, but she had also known better than to inquire too deeply into the matter. Lord Wrotham's family had always been a thorny topic of discussion.

"I knew the financial situation was tenuous but I was not aware of the extent of the debts owed," Ursula confessed.

"We have reason to believe that money may have been funneled to Lord Wrotham through accounts in both Ireland and Germany—were you ever aware of any transactions of this nature?"

"I am not privy to Lord Wrotham's financial affairs, and before you ask, Lord Wrotham has never asked for money from me. As my guardian, however, he has always treated my inheritance with due propriety. I know my accounts are all in good order but I am not aware of any of his dealings with Ireland or Germany."

"But you are aware that the Wrotham family has German business interests and that Lord Wrotham visited the continent on a regular basis."

"Yes," Ursula admitted reluctantly.

"And yet you maintain he never discussed the nature of these visits . . ."

"As you know, Lord Wrotham keeps his business affairs private," Ursula replied, leveling her gaze at Harrison.

"And his past?' Harrison asked quietly.

Ursula bit her lip before answering. "He certainly never discussed his time at Balliol," she said.

"Or, I take it, his time in Guyana?"

When confronted with Harrison's question, Ursula averted her gaze before answering, in a voice that had lost all semblance of equanimity, "No . . . he did not."

"Sir Buckley," Ursula asked as Chief Inspector Harrison escorted her to the door. "I was wondering if I would be permitted to speak to any of the crown witnesses in this case—specifically Count von Bernstorff-Hollweg."

"Certainly not," Sir Buckley responded with a harrumph. "Lord Wrotham's lawyers may interview him at an appropriate juncture in the case, but you have no right to contact him directly."

"But the Count is still in England?" Ursula pressed.

"No . . ." Sir Buckley hesitated. "Not anymore." His face was starting to grow red. "He's a very busy man, Miss Marlow and has returned to Germany. We have assurances of his continued cooperation, of course."

"Of course," Ursula echoed as she took her hat from Sir Buckley's secretary and tugged it on. "What about the other witnesses?"

"Pemberton has the list of all pertinent witnesses and documents," Sir Buckley replied stiffly. "I suggest you take the matter up with him."

Ursula adjusted her hat and pulled on her gloves, slowly, one at a time.

"Miss Marlow," Harrison intervened. "You may as well accept the fact you will not be allowed to talk directly to any of the witnesses in this case. Nor will you be allowed to conduct your own form of investigation. You must also keep us apprised of all your movements, both here and abroad."

"Why?" she demanded. "Am I under suspicion now?"

"No, of course not," Harrison responded. "But we may still need to contact you regarding questions in the case."

Sir Buckley's secretary held open the door for her, his face etched with disdain.

"I should keep my head down if I were you, Miss Marlow," Sir Buckley said as straightened his frockcoat and tugged his waistcoat down over his bulging stomach. "Put this whole unfortunate incident behind you"—he paused to clear his throat—"why a woman of your considerable means could easily find herself another husband."

Ursula regarded him with a look she hoped conveyed withering contempt but, like many things, it was lost on Sir Buckley. She saw Harrison though, his eyes thoughtful, regarding her with an expression she had never seen before—at least not for her.

Pity.

CHAPTER EIGHT

DESPITE LORD WROTHAM'S WARNINGS, Ursula returned to Brixton prison on Monday to visit him. The newspapers by now had already reported Admiral Smythe's death but Ursula was intrigued to note how few details were reported. There was no mention of cyanide or the possibility of murder. The cause of death as far as the press was concerned was drowning. Ursula surmised that Chief Inspector Harrison was keeping a very tight rein now on any information relating to the case and she was relieved, for it also meant at least one less reason for speculation and scandal. She had been involved in enough murder cases by now to know the insatiable public appetite for gruesome details.

Ursula bought with her to Brixton a basket of food that Cook had prepared—untried prisoners were allowed to supply their own food as well as wear their own clothes as they awaited trial. Despite this, the deterioration in Lord Wrotham's appearance was shocking. He had clearly not been allowed to shave and his blue-grey eyes seemed edged with weariness. On his forehead was a bandage through which the stitches were clearly visible.

"Whatever have they done to you?" she exclaimed.

"It seems some of my fellow prisoners aren't too keen on having

87

a traitor in their midst," Lord Wrotham replied, wincing as he eased himself into the chair. "And I thought I told you not to visit."

"We have to file a formal complaint," Ursula said, ignoring his last comment. "Whatever happened to being innocent until proven guilty?"

"I'm starting to believe that Hobbes was right," Lord Wrotham said. "Life really is just nasty, brutish and short."

Ursula stared at him in dismay. "Don't say that . . ." she responded hoarsely. "There is always hope."

"Is there?" he answered and the weariness in his tone concerned her almost as much as his physical deterioration. Ursula reached out her hand but he remained slumped in his chair, refusing to accept her comfort.

"Sir Buckley and Chief inspector Harrison interviewed me yesterday," Ursula said, hoping to provoke him into irritation at least.

"That must have been most unsatisfying," Lord Wrotham said.

"Yes," Ursula answered, "for all concerned."

Lord Wrotham raised an eyebrow.

"Why have you never told me about your days at Balliol?" Ursula demanded. "Were you afraid that I would find out that your politics were originally not so dissimilar to mine?"

"Is that what you think?" he asked.

"That's no answer." Ursula replied flushing.

Lord Wrotham ran his fingers through his dark hair. She detected the old sense of trespass—the old sense that she was treading close to old wounds. In the past she found the prospect of unnerving him electrifying. Now it prompted only anguish.

"I am not the same man I was at Balliol," Lord Wrotham replied. "Perhaps I didn't want to deceive you into thinking that I was."

"Not the answer that I wanted . . ." Ursula admitted. "But it was honestly given and I cannot fault you for that. Honest answers seem few and far between at the moment."

Lord Wrotham registered her reply in silence. The strain between them was almost unbearable. She wanted, no needed, to see the man beneath and yet still he ignored her pain. Ursula felt a spasm of grief convulse through her. Lord Wrotham sat across the table from her, his face as immutable and hard as a gravestone.

"In the interview, Sir Buckley showed me a black bound notebook,"

Ursula finally said. "He told me it belonged to Admiral Smythe but he seemed to think you also carried something similar. The notebook was filled with some kind of numeric code, though I'm guessing you already know that."

Lord Wrotham still said nothing.

"You know Sir Buckley sent Chief Inspector Harrison to my house a few nights ago, trying to draw me out," she said. "He thought I might be persuaded to testify against you. That would, of course, presuppose that I knew anything of value"—Ursula bit her lip, getting angry was not going to achieve anything and she exhaled slowly before continuing—"Why did you not at least tell me that Bromley Hall was in danger of foreclosing?"

"Is that what Sir Buckley told you?" Lord Wrotham asked.

Ursula nodded, her eyes not leaving his.

Lord Wrotham looked away and signaled to the guard. "Do you have a cigarette, by any chance?" he asked him.

Ursula drew a silver case from her skirt pocket and pushed it across the table. "Don't be ridiculous," she chided, "take one of mine."

She knew, however, that he was just stalling for time.

"Well?" she prompted.

He struck a match and lit his cigarette. "Is it true about the debts?" he finished the question for her and then paused. "Yes," he said.

"You should have told me," Ursula insisted. "I could have—"

"Could have what? Given me money?"

Ursula's hands clenched in her lap.

"You need to stop feeling guilty," Lord Wrotham said. "You are not, nor ever can be, my savior."

"Why does my halo not match my dress?" Ursula snapped.

"Ursula, you need to be serious . . ."

"That's what I have been—perfectly serious—why do you insist on avoiding discussion on the very things that matter?! Why, if you are bound by some kind of obligation to Admiral Smythe, do you not tell me how I might decipher his notes? Why hinder me from finding evidence that may exonerate you?!"

"Deciphering Admiral Smythe's notes may not be in anyone's best interests," Lord Wrotham replied.

Ursula bit her lip again as she tried to hold back her frustration.

"Tell me about Guyana then, at least," she said.

"Why would you want to know about that?" Lord Wrotham said and the cigarette in his mouth dangled precariously from his lips. His surprise seemed genuine.

"What happened to the woman who died?"

"The woman who?" Lord Wrotham stopped. "Oh, you mean the woman who was pulled from the river."

"Yes, the one who died of cyanide poisoning, just as they suspect Admiral Smythe did."

Lord Wrotham rubbed his temples with his fingers. "There's no connection so don't start thinking that there is . . ." He stubbed his cigarette out in the small ceramic ashtray. "What has James been telling you?" he demanded.

"James?" Ursula queried. "Surely you must know that James has not been sighted since your arrest? It was Harrison who mentioned Guyana to me."

The muscles around Lord Wrotham's mouth visibly tightened. "Why would Harrison be speaking to you about Guyana?"

"He showed me an old file that was found in Admiral Smythe's office," Ursula said. "I want to understand what happened back then . . ."

"What happened in Guyana has no bearing on my case," Lord Wrotham replied swiftly. "I will not be drawn out on it any further. As far as I'm concerned the matter is closed."

Just like a lawyer, Ursula thought angrily, to treat the past as if it were little more than a case to be closed. She knew him better, though, than to continue this line of questioning and risk further friction between them. She also suspected that James' continued absence troubled him more than he wanted her to know.

"You very conveniently skipped over the fact that I said that James is missing," Ursula said.

"Did I?" Lord Wrotham replied.

"You're not worried about him?"

Lord Wrotham's eyelids flickered. "No."

"Yet the afternoon of your arrest, you distinctly wanted me to ask him to drive me to Bromley Hall," she probed further.

"Did I?"

"Yes," she said. "And it's made all the more intriguing by the fact that you are trying to pretend his disappearance doesn't bother you . . . when it does, more than you like to admit."

Lord Wrotham shrugged. "I'm sure he'll turn up, he always does."

Ursula was not to be appeased but as she opened her mouth to question him further, she caught his gaze and it stopped her cold. Once again she found him and his past an impenetrable fortress.

"What about your own notes or notebook? Won't these explain what really happened in Germany?" Ursula asked. "If I could show these to Chief Inspector Harrison at least . . ."

"As I've said, without Admiral Smythe alive I cannot clear my name," Lord Wrotham answered.

"But surely there must be others in the government that knew what you and he were doing?" Ursula protested.

"Given the circumstances they will most certainly disavow any knowledge of our mission."

"But why?" she asked.

"Covert intelligence missions are hardly considered the 'done thing', my dear, least of all for a gentleman like me. There are many in the government who cannot stand to think of the British sullying our hands with anything as sordid as espionage. The thought that I may have used my business contacts abroad to gather enemy intelligence in one thing—but that I may have been masquerading as a traitor to draw out a treasonous conspiracy—well, that's almost as bad as having been a part of it for real."

"But"—Ursula started to object. Lord Wrotham reached out and held her hand for a moment. The gesture silenced her immediately.

"We just have to wait and see how the game plays itself out," Lord Wrotham said with deliberate emphasis.

"Game?" Ursula retorted, but she kept hold of his hand. "I'd hardly call this a game!"

"In many respects that is exactly what it is," Lord Wrotham replied, "and even I don't know who all the players are as yet—which is why we must wait—Admiral Smythe was murdered for a reason, by someone whose motivations aren't yet clear to me, so I need you to be patient, for your own safety."

"Patience is *not* one of my virtues," Ursula interjected.

"No—but patience may well reveal the truth."

"About who is really behind all this?" Ursula said.

Lord Wrotham nodded, his gaze suddenly intense, as his hand gripped hers.

"Exactly."

CHAPTER NINE

LORD WROTHAM'S BROOK STREET HOME,
MAYFAIR

THE AFTERNOON SHADOWS WERE ALREADY LOOMING, dark and cold, in the recesses of the buildings along Brook Street when Ursula unlocked the front door to Lord Wrotham's Mayfair home using the key he had given her less than a month ago. She was a stranger still to this place and, as she opened the door and stepped inside, she felt a strange thrill of excitement—as a child might feel intruding on forbidden territory.

She closed the door quickly and flicked on the electric hall light. The black and white flooring seemed stark but it was the presence of his coat and hat still hanging on the mahogany coat stand that caused a sudden pang of anguish. She reached over and let her hand travel across the smooth cashmere of his coat sleeve. No doubt the police had already examined the pockets when they searched the premises, but despite this Ursula still felt compelled to check the pockets herself. There was nothing but an old theatre ticket stub which, for Ursula, provided an agonizing reminder of how easily the normalcy of life could be snatched from her grasp. Less than ten days ago Lord Wrotham had accompanied her to the St. James Theatre to see *Turandot*, without any thought of what madness was to come. Ursula withdrew from the narrow entranceway abruptly—Such maudlin thoughts were ridiculous, she admonished herself. Lord Wrotham knew very well what was to come—of that she was now sure. Feeling a sudden twinge of resentment she passed through the high-ceilinged front hall and stood at the foot of the ornate carved staircase, tapping her lace up oxford shoes against the dark green carpet runner.

"Come on," she whispered to herself. "Surely there's something here that can help him." Although Chief Inspector Harrison and Sir Buckley had already supervised a thorough and exhaustive search of the house, Ursula felt duty-bound to come here. Perhaps it was Lord Wrotham's refusal to provide her with the satisfaction of any sort of answer that drew her here. Whatever it was it she was determined to keep looking.

She made her way up the stairs, fortified by a renewed sense of purpose, before pausing outside the door to Lord Wrotham's bedroom. A quiver of wistfulness ran through her as she pushed open the door. She stood hesitantly on the threshold for a moment and then turned away (telling herself not to let emotions get the better of her) to walk along the landing. She reached the front room that overlooked the street and peered inside. She had only been in this room once before but knew it was the small library and study that Lord Wrotham used when he was in London.

It was hard to believe, Ursula thought, as she walked over to turn on the lamp on the desk, that the room had been disturbed. Everything was neatly arranged and perfectly positioned—from the fountain pen that lay at a perfect right angle, to the orderly stack of paper on the desktop, to the cushions set out in a row on the bench seat beneath the window. The books on the bookshelf were similarly neat—only the lack of dust betrayed that they had recently been removed, examined and replaced.

Ursula used her finger to glide along the spines of the books as she took note of the familiar titles: Arnold Bennett's *Clayhanger*. Joseph Conrad's *The Secret Agent*. Anthony Trollope's *Eye for an Eye*. She hesitated when she reached the bottom shelf—for there were two books—that surprised her and she smiled, despite herself. Zane Grey indeed.

Ursula peered in each of the desk drawers, even getting down on her hands and knees to look for hidden recesses. As expected, there was nothing. Lord Wrotham was as skillful at hiding his past as he was able to twist a legal argument. There would be no photographs or journals, no long lost letters or accidental receipts. The house appeared to have been sanitized to the point that she almost believed Lord Wrotham had expected the place to be searched at one time or other. Drumming her fingers impatiently along the wallpapered walls, Ursula returned once more to the landing. The stairwell was silent and cool—like the interior of a medieval church. Ursula stood for a moment mulling her options, but, even as she decided which room to look in next , there was still the nagging question of what had happened to Lord Wrotham's chauffeur, Archibald James.

Ursula mounted the rear servant staircase and slowly climbed her way to the top floor rooms. Lord Wrotham only brought James with him from Bromley Hall and employed a part-time housekeeper to maintain his London home. Accordingly, there was need for only one servant's bedroom and this, Ursula soon discovered, was deserted. It certainly looked as though James had packed his affairs and left permanently for there was no indication, except for the folded linens at the base of the single bed, to indicate that anyone had ever occupied this room. There were no personal effects, no clothes or other mementos—nothing save a photograph hanging on the wall near a narrow attic window. Ursula walked over and examined the photograph. It was of a rifle regiment in full regimental uniform. She recognized James standing at the back, even though he must have been no more that eighteen when the photograph was taken. The caption read *Kings Royal Rifle Corps. (21st Finsbury Rifles), 1902.*

After a search of the small austerely furnished room revealed nothing further, Ursula went back down the servants' stairs and crossed the landing once more, to enter Lord Wrotham's bedroom. Like the study it was immaculately tidy, and yet Ursula was sure that this too had been thoroughly searched.

She opened the tall mahogany wardrobe and gathered up the black and grey frock coats in her arms, just to feel the texture of his clothes against her cheek. The smell of his cologne—a mixture of bergamot and lime leaves—lingered still. Although she double checked she knew she would find nothing in any of the pockets. Lord Wrotham was too fastidious to have left anything, though, no doubt it would have amused him to think of Chief Inspector Harrison and Sir Buckley poring over every scrap, list or receipt in search of clues. Ursula sat on the bed and sighed, chiding herself for being naïve enough to think that she could have found anything of value here. She went over to the chest of drawers and drew out two fresh white shirts. The top drawer contained collars and cuffs and she took some of these too. She reasoned that if she could find nothing of use here for her own investigation, she may as well get him a fresh change of clothes. In the inlaid wooden box in which he kept his cufflinks and tie pins, Ursula found a small prayer card such as those one may expect to find at a Catholic mission. It depicted Saint Dismas, with the words for a *Prayer for the Penitent Thief* written underneath the garishly colored picture.

Lord Jesus, help us to be merciful as you are merciful.
O Sacred Heart of Jesus, make us love thee more and more!
Let us see that all are your children and remember that we are
*   not to judge.*
St. Dismas, the Good Thief, pray for us!

Strange, Ursula thought, for Lord Wrotham was not Catholic—nor was he even particularly religious. She turned the card over in her fingers. Why would Lord Wrotham keep such a thing? She took it and placed it on the stack of shirts, collar and cuffs and walked back into the study. Beneath the lamp light she studied the prayer card a little more closely. In the top drawer of Lord Wrotham's desk she found a small ivory-handled magnifying glass and looked at the small print at the bottom of the card. It read *St Ignatius Mission, Guyana*. She could well imagine Sir Buckley and Chief Inspector Harrison dismissing this as little more than a religious trinket but if Lord Wrotham kept this, and this alone, from his time in Guyana—then it must have some special significance thought Ursula. She felt sure that finding this prayer card, in a place where Lord Wrotham clearly wanted it to be found, was important. Lord Wrotham may not be Catholic, but Fergus McTiernay most certainly was.

Ursula looked up, startled to hear the slam of a motorcar door being closed. She parted the curtains and looked out to see Chief inspector Harrison emerge from a black taxi-cab below. Another man crossed the street to speak with him and Harrison looked up. Ursula, knowing it would irritate Harrison all the more, waved to him from the window.

Gathering up the shirts and collars in her arms, Ursula quickly turned off the lamp and made her way out of the study. She replaced the prayer card in the inlaid box—Harrison would undoubtedly notice and wonder about its significance should she have it with her. Hearing the front door open and close, Ursula she walked down the staircase to greet Harrison.

"What the hell do you think you're doing here?" Harrison demanded. "You must have known we would be watching the place."

Ursula held up the pile of clothes in her arm. "I thought Lord Wrotham could do with a fresh set of clothes," she said.

Harrison regarded her skeptically. "You're hardly the sort of woman who needs to worry about another man's laundry."

"Why, did you think I came here to extract some vital evidence that you and your men had failed to uncover?" Ursula asked.

"I know you're not the sort to sit idly by while we conduct our investigation . . . Did Lord Wrotham tell you to come here?"

"Since he spends almost every day at Scotland Yard being interrogated by you and Sir Buckley, I doubt he has the time. Besides, do you really believe Lord Wrotham wouldn't have guessed his house was under surveillance?"

"I'd hardly call it that," Harrison replied, "but I still want to know what you're doing here."

"Yes, yes . . . I know, you and Sir Buckley don't want me undertaking my own inquiries."

"Poking your nose around in this case could be dangerous—or didn't you read the case file I gave you?"

"I read it," Ursula said.

"But it didn't change anything did it?" Harrison's voice was quiet.

"No," Ursula replied, equally quiet. "I'm afraid it didn't."

Harrison shook his head. "I'm going to have to ask you to accompany me to Scotland Yard. You will have to be searched by one of our police matrons."

"What are you expecting to find on me—a cache of Irish armaments? A secret written confession by Lord Wrotham perhaps? Really Harrison, sometimes you treat me as if I'm a total imbecile . . ."

"Don't be ridiculous," Harrison said under his breath. "I've been trying to help you as best I can—but my actions must be above any form of reproach. When Sir Buckley hears you've been here he will demand to know why. I simply cannot afford to fall into Sir Buckley's disfavor."

"Your promotion—of course," Ursula replied. She shot him a sideways glance. "So tell me, Chief Inspector, how is that all working out for you?"

Harrison's baleful glare spoke volumes.

It was late into the night when Ursula was finally released from Scotland Yard to return to Chester Square. Sir Buckley had insisted the police matron conduct a thorough and ignominious search of Ursula's person so that by the time Ursula arrived home she was indignant, frustrated and in a thoroughly rotten temper.

As Julia helped undress her (for the second time that day) Ursula vented her frustration in a series of tirades against the idiots of the Metropolitan Police, Scotland Yard and the War Office as well as the arrogance of small-minded, pompous bureaucrats like Sir Reginald Buckley.

"And they think civilization will collapse if women get the vote!" Ursula cried as she plunked down on the upholstered satin stool in front of her bureau. "The Empire is already doomed if men like Sir Buckley can not only vote but hold high office!"

Julia made appropriately soothing sounds as she pulled the hairpins from Ursula's dark auburn hair.

Ursula leaned back and found some comfort in the rhythmic strokes as Julia brushed her hair.

"Julia?" Ursula said, yanking her head back up abruptly. "You grew up Catholic, didn't you?"

"Yes, Miss . . . why do you ask?" Julia said and she continued brushing with calm, even strokes.

"What do you know about Saint Dismas?"

"Why, he was the good thief crucified with Christ on Calvary," Julia replied. "He repented of his sins and Jesus promised he would go to heaven."

Ursula studied her reflection in the mirror. "What kind of person, do you think, would pray to him?" she asked.

Julia screwed up her nose in thought. "Perhaps someone who had been dishonest in his life who wants forgiveness before death . . . I've heard of those in prison praying to him, seeking restitution for the sins they have committed," Julia paused, "for Saint Dismas is the patron saint of those condemned to death."

Ursula fell silent. The prayer card seemed so incongruous, yet she could not ignore the sense that it offered an insight into the past—into the men that had gone to Guyana and whose friendship had been irrevocably altered by what had occurred there. All that she had read in Admiral Smythe's file suggested that there had been some kind of fraud involving The Imperial Gold and Diamond Mining Company, something unscrupulous enough to compel Lord Wrotham to suppress evidence regarding the murder of Bernice Baldeo. Could McTiernay have been both murderer and thief? Was it he who had given Lord Wrotham the prayer card?

The specter of McTiernay's involvement could also not be ignored. A Catholic and fiercely patriotic Irish man, he had been Lord Wrotham's best friend until the events in Guyana fractured their friendship. Yet now Lord Wrotham was accused of colluding with him once more. What really happened back in Guyana, Ursula thought, as she studied her reflection once more. If McTiernay was the one who gave Lord Wrotham this prayer card, was it offered as some kind of apology? A plea for absolution? Or had Lord Wrotham brought it out more recently as a reminder that there remains hope even for those condemned to death?

CHAPTER TEN

THE FOLLOWING EVENING, Ursula was once again forced to rely on Julia's good opinion. This time, however, it was on the necessity of fulfilling a social engagement.

"Julia, I hardly think attending a charity function is good idea at the moment." Ursula looked down at the sequined gown Julia had laid out for her on the bed in dismay.

Julia handed her Lady Winterton's invitation. "You did accept the invitation some weeks ago," she reminded her.

"Yes, but that was before . . . besides, she would hardly expect or want me to attend now!" Ursula protested.

Julia studied the wallpaper.

"You think I should go, don't you?" Ursula said as she sat down in front of the bureau with a sigh. "But why?"

"It might do you good to go out," Julia said.

Ursula picked up her silver handled hair brush and idly ran her fingers along the bristles. "Instead of moping around here, you mean?" she asked.

"I just think you should be out in society—showing them that you are still standing strong—that's all, Miss," Julia replied.

"But what if they shun me?" Ursula asked, her vulnerability suddenly exposed. "What if even Lady Winterton refuses to have anything to do with me?"

"But Lady Winterton's a friend, Miss," Julia said.

Ursula leaned on her elbows, put her head in her hands and closed her eyes.

"She's not Miss Stanford-Jones, I know," Julia said quietly as she started to unbutton the back of Ursula's blouse, "but perhaps she can still help."

Ursula's lifted her head and glanced across to Freddie's letter which lay open on the top of the chest of drawers. No doubt by now newspaper reports of Lord Wrotham's arrest would have reached San Francisco but Ursula had not been able yet to find the right words to express how she felt in a letter to her friend. Freddie's last letter was so buoyed with hope that Ursula hated the thought of her rushing back to England on Lord Wrotham's account (especially as he and Freddie rarely saw eye to eye on any issue). Ursula believed strongly that Freddie's place was in America promoting the ideals of universal suffrage and socialism but she also knew that Freddie was just as likely to cancel her lecture tour and return to England if she thought Ursula needed her. Although she dearly wanted to have her friend by her side, Ursula knew that there was little Freddie could do to help her.

"You're right, as always, Julia," Ursula said with a sigh. "I should stop my fretting and face society—I'll have to do it sometime and I may as well do it in the home of a friend. Lady Winterton did at least acknowledge me on Oxford Street—who knows, perhaps she can even shed some light on Lord Wrotham's past." Ursula stared at her own reflection moodily.

The door bell rang below.

"Ah," Julia said. "That'll be Mrs. Pomfrey-Smith."

"Julia?" Ursula warned. "What are you up to?"

"Nothing, Miss," Julia replied but her dimples were starting to show. "I must've just forgotten to say that Mrs. Pomfrey-Smith called this afternoon, asking about tonight . . ."

"And you and Biggs thought that I'd have to go if Mrs. Pomfrey-Smith thought she was accompanying me . . . Really Julia, you'd think I was a child!"

"Mister Biggs and I just wanted to see you all dressed up with a smile for once—"

"It's all right Julia," Ursula's irritation died as quickly as it had flared once she saw Julia's earnest expression. Ursula clasped Julia's hand. "I understand and, believe me, I appreciate the sentiment."

Julia gathered Ursula's auburn hair in her hands." Let's make sure you do Mrs. Pomfrey-Smith proud."

After a further ten minutes of tucking and pinning, Ursula's hair was tamed and curled into a simple psyche knot offset by a broad grey velvet headband and silver, sapphire and pearl encrusted dragonfly pin. Julia assisted Ursula into the loose fitting gown with its grey silk diaphanous silvery folds, and mother-of-pearl sequins. Finally she handed Ursula a string of grey pearls—the same ones her mother had worn when she was young. Ursula looked at them with sadness, even as she heard Mrs. Pomfrey-Smith's voice through the floorboards. She felt a pang of wistfulness—a longing for the past and all its innocence—but instead it was the ghosts of all those that she had loved and had lost that haunted her now: her mother; her father; friends like Katya Vilenksy. All gone yet ever present. It was a burden that at times seemed too much to bear.

Lady Catherine Winterton's Kensington home was bedecked with flowers—a testament to the abnormally mild weather for this time of year. She had blue primroses, irises and crocus, greenhouse roses and honey-scented hyacinths, all in vases or garlands used to decorate the strands of wound ivy that curved along the balustrade of the main staircase. A long buffet table had been strategically positioned in the center of the ballroom topped with canapés, plates of oysters, lamb and even quails stuffed with foie-gras. The focal point of the table was, however, a tall peacock made of marzipan and fruit. Although Ursula knew most of the guests by sight, there was no one, apart from Lady Winterton, who Ursula would call a friend. There were certainly no other members of the local branch of the Women's Social and Political Union that Lad Catherine and Ursula attended—Lady Winterton was much too savvy to commit that kind of social blunder. She was careful not to divulge her political views among the London society set and, unlike Ursula, shunned any form of radicalism.

102

As Ursula entered, Mrs. Pomfrey-Smith placed a reassuring hand on her arm. "Courage, dear girl," she whispered. "Courage!"

Ursula squeezed Mrs. Pomfrey-Smith's hand. "I'm my father's daughter," she said. "I never let myself forget that."

Mrs. Pomfrey-Smith, adorned in a ridiculous array of ostrich feathers on top of her black crepe-de-chine dress, smiled. "Remember," she said. "There are many eligible men here tonight and you, my dear, are only twenty-five!"

Ursula had to bite her lip but she let the comment pass as she extricated herself from Mrs. Pomfrey-Smith's grasp with the excuse that she had best find their hostess, Lady Catherine Winterton.

"I wasn't sure you would still want me to attend," Ursula admitted once she had found Lady Winterton circulating through the assembled crowd with a champagne glass firmly in hand.

"Nonsense," Lady Winterton said briskly. "As I tried to demonstrate on Oxford Street, this unfortunate event should in no way reflect badly on you."

"I wish you would tell some of my business associates that," Ursula replied, mindful of a particularly terse exchange with one her colleagues over the telephone that morning. She was only thankful that her business partner Hugh Carmichael had seen fit to take over most of their business negotiations. Although he had initially insisted on coming to London to see her, Ursula had managed to convince him that both their businesses were better served by him keeping his distance.

"You should treat tonight as a first step to your return to society," Lady Winterton said.

"I'm not sure I shall return at all unless Lord Wrotham's name is cleared," Ursula responded soberly. She felt all eyes turn to her, as some of the other guests overheard her speak his name.

"This way," Lady Winterton steered her towards the buffet table, casting a backward glance at a huddle of curious guests. "People just love to ogle when there's a scandal!"

"Please," Ursula said. "You really don't have to stay with me—I realized I'm persona non grata but you don't have to worry on my account, you should see to your other guests."

"Not before I've made sure you've bucked up a bit—I've known Lord Wrotham for many years, first through my husband, and then on my own account. I'm positive this is a misunderstanding." Ursula appreciated her conviction but could see it was not something shared by any of the other guests.

"I know your husband was once friends with Lord Wrotham at Balliol, but truly, you don't need to jeopardize your own reputation to demonstrate your loyalty," Ursula said.

Lady Winterton gave her a sympathetic smile. "Remember, I too know what it is like to evoke society's censure and approbation."

Lady Winterton's empathy roused Ursula from self-pity. She knew that Lady Winterton's elopement to Lord Nigel Winterton, an impoverished member of the lesser Irish nobility, had caused a fracas within her own family and, by extension, London society. His death may have mitigated some but not all of it and, although Lady Winterton now moved in the finest circles of London society, she still bore the scars of an imprudent and what many called a rash marriage. Ursula had only known Lady Winterton as a widow but it was still obvious how much she had loved her husband.

"I appreciate your concern. With Freddie in America I must confess I was feeling quite friendless . . ." Ursula hesitated, uncomfortable that she had revealed her frailties so quickly to Lady Winterton.

"Well you mustn't!" Lady Winterton said. "And I am not doing it just for Nigel—though he and Lord Wrotham were friends."

"I wish some of his friends from that time could explain Lord Wrotham's past to me—I feel as though I'm standing on little more than quicksand at the moment!"

"Chin up—you've got more backbone than to sink into it! As for the past—well I wish Nigel was here as much as you do, even though he and Lord Wrotham drifted apart after Oxford. They continued to maintain a correspondence, of course, but I'm not sure even Nigel could have told you much more than you already know."

"Why didn't he go to Guyana with the rest of them?" Ursula asked.

"I believe he had originally planned to do so," Lady Winterton replied. "But we—I mean Nigel and I—had just met around that time, and he didn't want to be parted from me. Besides he could barely afford the ship's fare as it was." Lady Winterton's expression grew clouded.

Ursula laid a hand on Lady Winterton's arm. "I am sorry," she said. "I didn't mean to bring up the past like that." She felt acutely conscious of Lady Winterton's sensitivity over the issue. It had been five years since her husband's death but, despite now having her family's approval (and access once more to their fortune), Lady Winterton was, in many ways, still grieving for her loss.

"Oh, I don't mind talking about him now—though, in the first few months after his death, I admit, I wanted nothing more than to be shut away from everybody and everything."

"It must have been very hard . . ." Ursula said. "Though it must have provided some measure of comfort to him, in his final days, to have at least one of his old friends in Ireland."

"You mean Fergus McTiernay?" Lady Winterton asked. "I hardly remember meeting him at all. Nigel always said he was more committed to causes than people."

"Still, I wish I could at least speak with him—maybe he could provide some answers . . ."

"Why, because he's a Fenian firebrand?" Lady Winterton asked dryly. "Ursula you should know not to trust those sorts of men."

Yes, Ursula said to herself, thinking of how her Bolshevik ex-lover had betrayed her last year. *Alexei, should have taught me that.*

"I wouldn't hold much hope for McTiernay my dear," Lady Winterton said. "I can't say he was close to Nigel—not at the end, but as I said, they all drifted apart after university."

"Do you know why?" Ursula asked.

"No, probably just natural after so many years—though Nigel told me he suspected the trip to Guyana had something to do with it."

Ursula frowned. "Did he ever tell you why he thought that was?"

"No," Lady Winterton said. "I'm not sure he really knew himself."

There was an awkward silence, until Ursula murmured. "I shouldn't have come out tonight."

Lady Winterton squeezed her arm once more. "Now you are being ridiculous, m'dear—We must all think to the future, not the past . . . that's what I must do, every day, when I'm tempted to think of Nigel."

Ursula fell silent. The pall of the past and all that had happened hung over her, so dense, so dark, that it was oppressive.

"I fear," Ursula said after a moment of reflective silence between them. "That I'm shamelessly keeping you from your other guests. Please—you should see to them. I shall be quite content to act the wallflower tonight."

"Hardly your strong suit," Lady Winterton replied with a semblance of a laugh. The dark shadow that had passed over her dissipated. With a light touch on Ursula's cheek and a swish of her stylish amber and gold flocked dress, she left her to mingle with the other guests.

Ursula spent the next half hour as an uneasy observer to the party. She longed to be at home, away from all talk of latest spring fashions or plans for the social season. Ursula took a glass of champagne from one of the waiters but felt disinclined to drink. She was falling prey once more to despondency when she noticed Christopher Dobbs enter the room and start to make his way over to where she was standing. Her misery swiftly turned to fury. Dobbs was responsible for orchestrating the murder of one of Ursula's friends, Katya Vilensky, last year, and it galled Ursula to think that his strategic value to the British government as an armaments dealer, meant he got to walk free among society. It was a fact that Ursula could neither forget nor forgive.

"Unexpected to see you here, Miss Marlow," Christopher Dobbs ('Topper' to his friends) said, taking a glass of champagne from a footman's tray and downing it in three mouthfuls. Ursula's eyes narrowed. With only the smallest tilt of her head, did she acknowledge his presence.

"How is Lord Wrotham faring in jail?" he asked. "I hear they don't take kindly to traitors."

Ursula's whole body stiffened.

She caught sight of Mrs. Pomfrey-Smith's worried glance from across the room, and was determined to maintain her composure. Although Mrs. Pomfrey-Smith, like everyone else in London society, had no knowledge of Christopher Dobbs' crimes, she was well aware of Ursula's antipathy towards him. It was clear from the look on her face that she feared yet another 'scene'. This time, however, Ursula refused to give Dobbs the satisfaction of seeing her provoked.

He regarded her with amusement. "You may not realize it," he said. "But I'm one of few men who can help you."

"Really?" Ursula was unable to restrain her sarcasm.

"Yes," Dobbs replied with the arrogance of one relishing his position. "I can tell you all you need to know about the people behind this so called 'traitorous' scheme including the Crown's key witness, Count von Bernstorff-Hollweg."

"I would have thought you would have already run to you new masters, the British government, and told them all of this information already."

"Perhaps I thought I might get greater satisfaction out of telling you," Dobbs said and his leer made Ursula's skin crawl. Although Christopher Dobbs ('Topper' to his friends) was the son of one of Ursula's father's erstwhile business associates, the man who now stood before her bore little resemblance to the boy she had once known.

"I have no doubt of that," she responded. "But I don't feel like paying the price for it."

"Not even to help your true love?" Dobbs said lightly. "Tsk, tsk . . . Miss Marlow, I expected better of you."

"I'm glad you're disappointed."

"I doubt I'll remain that way," he said, leaning in. "Disappointed that is, because you will come to me for help. Eventually."

Ursula fingers gripped the folds of her dress, threatening to rip the fabric. "I will never be willing to give you money—no matter what information you have."

"You are a fool then—a fool for thinking that I would be seeking money in exchange for what I know. I make it a goal of mine to keep up to date with both you and Lord Wrotham's business affairs. If you want to know the real reason the Count is testifying against Lord Wrotham then you'll have to come to me."

"If you don't want money, then what else?" Ursula asked. She had to wet her lip with her tongue for her mouth had gone suddenly dry.

Dobbs smiled. "Oh, the taste of what his Lordship has already sampled would be enough for me," he said. His face was now close enough that she could see the veins in his neck, blue and bulging. "I have no doubt he has already sampled his marital wares."

Ursula could no longer restrain herself. With a violent jerk of her wrist she threw the contents of her champagne glass at him, before hurling the glass to the floor where it smashed with such force that splinters of glass flew across the parquetry floor like ice shavings.

As guests turned and stared, the room fell slowly, disapprovingly, silent. Dobbs took his handkerchief out of his dinner jacket pocket and mopped his face. He smiled tightly. "You'll be willing to pay the price," he said. "Once you realize that Lord Wrotham will hang unless you accept my help."

"I'd rather join Lord Wrotham in hell if that is the case," Ursula replied.

"That," Christopher Dobbs said, "can also be arranged."

CHAPTER ELEVEN

IT WAS WITH A COMPLETE DISREGARD FOR ETIQUETTE that Ursula and Gerard Anderson met with Pemberton the following morning at his chambers in Temple Inn. Anderson, apart from being her father's long time financial advisor, was now one of the few men, apart from her business partner Hugh Carmichael, who knew the extent to which Lord Wrotham's arrest threatened Ursula's business empire. Having taken over the helm of her father's textile companies after his death, Ursula had, until now, relied on Lord Wrotham's good will as her appointed guardian in allowing her the financial freedom she required. Since his arrest that freedom was in jeopardy and speculation regarding her ability to continue to run her father's business empire was reaching fever-pitch.

"I received good news this morning, Pemberton managed to secure a court order yesterday," Anderson said as he accompanied her up the wooden staircase to Pemberton's chambers. "I am now your guardian—at least in name."

"So long as you maintain the freedom that Lord Wrotham afforded me regarding my inheritance, I am content," Ursula replied. The fact that her father's will stipulated that she need a guardian to manage the money she inherited until she attained thirty years of age or was married, still galled her.

"I will continue to advise you as I think best," Anderson replied earnestly. Ursula reminded herself that, not so long ago, Anderson had urged her to consider Christopher Dobbs' offer to buy Marlow Industries. Despite their differences, however, Ursula still trusted Anderson—and at the moment there were few men in her life she could say that about with any degree of confidence.

Pemberton's clerk, a fustian specimen with the sagging jowls and eyes of a bloodhound, met them at the top of the stairs and trudged them into his chambers with grumbling reluctance. Legal propriety demanded that a solicitor accompany them, but Ursula, never one to abide by the rules of etiquette, had insisted on calling on Pemberton with Anderson alone.

"Ah, Miss Marlow and Mr. Anderson," Pemberton greeted them with jovial good humor. Unlike his clerk he seemed unfazed by the irregularity of such a meeting. Ursula removed her light 'duster' coat, small brimmed brown hat and kid-leather gloves before sitting herself down in one of the leather armchairs.

"I'm afraid I still haven't got to that little summary of yours on the law of treason, m'dear . . ." Pemberton said with a half-apologetic smile, "case-load is frightful at the moment." He took his place behind the imposing deep-set desk and adjusted the papers in front of him into a tall neat stack.

"If you're too busy, I can always arrange for another barrister to take over," Ursula replied.

Her bluntness took Pemberton off guard.

"My dear, my dear . . ." Pemberton stammered. "I am delighted by your interest and support in this case. Clearly it is a most terrible miscarriage of justice—an error which we shall soon rectify in court."

"I wish it was that easy, Mr. Pemberton," Ursula said. "But I think we can dispense with the pretense and get down to the real issues at hand." She ignored Anderson's hesitant sideways glance and continued. "The Crown is pursuing this case based, I believe on at least two witnesses as well as documentary evidence—am I right?"

"Yes," Pemberton replied, quickly recovering. "The laws of treason require at least two witnesses and the Crown has specified that the charges are reliant on the testimony of Lord Wrotham's second cousin Count von Bernstorff-Hollweg, and an Irish informer by the name of Padraig O'Shaunessy who was apparently at the alleged meeting in Germany and was privy to plans to assassinate members of the Royal family. I also received word just this morning of an additional witness in the case, Mr. Christopher Dobbs"—Ursula caught Anderson's glance this time—"It appears he was initially asked to assist with the procurement of arms via his contacts in Germany."

"So Mr. Dobbs is now one of the Crown's key witnesses?" Ursula asked and her jaw clenched involuntarily at the thought.

"Yes, though, as the case progresses I expect we will receive details with respect to other witnesses in due course. Do you have cause to know if Christopher Dobbs has had much dealing with Lord Wrotham?"

"There is certainly no love lost between them, if that's what you mean," Ursula replied, trying to maintain her composure.

"I should inform you," Anderson told Pemberton quickly, "that Dobbs once expressed an interest in acquiring Marlow Industries. Miss Marlow has already asked me to investigate any links or financial interests that Mr. Dobbs may have respect to the Wrotham family."

"You mean the family debtors, I assume . . ." Pemberton asked and his voice dropped to little more than a murmur.

"You needn't both try and shield my sensibilities," Ursula interrupted. "I am well aware of Lord Wrotham's precarious financial situation, though he is hardly to blame for the deplorable state in which his brother left the estate."

"No, no, of course not," Pemberton hastened to assure her. "No one could have impugned Lord Wrotham on that score."

Anderson cleared his throat. "I think Miss Marlow may be justifiably concerned that Dobbs' interest in this case is personal as well as commercial, so I have widened my inquiries to ascertain the nature of all Dobbs business interests to see if whether any of them impinge on Lord Wrotham's affairs." Anderson had discreetly avoided mentioning the animosity clearly felt between Lord Wrotham, Dobbs' and herself.

"Mr. Anderson is looking at both families' commercial interests in Germany, Britain and Ireland," Ursula said.

"I see," Pemberton answered. "Are you planning to hire a private investigator by any chance?"

"Not for now, I'd rather not risk it," Ursula replied. "I think it's best that only the three of us in this room are privy to any information that may be unearthed though our inquiries. The last thing we need is an unscrupulous investigator leaking stuff to the newspapers."

"Agreed," Pemberton said with a barely suppressed shudder.

"One company I am particularly interested in The Imperial Gold and Diamond Mining Company—are you aware that Lord Wrotham once acted in a case involving this company?"

"No, I can't say that I was."

"Well, I would like help finding the case report"—Ursula dug out a piece of paper from her pocket—"The case is called *El Dorado Investments v. The Imperial Gold and Diamond Mining Company.* I think the High Court heard the appeal in 1907."

"I suppose I could get my clerks to look the case citation up if you'd like," Pemberton offered, after a pause. His expression was faintly bemused.

"That would be most helpful," Ursula replied.

"May I ask why you should be so interested in this case?" Pemberton said.

"Have you not considered that someone may wish to injure Lord Wrotham in this way?" Ursula responded.

"What do you mean?" Pemberton stared at her.

"Let's assume, for the sake of argument say, that the charges made against Lord Wrotham are a fabrication and the witnesses statements a lie . . . Can you think of anyone who would wish to see Lord Wrotham humiliated in this manner? Perhaps someone in power who has borne him a grudge?" Ursula kept her tone brisk and her expression deliberately neutral before Pemberton's obvious incredulity. Nonetheless, she could hear Anderson rock back and forth on his chair with apparent unease.

"You can't be serious Miss Marlow!" Pemberton spluttered. "Such a person would have to be diabolical in the extreme and if that was the case why doesn't Lord Wrotham deny the charges most vigorously rather than remaining silent as he has? I hardly think that theory has any serious merit to it . . ."

"Really, I would have thought it was obvious," Ursula responded. "Lord Wrotham's actions may well have been manipulated to appear treasonous."

"That as may be"—Pemberton's skepticism remained undiminished—"but I have to proceed on the assumption that the crown case is based on facts and the application of the law—not some vast and, dare I say, ludicrous conspiracy theory."

"I see," Ursula replied, but she was not one to be brow beaten by any man, least of all a lawyer. "Nevertheless would you indulge me?" Ursula turned to speak to Anderson.

"Perhaps," she began. "We should try and identify the investors involved in that legal case as well as any companies which once had direct ties to The Imperial Gold and Diamond Mining Company. It's a starting point at least. I would also like a list of all of Lord Wrotham's most controversial cases," Ursula turned back to Pemberton. "No, I haven't completely lost my senses, I just haven't discounted the possibility that someone with a grudge against Lord Wrotham is instigating this."

Pemberton's eyebrows lifted but, after exchanging glances with Anderson, he finally nodded his acquiescence.

"What about the documentary evidence in the case?" Ursula asked. "Do you have copies of the files or Admiral Smythe's notebook as yet?"

"In time we will get access to all the documents—but Miss Marlow, it is still early days, we are only in the preliminary stages of the case and, as you well know, the law does not charge forward apace—unfortunately it is very much inclined to dawdle."

Ursula leaned back in her chair with a disgruntled sigh. She was getting increasingly frustrated by her inability to move forward in her inquiries.

"Have any further charges been laid with regard to Admiral Smythe's death?" she asked.

"Has Lord Wrotham been charged with his murder, do you mean? No"—Pemberton shook his head—"not yet . . ."

"But Lord Wrotham still refuses to offer any evidence in his own defense . . ." Ursula prompted. Her voice was hollow. She knew the answer.

"Yes," Pemberton admitted. "I'm afraid he does."

"I am sure . . ." Anderson offered uncertainly into the silence. "His lordship has his reasons . . ."

Pemberton gave an unsatisfied sniff. "That as may be, but he's placed us all in a most damnable position."

Ursula noticed Pemberton furtively glance at the wall clock, and she gathered up her gloves and purse. "Well," she said briskly. "We won't get him out of jail by sitting around here!" She got to her feet. "Just let me know when your clerk has found the Imperial Gold and Diamond Mining Company case."

"I will make suitable arrangements for you to be able to visit the law library to read it," Pemberton replied and he too got to his feet. Ursula saw the hesitancy and she suddenly understood that there was at least one matter that they had not yet covered: One of extreme delicacy given Lord Wrotham's precarious financial situation.

"I am, of course, planning to pay all legal expenses necessary to clear Lord Wrotham's name—so if we require background searches, additional witnesses—anything like that—you must spare no expense . . ."

Pemberton averted his eyes with an embarrassed cough. "Thank you . . . that certainly . . . yes . . ." he stumbled over the words.

"I am well aware of the precariousness of the Wrotham family finances," Ursula said. "So please, let us say nothing further in the matter only rest easy, Marlow industries will be covering all costs in this case." Ursula gave Anderson a nudge. As her new appointed guardian he would have to also agree. He looked up and gave an eventual, though not entirely convincing, nod.

"No need to see me out," Ursula said briskly as she tugged on her hat and gloves. "I know my way around Temple Inn quite well by now." And with that she exited Pemberton's chambers with what she hoped conveyed a confident, yet steely determination.

Once in the quadrangle, Anderson stopped Ursula in mid-step. "Are you sure?" he asked. "Are you sure you want to go through with all of this—delving into these cases and companies? You may find out things that about Lord Wrotham that you would rather not have known . . ."

"I know," Ursula replied. She knew all too well what it was like to uncover the secrets of the past—it was what led her to discover her father's killer after all. "It's a risk," she admitted, "but it's one that I have to take."

They walked the rest of the way in silence and, as they exited Inner Temple Lane onto Fleet Street, Ursula spied Samuels leaning against the bonnet of Bertie, reading the *Daily Mail* newspaper as he waited for them to return.

"Is a German invasion still imminent?' Ursula asked. The proprietor of the *Daily Mail*, Lord Northcliffe, was notorious for warmongering.

"Any day now, Miss," Samuels replied with a grin as he opened the rear door and assisted Ursula inside. Anderson clambered in alongside her while Samuels cranked the engine. As Samuels navigated the motorcar along the busy streets towards Belgravia, Ursula turned to Anderson and asked: "My father didn't know Admiral Smythe, by any chance, did he?" she asked.

"No, Anderson replied. "He moved in quite a different social circle. I believe your father may have met him once and you know how close he was to Lord Wrotham."

"Pity," Ursula mused. "It would have been useful to have some independent account of what the man was like."

"Yes," Anderson agreed. "Though what little I've heard suggests he valued his secrecy. There have certainly been no rumors of whispers of scandal—though he had little in the way of business interests."

Ursula fiddled with the one of the cuffs of her shirt as she rested her arm on the passenger door.

"Did my father ever mention that Lord Wrotham had once been in Guyana?" she asked.

Anderson shrugged. "He may have, but I don't recall anything of significance. I believe your father met Lord Wrotham on the return journey from there—they were on the same ship from New York to England."

"Yes, I knew that . . . I just wondered if my father ever said"— Ursula paused. She felt a sudden stab of grief. If only her father was still here, she could have had someone to talk to about Lord Wrotham—someone who probably knew more about his secrets than anyone else.

"I know," Anderson said gently. "I still miss him too." His face bore the same wistfulness as Ursula, for he had been a good friend to her father. Ursula bit her lip to keep her tears in check. Although Anderson's children had been spared the murderous vengeance wrought by the man who had killed Robert Marlow, the tragic events of 1910 still reverberated among all of Ursula's father's friends. Ursula suspected that the bonds of friendship between Robert Marlow and his long-time business associates were not unlike those that bound Lord Wrotham and his friends from Balliol. They were borne out of history of shared secrets—of past betrayals and bitter recriminations.

"It's frustrating," Ursula said as she leaned her head against the window glass. "Chief Inspector Harrison won't even let me in to see Admiral Smythe's office or home—or speak with his housekeeper. I know they are handling the investigation but I can't help feeling that they are missing something crucial—something that a man like my father could have known."

"I think you assume too much, Ursula," Anderson said, slipping into informality. "I'm not sure even your father could have helped Lord Wrotham."

Ursula took a deep breath "No, perhaps not . . ." she murmured as she returned her gaze to the window.

After a moment's hesitation, Anderson asked. "Do you really think Christopher Dobbs could be involved?" Christopher Dobbs' father, Obadiah had once been a close friend of Anderson's but, after he had tried to blackmail them all following Robert Marlow's death, friendship between the families had cooled. Anderson was ignorant of Christopher Dobbs' involvement in the death of Katya Vilenksy and her sister the previous year, but he was nonetheless wary of the power and influence Dobbs' companies now wielded. With the possibility of a war with Germany fast approaching, Dobbs' shipbuilding, munitions factories and supplies were in ever increasing demand.

Ursula knew if she told him of the conversation she had with Dobbs at Lady Winterton's party, Anderson would warn her off investigating Dobbs any further. Avoiding the implication in his question, she merely answered: "I am my father's daughter. I never forget that without my fortune I am nothing."

As Samuels dropped Anderson off at his office on Threadneedle Street, and they continued on their way to Chester Square, Ursula reflected that there was more truth to those words than she cared to admit. Of course she wanted all this information as part of her investigation into the case against Lord Wrotham—and she wanted to clear his name above all things—but she was not so altruistic not to recognize the seriousness with which any diminution of her own monetary fortune would have on her standing in society. Tenuous as her position was, if she were to lose her fortune she would lose everything.

CHAPTER TWELVE

THE MORNING WITH PEMBERTON AND ANDERSON had made Ursula restless and uneasy and, after pacing the house for an unsettled few hours, Ursula decided she need to be doing something not waiting at home fretting about an investigation she had little control over. Donning a new navy and cream piped day suit Ursula decided to make her first social call since Lord Wrotham's arrest. When she arrived at Lady Winterton's house, she felt a nervousness that was alien to her—but she summoned the courage and rang the doorbell—casting an imperious look at a passerby who, recognizing her features no doubt from a newspaper photograph, dared to stare at her with unrestrained curiosity.

Ursula was soon ushered into Lady Winterton's front parlor.

"I'm so pleased you've decided to visit," Lady Winterton said, approaching her with a welcoming smile. "After the incident with Mr. Dobbs the other night I was afraid you might retreat into total seclusion."

"Oh, it would take bit more that Christopher Dobbs' vulgarity to do that," Ursula replied.

Lady Winterton took a seat and pulled the servant's bell for tea.

"I was actually thinking of calling upon you," Lady Winterton said.

"I was summoned to Scotland Yard to be interviewed yesterday by Chief Inspector Harrison and Sir Reginald Buckley."

"You were?"

"Yes, I guess because of my long association with Lord Wrotham," Lady Winterton replied. Ursula felt an unexpected stab of jealously.

"What did they ask?" Ursula inquired.

"Oh, it wasn't a very long interview I assure you. Once they discovered I knew very little about Lord Wrotham's business affairs in Germany or his movements abroad they soon realized I was of very little interest to them. They asked about Admiral Smythe of course, but since I last saw him two weeks ago at a gallery opening, I had little in the way of information for them."

Lady Winterton's maid Grace entered bearing the tea tray. "Daisy's taken poorly again, Miss, so I thought I'd help out." Grace was obviously referring to one of the parlor maids and Lady Winterton's smile stiffened. "Daisy needs to take better care of herself," she said coolly.

Grace's light brown curls bobbed as she nodded vigorously. "I'll speak to her right away," she said and Ursula noticed the unspoken agreement that passed between them.

Once Grace had gone, Lady Winterton leaned over and confided: "we have observed that Daisy is rather a little too fond of Cook's sherry. I am only grateful that Grace at least has always been the model of discretion and loyalty—I only wish the rest of my staff could give me such comfort!"

Ursula murmured something inaudible but, she hoped, suitably approving. In truth, Ursula treated her staff with far less formality but she could appreciate Lady Winterton's demand for discretion.

Lady Winterton poured Ursula's tea and was soon sitting back in the plush armchair regarding Ursula thoughtfully as she sipped her cup of Orange Pekoe tea.

"You still look as though you are in much need of sleep," she observed.

"Yes," Ursula admitted. "In truth I have not been sleeping well."

"Understandable, but you must take care of yourself."

"I know," Ursula smiled wanly as she took a sip of tea. The two of them fell into an easy, contemplative silence before Ursula said. "I wonder did Admiral Smythe say anything at the gallery opening to suggest anything was amiss?" Ursula asked.

"Not to me, he didn't," Lady Winterton answered. "He seemed in tolerable good humor that evening. He has never been one for idle chit-chat but I can't say I suspected he was concerned or worried about anything."

"I asked Harrison if I could speak to Admiral Smythe's housekeeper but he refused."

"I'm not sure she would have been much help anyway," Lady Winterton said. "I believe she only came three days a week or so. Admiral Smythe preferred dining at his club and besides, I don't think he had the money to afford full time domestic staff. Pity he never married into money—but he's been a confirmed bachelor for as long as I have known him—or indeed for that matter, for as long as Nigel knew him."

"Did Admiral Smythe ever have any female companions?" Ursula inquired.

"Certainly not," Lady Winterton responded. She eyed Ursula curiously. "Whatever made you ask that?"

"I was just thinking that it seemed a little sad that was all. I mean from the photograph I saw in Oxford, he was not an unhandsome man—surely you would expect him to have female 'friends' shall we say?"

"He was a man . . ." Lady Winterton conceded. "No doubt he had the kind of urges men have—but if he frequented brothels he was discreet about it—I never heard any hint of impropriety or, improper relations of any kind."

Ursula put her cup down with a sigh.

"Sorry," Lady Winterton said. "Not much help am I?"

"Oh it's not that," Ursula said. "I just cannot stand the fact that I don't have access to more information regarding the case. I feel as if I'm groping around in the dark."

Lady Winterton sipped her tea.

"Did Harrison or Buckley show you any of the files they found in Smythe's office?" Ursula asked.

"No, they said nothing about any of the evidence. They seemed more interested in what I knew about Lord Wrotham's past than anything to do with Admiral Smythe."

"When I met with them they brought out all sorts of stuff from Lord Wrotham's Balliol days—just to make me doubt him I suspect. Did they ask you about a notebook by any chance?"

"They asked me if I ever saw Lord Wrotham write in one, and I said no. Though now you mention it, they did ask me about whether I had ever had any conversations with him regarding ciphers or codes which did strike me as rather odd at the time—though I guess they know about our work with the WSPU."

Both Ursula and Lady Winterton had worked with the WPSU on trying to implement a coding system for messages sent between branches. This had originally arisen out of concerns that people were infiltrating the organization and tipping off police as to expected protests or other militant activities.

"I expect they asked you because of Admiral Smythe's notebook," Ursula said.

Lady Winterton cocked her head. "Notebook?" she queried.

"Yes, they apparently discovered it in some hidden wall safe at Admiral Smythe's house. It's encrypted using some kind of numeric code which Sir Buckley is desperate to break. He's convinced Lord Wrotham had a similar notebook and that he and Admiral Smythe used a book code of some kind to encrypt their notes regarding their missions for Naval Intelligence."

"I didn't know Admiral Smythe kept a notebook of his missions," Lady Winterton said.

"Sounds very clandestine and rather exciting, doesn't it?" Ursula admitted.

"Though less exciting when you think it may be used to convict Lord Wrotham," Lady Winterton added.

"True," Ursula conceded and the atmosphere in the room again turned somber.

"I wonder if we will discover Lord Wrotham kept a notebook too?" Lady Winterton mused.

"If he did, he hasn't told me about it," Ursula said and she could not disguise her bitterness. Lord Wrotham's silence continued to frustrate her—at times it depressed her to think he had such little faith in her.

"You know," Lady Winterton said suddenly. "I still have some of my old photograph albums, would you like me to get them out for you? There may be a few of Lord Wrotham and perhaps even that firebrand, McTiernay. I have some of Nigel's old photographs too—though most of these remain on his estate in Ireland."

Ursula's mood brightened. "I would indeed like to have a look," she said.

Lady Winterton left and soon returned bearing two leather bound photograph albums. Ursula sat next to her on the couch and peered over as Lady Winterton showed her the photographs.

"Here's one taken just after Nigel's funeral," Lady Winterton pointed to a somber party of men clad in mourning suits. "That's Count von Bernstorff-Hollweg, next to Lord Wrotham. You can see McTiernay on the other side." Ursula noticed McTiernay wore what appeared to be a medallion off his fob watch chain. She looked closely but could not make out anything further.

"It's a Saint Dismas medallion," Lady Winterton said, her voice quiet. Ursula jerked back and Lady Winterton regarded her with mild surprise. "Does that mean something to you?"

"No . . ." Ursula responded quickly. "It's nothing . . ." She was not prepared to disclose everything to Lady Winterton yet—particularly one that merely suggested greater complicity between McTiernay and Lord Wrotham.

"Did any of the others wear one?" Ursula asked.

"None of the others were Catholic, my dear," Lady Winterton reminded her.

"No, of course not," Ursula said.

Lady Winterton continued to turn the pages. "These are just all of the estate . . . so nothing of interest really here." Ursula saw a series of grainy pictures of a squat, uninspiring country house as Lady Winterton flipped the pages over. "They were taken of course before we fell on hard times—the estate's not much to look at now I'm afraid."

Ursula knew better than to bring up the issue of Lord Winterton's financial affairs. It was no secret that his impecuniosity had caused much of Lady Winterton's family's resistance to the marriage.

"Ah, here's one of Nigel's old photographs from Balliol," Lady Winterton said and Ursula leaned over eagerly.

In the picture all four men were in cricket whites. McTiernay held his bat nonchalantly tucked under his arm and his stance was one of natural arrogance and ease. Lord Winterton and Count von Bernstorff-Hollweg were standing next to him, their cricket jumpers knotted round their necks, sleeves rolled. Lord Winterton's pale hair looked silvery and provided a sharp contrast to the dark haired McTiernay and Wrotham. Lord Wrotham, who stood a little behind McTiernay, had a tall ice-filled glass in one hand and a cigarette in the other. He stared at the camera with the haughtiness of youth and Ursula reflected how idyllic the scene seemed to be—although she had to admit they all looked rather hot and impatient from posing for the photograph beneath the glare of the sun.

"I can't help but wonder," Ursula said, as Lady Winterton closed the photograph album. "What really happened between these men— what prompted them to become involved in this case?"

"I'm afraid only Lord Wrotham can answer that," Lady Winterton said, "or perhaps the Count, if you find him."

"If Admiral Smythe really was murdered, I feel certain that it must have been someone he knew, someone close enough that he would never have suspected . . ." Ursula's voice trailed off distracted by her thoughts. "Poisoning seems so personal somehow . . . and the timing too, so that it would look as if Lord Wrotham was responsible. It makes me wonder whether the person we're looking for didn't also have a grudge against Lord Wrotham . . ."

"Such a theory sounds a trifle absurd," Lady Winterton said quietly.

"I know," Ursula replied, rubbing her eyes. "When I see those photographs it makes me doubt that any of this could be even possible . . . but then . . ."

"Then?" Lady Winterton prompted.

"I remember what happened to my father," Ursula replied. "And I know that though the past can bury secrets, it can never hide them forever. One day, the sins of the past always come back to haunt you."

CHAPTER THIRTEEN

URSULA RECEIVED WORD FROM PEMBERTON by the first post the following morning, that the citation for the case she was looking for had been located, and she had permission to go to the Temple Library to peruse the case at her earliest convenience.

Ursula scrambled to finish her breakfast while Julia got her clothes ready, and by half past nine Ursula was striding down Temple Lane towards Church Court and the Temple library, ready, she hoped, to discover a little more about Lord Wrotham's enigmatic past.

As Ursula entered and took the volume of King's Bench reports that had been left for her to her seat, she could feel the stares of the other members of the Temple Inn—for it was hardly usual for a woman to be gracing their library with her presence, let alone actually reading a law case. Ignoring their disapproving looks, Ursula opened up the volume of the King's Bench reports to the place that Pemberton's clerk had marked. In the glow of the green and brass table lamp she started turning the pages, her initial excitement fading. The more she read, the more she worried that she was wasting her time—what possible relevance could a commercial case that was almost a decade old have on Lord Wrotham's arrest for treason?

Nevertheless she gritted her teeth and continued. The case must have arisen soon after Lord Wrotham 'took silk' and was appointed King's Counsel. It was an appeal to the High Court in the King's Bench Division pertaining to an alleged breach of contract between a company established for speculative investments (El Dorado Investments) and the Imperial Gold and Diamond Mining Company. Although most of the discussion centered on the arcane distinction between conditions and warranties and allegations of oral promises made, Ursula was able to grasp that the dispute fundamentally came down to an issue of expectations. El Dorado investments (as per its name) represented a group of investors who had hoped to get rich from gold and diamond mining in Guyana and, when these riches failed to materialized, they sued the Imperial Gold and Diamond Mining Company. Ursula was not surprised to see reference to two directors of the company, Fergus McTiernay and Count von Bernstorff-Hollweg, but she noted that neither Admiral Smythe nor Lord Wrotham's association with the company was mentioned. Ursula was unfamiliar with the legal issues discussed, but it was obvious as she read the decision of the Lord Chief Justice (who represented the majority opinion), that Lord Wrotham had not only destroyed the claimants' arguments in the lower courts, he had also managed to dash all grounds of appeal. Accordingly, El Dorado Investments not only lost the appeal but was also forced to pay all legal costs associated with the case—grounds enough for resentment no doubt—but motivation to contrive evidence against Lord Wrotham for treason? Unlikely.

"Damn and blast!" Ursula muttered under her breath as she put the heavy tome aside. An elderly barrister clad in black gown and grey wig shot her an outraged look as he passed. Cheeks reddening, Ursula sighed, frustrated that so far she had made little progress. Had Harrison given her the file about Guyana merely to divert her attention from the real issues? In her current state of mind, she could not be sure. All the information she had so far obtained seemed to obfuscate rather than illuminate the truth, but then, Ursula reflected ruefully, the same could also be said about almost everything in Lord Wrotham's past.

Ursula was relieved to find the Inner Temple all but deserted as she crossed Church Court and hurried along Crown Office Row. Today, at least, she had been granted a respite from the constant hounding of reporters eager for information on Lord Wrotham's case. As she walked through the gardens towards the Victorian Embankment and the place where Samuels had been instructed to wait, a short man in a brown sack suit approached her. He bowed, tipping his bowler hat as he did so, before handing her a piece of folded paper. Ursula took and opened it reluctantly.

On the piece of paper was a handwritten message: *Ask Christopher Dobbs about his dealings with Major Frederick Hugh Crawford. This should be sufficient to get you the information you seek. If not, tell him you know about his secret dealings with both Narodna Odbrana and the Serbian society known as The Black Hand.*

The man who had handed her the paper, flashed a crooked smile before saying: "with the compliments of Mr. Fergus McTiernay." The lilt of his Irish accent was unmistakable but no sooner had Ursula's glance flickered back the letter than the man disappeared from view with the same disarming alacrity as he had arrived. She studied the message turning the piece of paper between her fingers thoughtfully before placing it in her skirt pocket. Clearly McTiernay knew about Christopher Dobbs—but was he and his message to be trusted? Ursula wondered just what kind of game McTiernay was playing at in helping her—but regardless, she had to pursue whatever information Dobbs may have. Ursula made her way over to the 'Bertie' and climbed in the backseat, knowing that no matter how much she despised Dobbs she would have to confront him. Of that she was sure. Ursula gritted her teeth. *Tomorrow*, she thought, *I will do it tomorrow*, but in the meantime she would check on the progress of Gerard Anderson's inquiries. When it came to Christopher Dobbs, it was always prudent to be well-armed.

CHAPTER FOURTEEN

THE BRASS PLAQUE on the black lacquered door read: *Dobbs Shipping Company Ltd. By Appointment to His Majesty, George V.* Ursula turned the doorknob and entered a green and black marble-lined entrance foyer. She sniffed in disgust as she saw the long list of Dobbs' acquisitions posted on a further series of brass plaques just inside the doorway. *Madison Steel and Plating Ltd., Liverpool Shipbuilding and Shipyards, Dobbs Munitions and Ammunition Supplies . . .* the list went on, but at least, Ursula reflected, she had prevented Marlow Industries from suffering the same fate. She would rather die than hand over any of her father's business empire to Christopher Dobbs.

On the opposite wall, above the secretary's desk, was a magnificent mural depicting a map of the world, complete with details of all the Dobbs' companies' shipping routes. From the cut crystal chandelier that swung from the high ceiling above, to the sleek modern typewriter sitting unused behind the secretary's high backed chair and the Marconi wireless receiver strategically displayed on a pedestal beneath the window, Christopher Dobbs was determined to display the extent of his power in every expensive detail. It sickened Ursula to see his success displayed so ostentatiously. By all rights he should have been hanged for his role in the deaths of Katya Vilenksy and her sister

Arina, but his usefulness to the British government kept him immune from justice.

Steeling herself for what she must do, Ursula approached the secretary with long deliberate strides. Her boots struck the polished floor with each footfall, creating an illusion of almost masculine authority which Ursula, inwardly nervous, was grateful for. As Ursula reached the high polished front desk with its carved, ship-like details she nodded to the secretary.

"Kindly inform Mr. Dobbs that Miss Marlow is here to see him," Ursula instructed with calm assurance. She pulled off her navy blue velvet hat and soft leather gloves as she spoke and regarded the young red-headed secretary with cool appraising eyes. It was not difficult to see why Christopher Dobbs had hired this young woman. She was petite and pretty, with violet eyes and a small pout of a mouth. It was also obvious from the bat of her eyelashes and the tap-tap of her fingernails on the shiny desk top that she posed little intellectual threat to him or anyone else.

"Have you an appointment?" the secretary asked. She looked down at her desk calendar, already flustered.

"No, I have not," Ursula replied.

"Well I'm afraid . . ." the secretary began hesitantly before Ursula insisted. "Please tell Mr. Dobbs that I am here. I'm sure he will rearrange his schedule if necessary."

The telephone rang and the secretary bobbed up and down on her seat before taking the call, her face reddening with a mixture of embarrassment and uncertainty.

Ursula merely raised an eyebrow. The secretary put the telephone ear-piece down and quickly got to her feet once more. "I will just go and ask him, Miss Marlow."

"Much obliged," Ursula answered.

The secretary disappeared behind an imposing oak door off to the right. It led, Ursula could only assume, to Christopher Dobbs' office. It was a far cry, Ursula thought, from the man who just two years ago had taken over his father's shipping company when it was in dire financial straits. Dobbs now had the money and the influence to own an office in the heart of London's financial district and he was clearly determined to impress all who entered. It was no secret that Dobbs, convinced a war with Germany was inevitable, was building an armament empire worthy of competing with Vickers and Krupp.

The secretary emerged quickly from Dobbs' office.

"Please come on through," she said with a squeak. "He will see you right away."

"I thought he might," Ursula muttered under her breath, but still, the palms of her hands were clammy. It was never prudent to underestimate Christopher Dobbs.

"Miss Marlow," Dobbs welcomed her from the doorway with a crocodile smile. "I'm surprised it took you this long to come and see me."

"I've been busy," Ursula replied.

"But of course," Dobbs said as he closed the door behind her. She heard him turn the key in the lock.

Ursula quickly examined her surroundings, taking note of the tall cabinets and bookshelves, the framed photographs of Dobbs with an array of powerful men, and the large replica navigator's globe on a wooden stand in the corner. Everything was designed to impress, but, she suspected, Dobbs was also sending a message to those like her who dared to challenge him. Opposition, this room said, was not only futile—it was dangerous.

Ursula took a seat on one of the leather armchairs in front of Dobbs' oversized desk. She crossed her legs and arms to conceal her nervousness and watched as he walked round to take position behind the large mahogany desk. The swagger in his step was galling.

"I've been looking into some of your Irish friends," Ursula said as he inched forward on the wooden swivel chair. She set her hat and gloves down on the chair beside her.

Dobbs regarded her with amusement. "Really?" he said.

"Yes, Major Frederick Hugh Crawford, to be exact," she replied and was gratified to see that his smile faded a little.

"What of it?" Dobbs asked.

Ursula dug out her notebook from her skirt pocket. "Seems that one of your shipping companies has done quite a bit of business with the major. Even more interesting is that one of your armament firms also seems involved." Ursula made a show of finding a page in her notebook, grateful that Anderson had discovered this much, at least. "Now, let me see," she said, "Ah yes, a shipment of rifles was made just last week." She glanced up quickly.

Was she imagining it or did Dobbs' eyes narrow for a moment? There was certainly a dangerous glint in them. Ursula knew she would have to tread carefully.

"I was surprised," she said, closing her notebook. "I would have thought the British government would have taken a dim view of gun running for the Ulster Unionists."

Dobbs said nothing but continued to watch her warily.

"Oh, I know the Unionist cause has the support of many in parliament," Ursula said. "But I feel sure that there are many in the government who would consider arming Ulster for a possible revolt against Home Rule as tantamount to treason . . . You wouldn't want the wrong people to learn about your involvement, would you? You are, after all, only alive because the government deemed you to be a useful lackey to have on its side." She paused and saw the flush of anger rising on Dobbs face. "If I had my way," she added, "you would have been hanged for murder"—bitterness crept into her tone—"But if I can't have that satisfaction, the least I can do is see you hang for this."

"Only one man is likely to hang, my dear," Dobbs responded, his composure returning with all its icy arrogance, "and I am happy to testify in court to ensure that he does."

Ursula guessed that Dobbs could count on the tacit support of some of the conservative members of parliament and her knowledge of his Unionist activities was not, as yet, a sufficient threat to his position. She would need to use all the information McTiernay had provided her if she was to succeed in drawing him out, even though Anderson had found no evidence linking Dobbs to the pan-Serbian organization known as The Black Hand.

"Your chums at Whitehall would perhaps be less supportive if they knew about some of your other little side deals," Ursula said smoothly. "I can't imagine they wish to see organizations such as Narodna Odbrana or The Black Hand receiving British armaments or intelligence—especially not from a man whose fortune and freedom rests on doing exactly what the government wishes."

Dobbs edged his chair away from the desk. His eyes bored into hers but Ursula remained calm. She sensed his uncertainty—that he was worried exactly how much she knew about his activities. In truth, Ursula only had McTiernay's note to go on and there was always a chance that Dobbs would call her bluff. Ursula maintained eye contact with Dobbs with what she prayed appeared to be calm indifference.

"Perhaps," she offered, forcing a confident smile. "I could forget all that I know about your little side deals, if you provided me with the information you have regarding Lord Wrotham's case."

Dobbs rocked back on the swivel chair and watched her closely.

"It's up to you," Ursula said, getting to her feet as if to go. "The satisfaction I will get from thwarting you is almost enough to outweigh helping Lord Wrotham. Believe me, I won't hesitate to use what I know against you."

"I have no doubt of that," Dobbs responded gesturing for her to sit, "and I will give you what you want on the proviso that you keep your mouth shut."

"Your sordid dealings are of no further concern to me," she answered coolly.

Christopher Dobbs rose to his feet and crossed the room. Hidden inside one of the lower cabinets of the bookshelves was a large wall safe. With his back turned to her, Dobbs quickly opened it and rummaged for a few seconds before extracting a single piece of ledger paper.

He walked back and tossed it to her across the desk.

"This is it?" she asked, regarding the sheet with skepticism.

"That's all I have at the moment," he answered. "A closer examination will reveal it to be a summary of the financial accounts for the Imperial Gold and Diamond Mining Company dated 1907 with corresponding links to investments made by Count von Bernstorff-Hollweg and Fergus McTiernay. You don't need to be certified as an accountant to work out that both men were defrauding the company. I'm sure by now you know that Lord Wrotham defended the company in a court case brought by disgruntled investors."

Ursula gave a short sharp nod and continued to watch Dobbs suspiciously. She knew better than to take anything on face value from him.

"I just happen to know that the reason the Count von Bernstorff-Hollweg is testifying against Lord Wrotham is because someone threatened to divulge where the money is to the Count's extremely long list of creditors. Now the Count may be a fool but he's not stupid enough to allow wind of this to reach the ears of men like those associated with The Black Hand. If they were to learn the truth about the money from Guyana then they might start getting suspicious—and if they delve deeper they are likely to discover a number of unsavory business practices from their dear friend the Count . . . He is worried not just about his safety but also his reputation among Germany high society. The last thing he wants is for anyone to discover what really happened in Guyana."

"Why were you originally offering to tell me this?" Ursula asked. "There must have been something you were hoping to get in return."

"What, apart from the enjoyment of bedding you?" Dobbs said and she flushed at the reference to their conversation at Lady Winterton's party. Dobbs really was a brute, but Ursula was not about to give him the satisfaction of another outburst. Instead she merely raised an eyebrow enquiringly.

"Your investigations into Lord Wrotham's case will undoubtedly uncover information regarding potential rivals in the armaments trade," Dobbs replied briskly. "Information that may prove useful to me one day."

"And you really thought I would be willing to share this information with you?" Ursula said.

Dobbs smirked. "If I know you, it will end up on the front page of every newspaper in the country."

Ursula felt uneasy, now she had played the hand McTiernay had given her, she was not at all sure that Dobbs was not still holding something back.

"There is still one thing I'd like to know," Ursula said.

"And that is?" Dobbs regarded her insolently.

"Who exactly used the information you've given me, to compel Count von Bernstorff-Hollweg to testify against Lord Wrotham?"

Dobbs smiled. "Ah, that little piece of information would require further payment . . ."

Ursula felt a surge of anger. She snatched her hat and gloves and quickly rose to her feet.

"Don't tell me your scruples are now suddenly offended," Dobbs said with a laugh. "Remember my dear, you came to me . . . as you will come to me again when you realize you still need my help."

"Kindly unlock the door," Ursula said stiffly, trying to maintain a tenuous hold on self-control, "so that I can leave."

"As you wish," Dobbs replied. He slowly got up out of his chair, stretched his neck and walked around from behind the desk. Ursula was still standing, holding the back of the chair to steady herself as she waited for the rage to subside. She turned go but as she did so, Dobbs gripped her wrists and forced her back down on the chair to face him. He pinned her arms behind her easily, pressing his weight down upon her.

His hot breath was on her cheeks even as she struggled to turn her face away, even as she kicked and writhed beneath him. "You don't seriously imagine that your petty threats will ever succeed against me—and please, there's no point in screaming," he said in a low voice in her ear, "all my employees know when to be discreet."

Dobbs' strength took Ursula by surprise. She had been under his power once before, when he had threatened to kill her over her discovery of his part in the death of Katya Vilensky, and she was under no illusion that he would have any qualms about doing the same now.

"Soon," Dobbs said, "you and I are going to have a long overdue chat about gratitude and respect—"

Ursula arched her back trying to cause him to lose his balance but all he did was press his hands against her wrists more tightly. "Although I grow impatient with our conversations," he murmured in her ear, "I must confess I'm beginning to find the challenge . . . exciting . . ."

His tongue licked the tip of her ear and then slid down along her neck. Ursula tried to kick him in the shins but Dobbs pinned her legs down with the full weight of his body.

"Hmmm . . ." he said, his voice muffled by the folds of her shawl style collar. "I always knew you would smell good. I bet you taste even better." He moved his head down to where her jacket parted and the cut of her silk shirt revealed the swell of her breasts. With the tip of his front teeth glimmering in the overhead electric light, he lightly bit at one of her nipples beneath the fabric. Ursula's body froze with the shock of such a chillingly intimate and abhorrent act. She could not move. Could not fight him. Her body was too numb to react. A small dark patch of saliva remained on her blouse as Dobbs pulled away from her with a smile. Her senses finally awoke and she tore herself free from his grasp. But by now Dobbs was satisfied; he made no attempt to continue to hold her down. Nauseated, Ursula stumbled to her feet as Dobbs calmly walked to the door and unlocked it.

"I look forward to seeing you again, Miss Marlow," he said. "When you return, as no doubt you will, begging me for further answers."

As she passed him, Ursula faced him with such ire she could barely control the rage in her voice. "If I had a gun," she said, "I would have killed you for that."

"If you had a gun. Miss Marlow, I would have wrested it from you." Dobbs leaned in towards her. "Then," he said, "I really would have been able to have everything his Lordship has had."

Ursula got into the back seat of Bertie and struggled to pull a handkerchief out from her skirt pocket. She kept her jacket buttoned tightly to hide the stain on her blouse.

"Are you all right?" Samuels asked anxiously as Ursula retched.

She nodded weakly. "Just take me home." She could barely speak, the disgust was so great.

Samuels faithfully drove her home as quickly as possible, weaving his way through the London traffic with one eye open for any reporters who might still be hoping to catch a glimpse of her for their latest story. Thankfully there were none waiting for them outside Chester Square and Ursula was safely escorted by Samuels up the stone steps and inside before the neighbors' curtains even parted.

Once inside, Julia bundled Ursula upstairs and stood by in stunned astonishment as Ursula tore off her jacket and shirt as soon as she entered her bedroom. Ursula threw them both to the floor before collapsing on her bed. Her breathing was still ragged and the sour taste in her mouth remained—even as she tried to drive the image of Christopher Dobbs from her mind.

"Can I get you anything, Miss?" Julia asked anxiously.

Ursula shook her head. "Just burn it," she said, pointing to the offending silk shirt that lay crumpled on the floor.

"Burn it?" Julia echoed.

"Yes," Ursula said as she laid her head back to contain the nausea that rose once more. "Burn it and then send Hugh Carmichael a telegram. Tell him I need to buy a lady's gun."

That night Biggs delivered a note from Chief Inspector Harrison. It was brief and to the point. No fingerprints could be obtained from the files found on Admiral Smythe's desk. We are proceeding on the assumption that they are not forgeries. You should reconsider your position. Any information you provide me I can use to plead for clemency in His Lordship's case.

Ursula tossed the note into the fireplace but as she leaned her head against the mantel she closed her eyes. She could see the photograph of the four men in her mind—captured on that idyllic summer's day at Balliol—and was reminded of Tennyson's words in the poem "The Princess": O Death in Life, the days that are no more. It was all she could do to keep from weeping.

CHAPTER FIFTEEN

BROMLEY HALL, NORTHAMPTONSHIRE

"WHAT NEWS DO YOU HAVE THEN?" Lady Wrotham asked, flicking the crumbs from her lap onto the floor where they were hastily licked up by one of the collies. Her tone remained petulant. No doubt, Ursula reflected, she wished to be in London where she could milk the drama of her son's arrest for all it was worth, but Ursula was not about to install Lady Wrotham in her Chester Square home and Lord Wrotham had vowed long ago that his mother was never to step foot in his Mayfair abode. So Lady Wrotham had to be content sitting in the Green Room, but she did not have to pretend to be happy about it. Biding her time in the shadows of Bromley Hall was hardly the dowager's style.

For her part, Ursula felt compelled out of a sense of duty to visit Lady Wrotham and relay to her what news she could of her son's condition as well as progress in the case. Needless to say, Ursula told her nothing of her own enquiries, Christopher Dobbs, or the file on Guyana that Harrison had shown her.

"After all the grief he's given me of late my nerves are in shreds! I tell you, if I never hear from my son again it will be too soon."

"Lady Wrotham," Ursula said gently. "I know you don't mean that."

The dowager pulled a lace handkerchief from the pocket of her chiffon blouse and dabbed her eyes. Ursula, unmoved by Lady Wrotham's feigned sensibilities, reached out to stroke one of the collie's ears (who were still hoping for further tidbits from Lady Wrotham's plate).

"I'm sure it will all blow over in good time," Ursula said as if comforting the dog. "You'll see . . . It will all turn out to be a grave mistake, that's all."

Lady Wrotham stuffed the handkerchief up her sleeve. "From what I hear, that's the last thing it will turn out to be," she replied caustically. "How, pray tell, can I be expected to restore the family's good name if I am not in London but stuck out here in the middle of Northamptonshire?! How can I disavow all knowledge of Oliver's indiscretions—rebut the whispers and insinuations, if I . . . am . . . not . . . there?" The last four words were stressed with an emphatic shake of an index finger.

"It cannot be helped," Ursula replied. "Believe me you are better off here where you cannot be hounded by the press."

Lady Wrotham harrumphed. "I assure you, there are quite a few things I would like the press to hear . . ."

Ursula was not sure how much longer her irritation with Lady Wrotham could remain in check.

"Unless you have anything good to say about your son, I suggest you keep your opinions to yourself," Ursula snapped. To her surprise Lady Wrotham actually looked abashed for a moment.

"I'm sorry," Ursula apologized. "I shouldn't be taking out my frustration on you. I just wish I could put the pieces together and begin to understand what's going on."

"When it comes to Oliver, I gave up trying to do that years ago," Lady Wrotham responded with a sniff. "After Guyana the man was more private than ever—if that was humanly possible."

"So he never told you anything about what happened there?" Ursula asked bleakly.

"No. Though I noticed that he no longer invited his Balliol friends to the estate—no loss, I assure you. But by then he hardly ever came up here anyway—always holed up in London with his legal work and his time in the House of Lords . . . Never took me to the continent did he? No—I was always stuck away here, forgotten . . ."

"I think I'd better go see if the library is back in order," Ursula said, getting hastily to her feet. She had just about enough of Lady Wrotham's selfishness for one day.

Lady Wrotham glared at Ursula as she gave the servants' bell a short sharp tug. "At least Ayres continues to show me a little respect!" she said, drawing her head back imperiously.

Ursula hurried out of the room before she said something she would be sure to regret. In her rush, she almost bumped into Ayres in the hallway.

"Ah, Miss Marlow . . . was it you that rang?"

Ursula shook her head. "No, it was her Ladyship. I'm just escaping . . . I mean, on my way, to see how the library is holding up."

"May I recommend that you avoid that Miss Marlow," Ayres said. "I fear what you see there may . . ."

"Induce a fit of apoplexy?" Ursula supplied.

Ayres exhaled loudly "The Metropolitan Police have, I fear, failed, to respect our wishes and the place is in disarray. We are still trying to rectify the situation, I'm afraid."

"Don't worry, I will steel myself for what's in store," she reassured him. "Though, Lady Wrotham, I'm afraid, may require some fortification of her own . . ."

Ayres lifted up his tray. "I thought this fine sherry that you sent from Fortnum's could be just the thing to lift her ladyship's spirits."

Ursula tipped an imaginary cap at Ayres with a smile and continued on her way down the hallway towards the picture gallery.

As she passed beneath the long row of pictures depicting the lineage of the Barony of Wrotham at Bromley Hall, she paused for a moment, and looked back with a frown. She turned to retrace her steps, her pace quickening as she saw Ayres returning from Lady Wrotham's parlor.

"Ayres," she called out as she drew near.

"Yes, Miss?"

"Where did you say sherry came from?"

"Fortnum's Miss. Your hamper arrived this morning."

"But I didn't send any hamper . . ." Ursula started to say before her words were interrupted by a cry from the parlor.

Ursula and Ayres rushed back down the hall and threw open the door. As they entered Ursula saw Lady Wrotham admonishing one of the dogs.

"I swear," she said turning to them. "My son is determined to drive me to an early grave—even his dogs are in on it! Just look what they made me do? Always getting in the way and tangling up my skirts . . ." she reached down to pick up the sherry bottle that had tipped over on its side.

"No!" Ursula cried out. "Don't touch it!"

Lady Wrotham recoiled sharply. "What on earth is the matter with you, girl?!" she said. "It hasn't all spilled you know!"

"I don't think we should touch anything until we've called the authorities," Ursula replied, her voice shaking.

"The authorities?! Are you completely mad?" Lady Wrotham retorted.

"Possibly," Ursula conceded. "But I didn't send any Fortnum's hamper."

"The hamper had your name on it, Miss, quite distinctly," Ayres said, He paused as the implications of the situation sank in.

Lady Wrotham, however, ignored their concerns and shrugged. "I have many friends who may have thought to send me some sustenance in my hour of need."

"Maybe," Ursula responded. "But after what happened to Admiral Smythe do you really want to risk it?"

"It was most certainly laced with cyanide," Chief Inspector Harrison said. "It's easily disguised in liquids of this kind . . . and once either of you had drunk it there was nothing anyone could have done."

Ursula was seated in one of the upholstered green and white armchairs in the Green Room while Lady Wrotham lay on the sofa, ashen faced, as Ayres placed a cold compress on her forehead. Once he had received Ursula's urgent message, Chief Inspector Harrison had wasted no time in taking the first train from London. Though it had taken him all afternoon to reach them, he had quickly made his determination.

"The tell-tale almond scent is definitely there—you were just probably not able to smell it Lady Wrotham. Not everyone can," Harrison said.

"But who would have done such a thing?" Lady Wrotham whispered. "I am beloved on the estate."

Ursula kept her eyes firmly on the floor.

"Of course you are," Harrison responded. Lady Wrotham opened one eye and fixed it upon his countenance.

"Do I know you?" she demanded.

Harrison coughed. "Your ladyship may remember my family—we lived on the estate many years ago. My father was one of your tenant farmers. We lived in the cottage at the edge of the Eastern meadows."

"Didn't your father move to London?"

"Yes," Harrison replied. "After that portion of the estate was sold. My father joined his brother in the East End. They operated a couple of stalls in Spitalfields market."

Ursula looked at Harrison curiously but she could sense his reluctance to say more. By now, Lady Wrotham closed her eyes—she had already lost interest in Harrison's family.

Harrison folded his arms and turned his attention to Ursula.

"I'm glad you saw fit to send for me," he said. "Whoever did this was indiscriminate—who knows how many people could have drunk that sherry. If you hadn't acted as you did, the circumstances could have been dire."

"The only two people likely to have drunk it," Ursula reminded him, "were Lady Wrotham and myself. The servants would have hardly partaken."

"Whoever it was, however, was reckless enough to risk others. What if there had been visitors?"

"Don't you think, whoever sent it knew that we were likely to be alone? I mean given the circumstances, no one's likely to come calling, are they?" Ursula responded, and though she tried to avoid sarcasm, some involuntarily snuck through.

"Do you think someone is targeting me because of my son's treacherous activities," Lady Wrotham interrupted, her voice hoarse.

"There has been a remarkable degree of publicity surrounding this case," Chief Inspector Harrison admitted. "But no details of Admiral Smythe's death have been reported. I know for a fact that no one in the press has been told about the cyanide. The official cause of death

---

issued was drowning—we deliberately suppressed any mention of cyanide poisoning."

"So it was probably Admiral Smythe's murderer who sent us the sherry . . ." Ursula said. "At least this helps eliminate Lord Wrotham from your investigations into Admiral Smythe's death."

"Unfortunately, nothing so simple as that, Miss Marlow . . . Fortnum & Mason's records state that the hamper was ordered by telephone under your account name and picked up by an unknown messenger boy yesterday morning."

"What, now you think I may have attempted to poison Lady Wrotham to move suspicion away from Lord Wrotham?" Ursula exclaimed.

"I'd not be much of a policeman if I'd leapt to that conclusion without first checking your movements and activities."

Ursula flushed. She should have known of course that she would have been under surveillance.

"Instead, I have men speaking with the staff at Fortnum's. I only hope we can trace the messenger boy and find out who sent him."

Ursula sank back against the cushions "Do you think whoever planned this wanted both of us to die?" she asked.

"Whoever it is may have not cared—either, or both of you may have been sufficient . . ." Harrison replied.

"But of course, the person who was likely to suffer the most," Ursula said slowly, "would have been Lord Wrotham?" She shivered. "What better way to seek revenge," she said, "than to kill the two women closest to him?"

"What better way indeed," Harrison replied, his face as inscrutable as a block of granite beneath the chisel.

Revenge. The word spoke volumes—about the past, about the motivation for murder or treason. But by whom? And for what? Ursula's thoughts were reeling. Did the answer lie in the past? In Guyana perhaps? Or was it more obvious than that—could she retrace Lord Wrotham's steps that led to his arrest and try and make sense of it? But where to start and where to go? Germany? Ireland? She only knew one thing—that she would see it through to the end—whatever end it may be.

PART TWO

GERMANY

CHAPTER SIXTEEN

BERNSTORFF-HOLLWEG SCHLOSS,
THURINGEN MOUNTAINS, THE GERMAN EMPIRE

THE CASTLE WAS LITTLE MORE THAN A BURNT OUT RUIN. As Ursula climbed the steep cobbled stone path, leaving the motorcar she had hired far below, she saw evidence of the speed of destruction everywhere. From the charred earth and bare trees, from the twisted iron that had melted in the ferocity of the fire, and the collapsed stone ruins that were already being overrun by vegetation. So much for finding Count von Bernstorff-Hollweg, or learning what truly happened at the meeting here in December 1911, thought Ursula ruefully. She was too late, whatever secrets had been kept here had been destroyed days, maybe even weeks ago.

Winded from the steep climb, Ursula stopped to catch her breath. She pulled a handkerchief from the pocket of her divided green 'hiking skirt' and mopped her brow. Disappointment clenched in her stomach as well as anger—coming to Germany had turned into little more than a wild goose chase. She gazed despondently across to what must have once been a thick pine forest—the little that remained was now a half charred and mottled bosket, looking forlorn in its brief glimmers of greenness, against the blackened earth and blue-gray boulders. Ursula made her way over and sat down on one of the smaller, wind-smoothed rocks. If she had thought she could pass herself off as a sturdy English rambling type then she was sorely mistaken. As she continued to gasp for breath she was thankful she had encountered no one on her walk here. She continued to wipe her face, the hearty breakfast she had enjoyed at the small gästehaus in Bad Liebenstein now sitting uneasily in her stomach.

Ursula had been in Germany just over a week. She and Lady Winterton had accompanied Lady Wrotham to the sanatorium at the historic spa of Bad Liebenstein under the auspices of helping the dowager recover from the shock of the recent attempt to poison her (not to mention the stress of her son's arrest). Ursula had never been more grateful than when Lady Winterton offered to assist her—the thought of having Lady Wrotham as a sole traveling companion had been a nightmarish one and Lady Winterton's valuable linguistic skills came in handy as Ursula knew no German. (Lady Wrotham's German seemed limited to commands that she would bark out randomly.)

Earlier that morning, Ursula had left Lady Winterton at the gästehaus they were both staying in near the sanatorium, while Lady Wrotham checked herself in to avail herself of the various cures available. The sanatorium was equipped with bathing houses for hydrotherapies and balconies from which patients could receive the 'resting cures' prescribed to them. Such cures sounded rather appealing now and Ursula, still short of breath and feeling queasy, had to lean against one of the disfigured black trees to regain her strength.

Once she had recovered, Ursula gingerly climbed over ash and rock, blackened beams and disfigured metal that appeared to have once been suits of armor. She felt the wind rise—cold and bleak on this ruined escarpment in the Thüringen Mountains. Yet there was, even amid the wail of the wind, the sound of firm footsteps, of boots crunching over cinders as if the remains of the castle were bones to be crushed. Ursula froze.

From over the rise of rock and ash came a figure, dark against the sky.

"James?!" Ursula exclaimed as she recognized Lord Wrotham's chauffeur. "What on earth are you doing here?!"

As James' presence here raised any number of intriguing and possibly disturbing theories, Ursula remained watchful as he approached.

"Miss Marlow," James said calmly. "As soon as my contacts, or should I say his Lordship's contacts in the shipping industry informed me that you had boarded a ship bound for Germany, I knew it was only a matter of time before you came here."

"You were expecting me?" Ursula queried, still keeping her distance.

"Of course, although I wish the circumstances were different," James replied. "Until now, I have been unable to carry out his Lordship's orders."

"His orders?" Ursula repeated. "But Lord Wrotham has been most concerned about your disappearance. He thinks you're still in England." Anxiety rose within her, making her already queasy stomach much worse. *Had Lord Wrotham deceived her in this respect too?* "What orders? What are you talking about?"

"Ah," James responded. As he started walking towards her, Ursula held up her hand. "Don't come any closer," she instructed him.

James halted in mid step.

"Please, Miss Marlow," he said. "I can explain. Lord Wrotham's orders were that, in the event of his arrest, I should immediately find you and get you out of England. His primary concern, as always, was for your safety. The morning before his arrest, however, I received specific instructions from Admiral Smythe to leave for Germany. It wasn't until I landed in Hamburg and heard of Lord Wrotham's arrest as well as Admiral Smythe's disappearance, that I began to suspect that the orders I received were false."

"If you suspected they were false, why did you not return to England?" Ursula asked.

"Miss Marlow, things are more complicated perhaps than they first appear. As soon as I heard who the crown witness was against Lord Wrotham I knew I had to stay in Germany and confront the Count. If you give me a chance to explain, then hopefully you can trust me . . ." James held out his hands as if to placate her, but Ursula continued to regard him warily.

"You do know that Admiral Smythe is dead," she said, watching his face closely. "His body was fished out of the Thames a week ago."

"Yes," James answered slowly. "It makes our next steps all the more difficult."

"Our next steps?" Ursula queried. "You mean in terms of my investigation into who is behind all of this?"

"No, I mean in terms of getting you to safety. I have also heard about the attempt on Lady Wrotham's life."

"You seem remarkably well informed—but if you are here then you must know that I am undertaking my own enquiries . . ."

"My orders are to see you safely out of harm's way, that is all."

Ursula ignored the implication that he would not assist in her investigation and said "I had hoped to speak with the Count, but it seems I am too late . . . Do you know what happened here?"

"A fire broke out in the kitchens about a week ago and it spread so fast there was nothing they could do to contain it. I happen to know one of the scullery maids and she told me the Count was lucky to escape with his life."

Ursula bit her lip. "Do you know where the Count is now?"

James shook his head.

"Lady Winterton was hoping she might be able to use her family connections, should my trip here prove unsuccessful. Perhaps she can help. She has quite the circle of continental friends . . ."

"You won't get anywhere near him," James replied emphatically. "Not now, and unless you're *hochgeboren* don't expect to be invited to any parties at which you might even see him by chance. Count von Bernstorff-Hollweg, like many of the German nobility, is a snob—he won't mix with the likes of you or me."

Ursula's eyes narrowed at the perceived insult.

"No point lookin' at me like that," James responded. "I'm not the one who makes the rules. As far as the Count's concerned, your family, seeing as how they were in trade, isn't of his class. Of course, the Count did make exceptions for anarchists, Irish rebels and the like. If he could profit then he'd meet with you, but now—he's no fool; he's not going to speak with you on any account."

Ursula flushed. "I suppose you think there's no point in me being here then!" she retorted. "But I'll not be giving up my enquiries that easily."

"I never thought you would," James said calmly. "But we'd best hurry before the Count's men discover we are here." His eyes were mercurial in the changing light. "We don't have much time."

Ursula held back, unsure whether she should trust him. "Who are you really?" she demanded. "For I find it hard to believe that you're *just* Lord Wrotham's chauffeur."

"Miss Marlow, we don't have time for me to tell you my life's history. There are armed men here to deter any locals poking through the ruins to see what they can salvage. The Count is nothing if not paranoid these days. If we are to find what we need, we need to do so immediately, and then leave."

Ursula crossed her arms. "What could there possibly be left to find here?" she asked, still unconvinced.

"You'd be surprised what secrets can be unearthed," James replied enigmatically. He signaled her to follow him towards another small copse of trees, singed black and surrounded by large boulders and rocks. Ursula followed cautiously.

"Why are you here? I doubt it was on the off chance that you'd see me today? What is it that you're looking for?" Ursula pressed.

"I'm looking for the man who probably started the fire."

"You think it was Fergus McTiernay, don't you?" Ursula said slowly as she steadied herself on one of the tree trunks. She really needed to improve her fitness if such a walk made her feel so bad. "You think he wants the Count dead because he's testifying against Lord Wrotham . . ."

"No, I think he wants him dead because the Count betrayed McTiernay," James replied. "He betrayed their friendship and for McTiernay that is unforgivable."

"What about Lord Wrotham?"—Ursula swallowed hard—"Does McTiernay think he betrayed him?"

"I'm not sure," James confessed. "McTiernay may still believe Wrotham is a fellow Irish patriot. Whether he now suspects Wrotham was double-dealing—that he was really acting on behalf of the British government, I can't say."

"Are you confirming that Lord Wrotham *was* acting on behalf of the government?" Ursula demanded. *Finally* she thought, *I might get some answers.*

James whirled around, as if he heard something and, turning back quickly, placed a finger to his lips signaling silence.

"I'm not confirming or denying anything," he whispered as he led her, half crouching, to what little cover there was—amidst the straggle of fir trees and rocks. "After all," he flashed an unexpected grin, "that's my job."

"If you can't answer my questions, you can at least tell me what on earth you possibly hope to find here!" Ursula gestured to the bare blackened earth.

James flashed another crooked half-smile as he pointed behind her, into the dim grayness between the branches and rocks. "Well, if you were to go through there for instance, you would find two shallow graves."

"Graves?" Ursula repeated, her mouth suddenly dry. "How did you know where they would be?"

"Why Miss Marlow," James responded. "I was here, of course. I dug the graves myself."

James instructed Ursula to remain concealed behind one of the boulders while he began digging and sifting through the dirt and ash using his bare hands.

"You're not going to exhume the bodies like that I hope?" Ursula said, feeling weak at the prospect of James unearthing bones before her very eyes.

"No, I'd have brought a shovel if I was planning on that," James replied. "I'm looking for something else." On his hands and knees he dug furiously with his hands. "Fire has a way of unearthing things that people wish to remain hidden," he said, briefly wiping his brow with the back of his hand. "I saw his Lordship come out here a couple of hours after we buried the two men and I have a feeling he placed what I'm looking for somewhere around here. I'm just not exactly sure where . . ." He continued his searching and sifting. "As you well know, his Lordship is good at playing his cards close to his chest."

"Is that what you'd call it," Ursula murmured.

"Shh!" James abruptly whispered. Ursula heard men's voices in the distance.

James renewed his search with renewed urgency. "Keep down," he hissed. "We'll just have to hope there remains enough cover to shield us for a little longer."

Ursula got to her hands and knees and crawled over, joining him in clawing through the dirt and ash and leaves.

In a small patch of earth, James appeared to find what he was looking for. He dug out a brown oilskin covered package and shoved it into the inner pocket of his jacket before pulling out his revolver. She heard one of the men speaking in low guttural German, his voice closer now. James gestured to her to retreat further into the copse of fir trees.

She had hardly gotten more than two yards before a shot rang out, so close that Ursula flattened herself against the ground.

"That was just a warning shot." James was suddenly beside her. "But they know we're here."

"Who are they?" Ursula asked.

"The Count's hired thugs—as I said there's been a fair few people scavenging what they can from the ruins. What I need you to do is follow my lead. Just go where I say and keep your head down. It's going to be a scramble but I'll get you down safely."

"And when you do," Ursula replied, with a rueful glance at her now dirt-streaked skirt and blouse, "you're going to teach me how to use one of these." She pointed to the revolver, thinking of how her father's life had been ended by just such a weapon. "I've had just about enough of being on the receiving end!"

James merely laughed before he took her hand and steadied her as they began their descent down the steep mountain side.

CHAPTER SEVENTEEN

"HOW DO YOU FEEL ABOUT AUSTRALIA?" James called out as he dashed between the trees and across the dirt road to where Ursula's motorcar was sitting idle.

"How do I . . . What on earth are you talking about?!" Ursula exclaimed. She scrambled to keep up with him. By the time she reached the car, James was already cranking the engine and before she could climb into the driver's seat, he was at the wheel, starting to maneuver the motorcar down the narrow mountain roadway.

"I am quite capable of driving, you know!" Ursula protested as she hoisted her skirt inside and shut the passenger door. She looked down at the oilskin package James had placed on the seat between them. "And what's all this about Australia?"

James took no notice, but, with a quick glance behind him, deftly navigated his way down the winding road.

"I was thinking Australia may be as safe a place as any at the moment," James finally said, his eyes never leaving the road.

"If you think I'm going to be bullied into complying with whatever plans you and Lord Wrotham concocted for my so-called safety, you're sadly mistaken," Ursula retorted, holding onto the inner door handle as the motorcar lurched and bounced.

James shot her a sideways look. "So the attempt to poison you and Lady Wrotham doesn't bother you?"

"Of course it does," Ursula replied. "But it also makes me more determined than ever to find out exactly what this game is all about."

"Game?" James prompted.

"That's what Lord Wrotham called it—he said he wasn't sure what the game was, but he that we needed to wait and see how it played out." She gripped the handle once more. "Could you also try and be a bit more careful; I'd rather not revisit the breakfast I had this morning!"

James, ignoring her last comment, said: "you're willing to risk your life for a game—a game you don't even understand?!"

"If it means clearing Lord Wrotham's name, then yes."

"Ah," James replied enigmatically before falling strangely silent. For the remainder of the drive back to Bad Liebenstein he said no more about her fleeing to Australia.

They entered the outskirts of the spa town as the afternoon shadows were lengthening. "What should I tell Lady Wrotham and Lady Winterton? About you, I mean?" Ursula asked.

"I would prefer that you said nothing," James replied. "The fewer people who know about me or where I am, the better . . ."

Ursula chewed her lip uncertainly.

"Don't worry," James said, as the motorcar drew up outside the Gästehaus Rosenhof. "I'm just as committed to seeing how this game plays out as you."

He unbutton his Norfolk style jacket and tucked the oilskin package he had unearthed inside.

"If I'm right, this contains Lord Wrotham's field book. He carried it with him on all our missions—I noticed, of course, that all his entries were written in a numeric cipher of some kind but he never divulged the key to it. So you see, Miss Marlow, he kept secrets, even from me."

"Can I look at his field book?" Ursula asked.

James shook his head. "It will be safe with me, don't worry."

"Perhaps I would be the best one to have it—who knows, maybe I can help decipher it?" Ursula resisted the urge to command James to hand the book over, suspecting he was likely to be unmoved by her pleas. James' self-possession indicated a determination just as great as hers, and his loyalties, it was clear, lay with Lord Wrotham not her.

"Chief Inspector Harrison and Sir Buckley think Admiral Smythe probably used a book key for the code he used in his notebook," Ursula offered. "Perhaps Lord Wrotham was using the same?"

"That wouldn't surprise me," James replied.

"Don't you think I might have a better chance of deciphering it than—" Ursula began.

"Lord Wrotham once told me, with more than a touch or irony I admit, that you were probably the only person who would be likely to guess the key," James replied.

"Then why not let me have the notebook so that I can try?!" Ursula urged.

James shot her a sardonic smile. "I never said I wanted it to be deciphered."

Ursula looked at him in confusion. "But surely—"

"Since I don't know what it contains, and since Lord Wrotham has chosen not to divulge the book key to you, I can only assume he wants it to remain as it is—encoded. As far as I'm concerned, my job is to keep the field book as well as you under my protection until Lord Wrotham orders otherwise."

"But—"

James' expression halted her protests. His face was set in a manner she recognized all too well. She would have to wait to win this particular battle.

With the ease of one used to acting as chauffeur, James hopped out of the driver's seat and came round to open the car door. "I will contact you in a few days," he said. "I'll see what I can uncover about the Count's present whereabouts. Since the fire, he has all but disappeared, afraid, no doubt of McTiernay."

"Surely Scotland Yard would have sent someone to protect him?" Ursula said.

James shrugged. "He chose to leave England and I doubt that anyone at Scotland Yard can help him now. Besides, as I said, he's had his own personal bodyguards for at least a year—the Count's been paranoid about his personal safety for a while."

"But you think McTiernay is in Germany, don't you?" Ursula asked.

"Possibly," James admitted. He looked at her intently for a moment. "You know McTiernay could have been behind the attempt on you and Lady Wrotham's life, so I wouldn't trust anything from him. If McTiernay is in Germany we should take all necessary precautions— in the meantime," James gestured to the sanatorium building nestled in the woods behind her. "You'd better see how the dowager's . . . er . . . treatments, are going."

With obvious reluctance Ursula turned and walked through the doors of her Gästehaus.

Ursula took the first opportunity she had—between entertaining Lady Wrotham's litany of complaints and avoiding Lady Winterton's inevitable questions regarding her excursion that morning to Count von Bernstorff-Hollweg's castle—to reflect on the sudden appearance of James and the discovery of Lord Wrotham's field book. Surely James must have some inkling why Lord Wrotham thought that she, of all people, would be able to guess the code used? Ursula glanced over to her trunk—on the top her favorite poetry books, many of which Lord Wrotham had purchased for her, lay prominently on display. If only she had the field book, then, at least, she would be able to start the process of deciphering it. But would it really be so obvious as to be the book of Tennyson's poetry that Lord Wrotham usually carried with him? That seemed unlikely. It would jeopardize the need for secrecy and Naval Intelligence would have already tried and, no doubt, discounted that theory. James would know all the books Lord Wrotham usually had in his possession, but he was refusing to help and, besides, Ursula doubted that Lord Wrotham would use any book so readily observable. He was too clever for that. Ursula sighed and, in her frustration over not having access the Lord Wrotham's field book, threw one of the cushions from the divan across the room.

Lady Winterton opened the door and had to duck as the cushion flew past.

"That bad, huh?" she observed.

"Sorry," Ursula apologized. From the harried look on her face, Ursula could tell Lady Winterton had just spent time with Lady Wrotham. "You look as though you could do with tossing a few cushions around the place—was the dowager really that bad?"

Lady Winterton sat down and grimaced. "Let's just say that I've had enough lectures from her on the benefits of dietetic treatment for her so called 'nervous afflictions'. She has also met some old friend of hers, Herr Hubert, I think he's called . . ."

"Oh, I remember him," Ursula said. "He gave a series of lectures in London last year."

"I thought I'd heard the name before—well, with any luck he'll take Lady Wrotham off our hands for a bit. She said he has invited her to come to his private clinic in the Southern Tyrol to 'purge herself of all worldly concerns.'"

"Hmmm . . . an extended private clinic visit could be just the ticket," Ursula mused. She got up and stood by the window. She knew both Julia and Lady Winterton's maid, Grace, were attending to their work in the laundry. Unlike the large sanitarium where Lady Wrotham was staying, their small gästehaus afforded them a measure of privacy and seclusion—though it was a mere half a mile walk along the path through the thick fir forest to reach the sanatorium. Ursula stared out across the trees now. Though there were still patches of snow on the ground, the climate was as mild as the brochure had promised. At least there was none of the damp fog that always made London so depressing in winter.

"How did your visit with the Count go?" Lady Winterton asked, seating herself in an armchair by the fire. "We haven't had a chance to chat really since you got back yesterday afternoon."

"No luck, I'm afraid," Ursula replied, moving away from the window. She walked over to join Lady Winterton by the fire. "His castle turned out to be little more than a burnt-out ruin. A fire apparently occurred last week and destroyed everything. The Count escaped, but no one knows where he is now."

"The castle was a ruin?" Lady Winterton asked.

"Razed to the ground I'm afraid," Ursula confirmed as she sat down.

"So was there nobody there? Nothing at all to be found?"

"Nothing and no one," Ursula lied. "It was a total waste of my time."

"Oh my dear," Lady Winterton sympathized. "What bad luck!"

"Isn't it just!" Ursula replied trying to keep her tone light.

"Don't lose heart, Ursula," Lady Winterton said quietly. "I'm still happy to see if any of my family contacts have heard where the Count may have gone, difficult though that may be given it's not the social season yet."

"Thank you," Ursula said, suppressing a sigh. "I'm not sure what to do really. I don't want to stay away from England too long."

"No, of course not . . ." Lady Winterton replied before asking, after a pause, "Have you heard anything from him?" She let the question linger.

Ursula shook her head. She'd had no letters at all from Lord Wrotham. "All I've got is Pemberton's telegram saying that a trial date has been set for June," Ursula said. She nodded in the direction of the small coffee table upon which the telegram lay open.

"That still gives you a few months, m'dear . . ." Lady Winterton reminded her.

"I know," Ursula said, but that fact failed to rouse her. A few months seemed little time enough to discover the truth. She felt as though she had already wasted too much precious time.

"And," Lady Winterton said, picking up her embroidery, "it's not as if Lord Wrotham's going anywhere."

CHAPTER EIGHTEEN

AFTER THREE LONG GREY DAYS, under skies that threatened snow then rain, James finally made contact with Ursula. She and Lady Winterton were returning from a morning walk and, as they unburdened themselves of coats and hats and sturdy walking shoes, the proprietress of the gästehaus informed Ursula that there was a note waiting for her at the reception desk. After handing all their outdoor wear to Julia and Grace, Ursula and Lady Winterton headed into the small front parlor. As she passed the reception area, Ursula took the note and folded it quickly into her skirt pocket.

"Aren't you going to read it?' Lady Winterton asked.

Ursula shrugged noncommittally but Lady Winterton only scrutinized her face more closely. "Why all the secrecy?" she asked.

They chose a table beneath the window and, after asking for 'kaffe und kuchen' for two, Ursula opened the note and proceeded to read it to herself under the watchful eye of Lady Winterton.

The note said simply: *He is now believed to be in Prague. Hope to know more soon.*

"Well?" Lady Winterton demanded.

"It's nothing," Ursula said. "Just a note from Herr Hubert, that's all . . ." but she could tell Lady Winterton was not deceived.

"Herr Hubert's handwriting is far more gothic," Lady Winterton said. "So spill the beans old girl and tell me what's really going on."

The waiter arrived with a tray bearing a silver coffee pot, cups, plates and a tiered silver holder of cakes. Ursula took the opportunity to consider her reply as she poured her coffee.

"The note is from Lord Wrotham's chauffeur, Archibald James," Ursula said.

"Really?" Lady Winterton replied, using her napkin to wipe up the splash of coffee that had spilt on the tablecloth. "I thought you said he had disappeared."

"Yes," Ursula hesitated, uncertain whether she should let Lady Winterton into her confidence. "Turns out he's here in Germany."

Lady Winterton raised an eyebrow.

"I suspect," Ursula confessed. "James may have been a bit more than just a chauffeur—I think he worked with Lord Wrotham on the . . . er . . . clandestine matters he attended to here in Germany."

"That would make sense," Lady Winterton replied. She placed two sugar cubes in her coffee using the silver tongs with an air of practiced composure. "He was once a policeman after all."

"You certainly seem to know a great deal about him!" Ursula exclaimed.

"Of course," Lady Winterton replied calmly. "I visited the Wrotham household often enough over the years to know all the staff gossip. My lady's maid, Grace, always tells me everything and James is, as you know, a handsome man."

"Can't say I'd noticed," Ursula admitted as she took a sip of coffee. "So what else do you know about James?"

"Oh," Lady Winterton said airily as she lifted her cup to her lips. "I know he was in the army before he joined the Metropolitan Police—and that while he was there he worked under Chief Inspector or, as he then was, Sergeant, Harrison."

The cup in Ursula's hand froze for a minute. Lady Winterton laughed. "I thought you knew!" Ursula shook her head. Lady Winterton's wiped her mouth with her napkin before continuing, in more somber terms. "Then you don't know the circumstances that led to him leaving the police . . ."

"No," Ursula replied, and she felt a tremor in her fingers. She placed her cup down quickly to hide her disquiet.

"Ah . . ." Lady Winterton responded and she seemed to prevaricate.

"If you know something you must tell me," Ursula urged.

"Well," Lady Winterton began slowly." All I know is that something happened during his time at the Met that caused him to leave police service and go to work with Lord Wrotham. To this day, none of the details have ever been revealed, although I've often suspected it involved Chief Inspector Harrison. Grace is convinced that Lord Wrotham saved James' and Harrison's lives"—Lady Winterton smiled—"She is, however, easily influenced by those lurid tales in the penny weeklies!"

"But James wouldn't leave the police just because Lord Wrotham saved his life . . ." Ursula's gaze was intent.

Lady Winterton shifted in her chair. "No," she conceded. "It was well known at the time—amongst certain circles at least—that James left the police, because"—Lady Wrotham swallowed quickly—"he killed a man, an *innocent* man, in the course of his duty."

Ursula felt numb as the words sank in deep.

"As I said, the details were never known but I suspect there must be more to the story, given that Lord Wrotham took James into service as his chauffeur."

"What did you mean when you said it was well known only among certain circles . . .?" Ursula asked.

"Among those of us who knew the Wrotham family intimately," Lady Winterton replied simply. Ursula's cheeks reddened at the implication.

"Naturally our families have known each other since Nigel was alive and so I was privy to many confidences . . . and . . . there was a time when Lord Wrotham would come by and pay his respects . . . quite often in fact . . ."

There was a momentary frisson between them. Ursula tried to ignore the jealousy uncoiling like a green snake within her.

"Although those days are, of course, long gone," Lady Winterton concluded with a smile that did not quite dissipate the tension.

"James killed a man and yet Lord Wrotham took him in?" Ursula said, "that hardly seems to make any sense."

"Hmm . . . perhaps you are right, but I'm sure Harrison was part of it all. What role he played we may never know. I'm afraid Grace was really only interested in James' affairs."

"I see . . ." Ursula said, though in truth she felt more unsure of herself than ever.

"Lord Wrotham believed in James," Lady Winterton said quietly. "Surely that counts for something."

"It does," Ursula said, trying without success to shake off her doubts.

"What does the note from James say?" Lady Winterton inquired, reaching for a cake with the silver tongs.

Ursula paused, considering how much she should disclose, before answering. "He has discovered where Count von Bernstorff-Hollweg has gone—Prague."

"Prague?" Lady Winterton seemed to savor the word as she chewed her mouthful of cake. "That isn't too far—we could easily get there by train."

"Maybe," Ursula answered noncommittally as she stared at her now empty coffee cup—she was already regretting having brought Lady Winterton into her confidence.

"Why the hesitation?" Lady Winterton asked. "Don't you trust James?"

Ursula looked up sharply. "What on earth made you say that?!"

Lady Winterton raised an eyebrow. "I would have thought it was obvious," she answered coolly. "Why should you trust a man who abandoned Lord Wrotham at the first opportunity? He's killed before, so who's to say he isn't the one who murdered Admiral Smythe?"

She pinned Ursula with her stare.

"Who's to say he isn't planning on killing you?"

CHAPTER NINETEEN

HOTEL PARIZ, PRAGUE,
KINGDOM OF BOHEMIA

THE WINTER WIND HAD AN ICY EDGE TO IT as it swirled across the Old Town Square. Ursula pulled up the collar of her black cashmere coat as she hastened after James, whose long, brisk strides outpaced the mincing steps she was able to take in her skirt, stockings and tightly laced black boots. The powder-tower, *Prašná Brána*, loomed ahead in all its medieval glory but their pace did not abate. They were not here on any tourist vacation—they were here to talk to the man whose testimony may very well condemn Lord Wrotham to the gallows.

They passed the municipal house and turned down *U Obecního domu* to face the magnificent Hotel Pariz.

"Well, you certainly wouldn't know that he had money problems," Ursula observed as she and James walked through the doors into the foyer of the hotel. A long red-carpeted grand staircase curved its way to the upper floors, its cast-iron railing and ceramic tiled walls a testament to the flourishing art nouveau movement in Prague just a few years earlier.

"No," James replied. "But then I believe the Count is an expert at evading his debts."

Ursula regarded him uneasily, feeling vulnerable and exposed now that Lady Winterton was no longer with them. Although James had initially expressed resentment that Ursula had felt the need to bring Lady Winterton into her confidence, he had reluctantly agreed to allow her to accompany them to Prague. Even he had to acknowledge that in the absence of Lady Wrotham (who was now enjoying Herr Hubert's attentions at his sanatorium in the Southern Tyrol), propriety demanded that Ursula be accompanied by a female chaperone. James fell easily back into the role of chauffeur, making it exceedingly difficult for Ursula to speak to him in private about getting access to Lord Wrotham's field book. The existence of the book was an aspect of the case that Ursula had, so far kept, from Lady Winterton. Knowing Lady Winterton's doubts regarding James, she didn't want to prejudice her even further—something that was sure to happen if Lady Winterton knew that James was refusing to allow Ursula to attempt to decode it. Ursula had also been unable to shake off her own doubts about James—and now, as they walked together across hotel foyer, she felt her anxiety surge once more. Could she really trust him?

Her only comfort was that Lady Winterton was only a few minutes away, strolling down the 'Regent' street of Prague, *Příkop*, probably already ensconced in one of the many shops selling embroidery dolls or Bohemian glassware. Ursula had little interest in such trinkets but Lady Winterton seemed delighted by them.

"You should wait here," James said, waving his hand toward one of the armchairs that graced the lobby, "while I go and assess the situation upstairs. The Count is obsessed about personal safety and security. I don't want us walking in unprepared."

"All right," Ursula agreed reluctantly. "But I do need to speak to the Count personally—whether he likes it or not."

"I am well aware of your determination, Miss Marlow," James responded. "Believe me, your reputation precedes you."

"That'd be right," Ursula murmured as she took a seat in one of the gilt and brocade armchairs that afforded a good view of both the staircase and the front hotel doors. Dressed in his dark green and black chauffeur uniform, James had to make his way to the servant entrance and stairs. In so doing, he looked as innocuous as any other servant making their way to their masters and mistresses via the route designated for servants and other 'tradespersons'.

Ursula contented herself with watching the guests as they made their way in and out of the hotel—it was a pleasant distraction from worrying about James or Count von Bernstorff-Hollweg. A young couple entered arm in arm and Ursula felt a sudden pang—that could have been her she thought, if things had only turned out differently. She turned quickly away, embarrassed as the young woman looked up at her curiously. Instead, Ursula focused on the elevator doors as they slid open and a bellman in a red uniform stepped out. He was followed by a man in a dark pin striped frockcoat and trilby hat. As the man approached he took off his hat, revealing curly dark hair that was unexpectedly unruly beneath such a polished exterior. He acknowledged her with a slight bow that seemed to have an edge of mockery to it, and Ursula lift her head to glare at him imperiously. This prompted a crooked half -smile, but as he passed, she noticed the expression in his vivid blue eyes change from amused disdain to a kind of wary recognition. Ursula tried to sift through her memories but she was sure they had never met before. As she watched him make his way out of the hotel through the revolving doors, she suddenly felt her skin prickle. She remembered the photograph in Professor Prendergast's study; the man next to Lord Wrotham—younger yes, but the same curly dark hair—the same droll stare . . .

"Oh my God," she said hoarsely. "McTiernay."

Ursula rose to her feat unsteadily, gripping the back of the armchair to regain her balance before she hastened across the granite floor to the main staircase, worried that McTiernay's men may be upstairs waiting by the elevator. As she saw the back of his dark-clad figure sauntering down the street, she was torn between running after him and going to check on James. After a momentary hesitation she started to climb the stairs—the dread she felt about McTiernay's presence convincing her that the safety of James and the Count must be her first priority.

Ursula dashed up the stairs, heart pounding. By the time she reached the third floor she was breathless and trembling. What, she worried, was she likely to find? It took all her self-control to rein in the panic that squeezed all breath from her throat. As she made her way down the hallway towards the rear of the hotel she eased off her boots and tied the laces together. Slinging them over her shoulders she continued down the corridor, her steps like a cat's—light and wary of discovery.

The long hallway was deserted. As James had not given her any specific room number, all Ursula could do was proceed slowly down the cool, dim corridor, her stockinged feet noiseless on the carpet strip that ran along the polished floor. There was no sound, except the whirr of the dumbwaiter cables behind her and the halting sounds of her own ragged breath. All the doors she passed were closed. She came to a junction framed by a small window that looked out on the rear lane behind the hotel. The window had been cranked open an inch and as she approached the heavy curtain billowed out for a moment with an unexpected breeze. She heard a door open behind her and spun around—her hand firmly clamped against her mouth for fear of what sound may burst forth. No sound came, only the hoarseness of her breath as she watched James hurry towards her.

Through the open doorway behind him, she could see the form of a man lying face down on the carpet. James blocked her path.

"You don't want to go in there," he said, in low, urgent tones.

Ursula could just make out the edge of a gold and red brocade bedspread lying next to the man, and what looked like a dark pool of ink on the floor beside him.

James grabbed her arm roughly. "We need to leave now," he urged her forward. "Before the Count's servants discover him and the others!"

"Others?" she asked in confusion.

"The Count and both his bodyguards are dead," James said quickly as he unceremoniously pushed her through the door leading to the servants' stairwell.

"Was it? . . . I mean you didn't . . . did you?" she asked.

"No, they were already dead when I arrived," James answered, apparently unfazed that she should suspect he killed them.

"McTiernay," Ursula gasped, in the shock of seeing the bodies she had almost forgotten. She caught her breath. "I think I saw him in the foyer."

James tightened his grip on her arm.

"McTiernay?" he repeated. "Are you sure?"

Ursula nodded, still out of breath. "I didn't recognize him at first. I've only ever seen a photograph of him and Lord Wrotham at Oxford but I'm almost certain it was him—he came out of the lift just a few minutes after you left."

James urged her down the stairs. When they reached the doorway at the bottom, James shoved her through. "Did he see you?" he asked.

Ursula swallowed hard before nodding.

"Do you think he knew it was you?" he asked.

Ursula shook her head. "We've never met but . . ." she stopped just outside the doorway. "But I'm sure he recognized me—that's partly why it dawned on me who he was—from the look *he* gave *me*. I guess with all the photographs of me in the newspapers it's hardly surprising."

"Damn!" James said, pushing back his blond hair with the palm of his hand in obvious frustration. The servants' stairs led out onto a dreary laneway at the back of the hotel. As they walked quickly along the lane and back to the crowded street, Ursula heard James mutter. "McTiernay's cleaning house . . ." under his breath.

"What do you mean?" Ursula demanded.

"I mean he's just killed the Crown's main witness," James said and, without any concern for propriety, grabbed her arm, urging her to continue walking apace. "The question is," James said as they hurried along. "Why? Is it to help Lord Wrotham or is it merely vengeance?"

"Does it matter?" Ursula asked.

"Of course," James responded angrily. "We need to know if McTiernay thinks Wrotham is still a patriot or whether he's found out he was a spy."

"What if he believes Lord Wrotham betrayed him?" Ursula asked breathless as they turned the corner.

"Then," James replied grimly. "McTiernay will stop at nothing until Lord Wrotham is dead."

CHAPTER TWENTY

TRAIN BOUND FOR CALAIS

THE THIRD CLASS CARRIAGE was teeming with people; bodies, hot and sweaty from the proximity, and grimy from the coal dust and steam, were everywhere. The air was thick with cigarette smoke and Ursula and Lady Winterton, on opposite sides of the carriage, both tried desperately to get some air near the window, amid the stifling heat and atmosphere of the crowded train. Given his concerns about McTiernay, James had insisted that they travel 'incognito,' which meant foregoing the luxury of their own first class sleeper car and traveling as inconspicuously as possible. Ursula wriggled in the dress James had insisted she wear, for the cheap linen was itchy and the seams were damp with sweat. She felt herself getting woozy as the heat and claustrophobia of the carriage started to take its toll. She cast a glance across to Lady Winterton who had apparently managed to fall asleep, one cheek pressed against the window pane. Ursula staggered to her feet and made her way awkwardly out of the carriage, trying to avoid outstretched legs, feet, baskets and bags, as she stumbled her way into the passageway. It was a good thing, she reflected, that both Julia and Grace had been sent on ahead to England, for she could just imagine their horror at seeing their mistresses looking so dirty and disheveled.

Ursula closed the carriage door with relief—though the train corridor was also crowded, at least most of the windows were open. She could feel the drafts of cool night air clearing her head. James was standing, peering out of one of open windows, a cigarette dangling from his mouth. He turned and acknowledged her with the briefest of nods as she walked over to join him. Ursula sucked in a few deep breaths of fresh air as she steadied herself, hands gripping the window frame.

"Are you all right?" James asked.

Ursula nodded. "It's just infernally hot in there. It felt like I was being smothered by a cheap dirty pillow . . ."

"I would not have inflicted this if I didn't think it was necessary," James reminded her.

"Oh, I can cope," Ursula replied quickly. "And as an ex-rifleman man I'm sure you've endured worse."

"I see Lady Winterton's wasted no time in giving you the potted history of my life," James observed.

"Just the highlights I assure you," Ursula replied, feigning levity. "Actually I saw the photograph of your rifle regiment in your room."

James looked inquiringly.

"Lord Wrotham seemed concerned about your whereabouts so, naturally, I took a look around his house."

"Naturally," James replied.

His gaze returned to the window and the pitch black sky beyond. "I can't help but wish you'd kept Lady Winterton out of all of this." His face was now brooding.

"Why?" Ursula asked. "Because she knows more about your past than you cared to tell me?"

James flushed. "I thought Lord Wrotham told you I was once a policeman . . . and that's not what I meant. I just don't want any more people being in harm's way than absolutely necessary."

"Oh."

James continued to stare out the window with a bleak look of resignation.

"I guess you must have known the Winterton household pretty well," Ursula prompted.

"As much as any servant of a close family friend would," James replied.

"Lady Winterton certainly seems to know a great deal about you," Ursula said. "Her lady's maid was apparently always eager to tell."

"Yes, Grace never was one to keep her mouth shut," James said and there was a savagery in his response that took Ursula off guard. She paused, uncertain whether to continue with her questions. An overwhelming need to be know, to be reassured about his past, however, compelled her to probe further.

"Tell me about Grace," Ursula said gently.

"There's not much to tell," James replied, taking a drag of his cigarette. "She's Lady Winterton's maid—has been since before Lady Winterton was married. I met her soon after I became Lord Wrotham's chauffeur . . . only that wasn't the first time we had met. I knew her from my days with the Kings Royal Rifles. I joined when I was fifteen—they were the Finsbury rifles then, before they became the London regiment in '08—Grace's brother was in my regiment. She was just a scullery maid at the time but we went out now and again. Her brother didn't stick with the Rifles though. He ended up working with his dad on one of the stalls at Spitalfields market. That's how they knew the Harrisons. When I got back from the Boer War I was pretty much done with the army, and it was them who arranged for me to meet Harrison. That's why I joined the Metropolitan Police. By then Grace had risen in the ranks and was Lady Winterton's maid."

"Why did you leave the police and go work for Lord Wrotham?" Ursula asked. She was treading cautiously now as James' face revealed the depth of his unwillingness to delve into this particular aspect of his past.

"No doubt Lady Winterton has passed on all of Grace's tittle-tattle," James replied bitterly.

"She said it was because you killed an innocent man," Ursula said, watching his reaction closely.

James took Ursula by surprise when he let out a short bark of a laugh.

Ursula looked at James with confusion. "So you didn't?"

"No, I bloody well did not," James replied, he was still laughing but, again, there was an edge of savagery to it.

"But you did kill someone . . ." Ursula ventured.

"Yes," James' expression changed instantly. "But then that's what the army trained me to do."

"And is it the reason you left the police?"

"Yes."

"Does it explain why you went to work for Lord Wrotham?"

"Yes—in part at least—both Chief Inspector Harrison and I owe Lord Wrotham our lives."

Ursula looked at him questioningly but James shook his head. "I'm afraid that's for Lord Wrotham, and him alone, to explain."

"But—"

"But nothing, I swore an oath and I intend to keep it," James replied.

"Spare me such loyalties," Ursula muttered under her breath. "For I am heartily sick of them by now . . ."

James frowned.

"I only mean that Lord Wrotham said something similar about Admiral Smythe and why he could not rebut the charges against him," Ursula explained with an exasperated sigh. "I'm sure he also feels some similar obligation to his erstwhile friends from Balliol for he refuses to divulge anything about his time in Guyana or what caused the rift between him and McTiernay."

"How do you know about Guyana?" James demanded.

"I read about it in one of Admiral's Smythe's file," Ursula said. "It provided an account of the death of a woman, Bernice Baldeo."

"How the hell did you get your hands on that?!"

"Chief Inspector Harrison showed it me," Ursula said after a pause. "He told me it was important that I know just the kind of man Lord Wrotham is . . ."

"Why because he covered up the mess McTiernay left behind?" James said, drumming his fingers along the sill of the open window. "I've seen the same file myself but at least I had the benefit of asking Admiral Smythe for a few more details. He and Lord Wrotham may not have been sure whether it was McTiernay or the Count who swindled the Imperial Gold and Diamond Mining Company, but they were convinced of one thing—McTiernay murdered Bernice Baldeo, by poisoning her with cyanide."

"What else did the Admiral tell you?"

James sighed. "Not a lot. Just that one of the aims of the company was to buy up the small holdings on the gold fields to help entrench British colonial influence in the region. Of course, thanks to the Count and McTiernay, the company ended up losing money. There were allegations of false accounts as well as fictitious gold and diamond claims, though nothing was ever proved."

"I read the legal case brought by the investors—If Lord Wrotham suspected McTiernay and the Count of fraud, why did he defend the company in the law suit?"

"Neither Lord Wrotham nor Admiral Smythe could risk exposing the government's original involvement in it all," James explained. "Apparently there was already a great deal of worker unrest and the government feared that airing the company's 'dirty laundry' could inflame the situation. It was the same reason why they covered up Bernice Baldeo's death. Smythe told me that at the time there were ongoing threats of worker unrest by Indians working on the large sugar plantations in Guyana. They had to ensure that Bernice Baldeo's death didn't ignite further violence. Apparently, she was significant enough that any rumor of her being murdered could have destabilized the whole country. As it was, her death was regarded as a tragic accident even though as far as Smythe and Wrotham were concerned, McTiernay was the main suspect."

"Yes," Ursula answered. "I read that in the file too."

"McTiernay was supposedly with her the night before her body was found. He's a passionate man, Miss Marlow, but he was also a married man. Who knows whether it was a lover's quarrel over him returning to his wife in Ireland or whether, as Admiral Smythe suspected, she had found out what was really happening with The Imperial Gold and Diamond Mining Company . . ."

"Do you think someone involved in the Baldeo case may be trying to punish Lord Wrotham and the others for what happened in the past?" Ursula asked. "Could someone have used information about Guyana to blackmail Count von Bernstorff-Hollweg into testifying against Lord Wrotham?"

The information Christopher Dobbs had provided her loomed

large in her mind, even as she tried to push aside the unpleasant memories of her visit to his office.

"This isn't about Guyana," James responded emphatically. "This is about Ireland and McTiernay's passionate belief in an Irish Free State. The Count was nothing but an opportunist. This is not about the past, Miss Marlow, this is about the sins of the present."

"How can you be so sure?" Ursula replied.

She pulled out the list that Christopher Dobbs had given her. "Here's proof that the Count and McTiernay defrauded investors in the Imperial Gold and Diamond Mining Company. I believe someone used this information to compel the Count to testify against Lord Wrotham. You may insist all you like that this is nothing but present day politics, but I think this is much more personal. I think this has roots going all the way back to the past—to Balliol. To Guyana. I don't know what it is or how deep those roots go but this is not just about armaments, Home Rule or the threat of a war of Germany. This is about betrayal."

Later that night, as the journey ground on and the carriage fell silent as the passengers slept, Ursula stared out at the blackness of the night, unable to sleep. Her mind kept trying to make sense of all she knew, and all she thought she knew, about Lord Wrotham, about James— even about Harrison. She glanced across to Lady Winterton, who sat opposite her leaning against the window, her face twitching as she slept. Ursula watched as her eyelids flickered but remained closed and Ursula felt a twinge of jealousy, for Lady Winterton's grief lay years behind her. How had she managed to move on? To cast that loss aside? The hot, heavy stillness of the carriage seemed to bear down on her as Ursula squeezed her eyes shut, praying that sleep would finally take her and numb her pain.

CHAPTER TWENTY-ONE

CALAIS, FRANCE

BY THE TIME URSULA and Lady Winterton reached Calais, they were feeling the absence of their maids and their usual first class accommodations acutely. The small pension that James had arranged for them to stay in overnight had little in the way of luxury. It was a clean, whitewashed cottage with a view of the channel but was without private bathrooms or running hot water. Ursula, having finished a very unsatisfactory (and cold) bath in the shared facilities was trying desperately to brush the knots from her hair, when she overheard Lady Winterton speaking with James on the stairs. Lady Winterton was on her way down to the dining room for dinner when she must have encounter James coming up the stairs.

"Archibald James," Ursula heard Lady Winterton's arch tone and edged her way to the bathroom door. She opened it till it was slightly ajar and peered through.

James was obscured from view by the banister but the back of Lady Winterton, in her pale blue dinner dress, was clearly visible.

"Lady Winterton," James replied. His tone was cool. Since Prague, Ursula had noticed how the thin veil masking the animosity between them had started to tear.

"What brings you upstairs?" There was no mistaking the undercurrent beneath Lady Winterton's words—his place was downstairs with the servants.

"I have a letter for Miss Marlow," James replied.

Ursula felt a surge of excitement—perhaps Lord Wrotham had finally seen fit to reply to the innumerable letters she had sent him. Until now, despite all her missives, she had received nothing from him, only two telegrams from Pemberton—the first advising of a trial date and the second indicating that, as Lord Wrotham continued to suffer harassment, Pemberton had petitioned his removal from Brixton to another prison while on remand.

"Who is the letter from?" Lady Winterton demanded.

James gave no reply and Ursula's hopes faded. She felt sure even James would have told Lady Winterton if the letter had been from Lord Wrotham.

"I see your manners have not improved over time," Lady Winterton replied. "But your chivalry towards Miss Marlow is certainly admirable. Grace always said you had a weakness for damsels in distress."

Another silence.

"Though you certainly treat women like Grace, women of your own class, as though they were little more than dirt beneath your shoes . . ."

"Have a care, Lady Winterton," James replied, his voice sinking to a low-throated warning. "For I might have to explain to Miss Marlow just how hard you really tried to come between her and Lord Wrotham. She has no idea how many times you visited or how many calling cards were left."

Ursula gripped the edge of the door.

This time it was Lady Winterton who remained silent.

The letter for Ursula was from Gerard Anderson. It had been sent two days ago in anticipation of her arrival—at least James had allowed Ursula to tell him that, if nothing else regarding her travels. The letter provided a brief summary of the findings of his latest investigation into Christopher Dobbs' links to the Wrotham family and its creditors. It also outlined the names of the investors that Anderson had managed to locate which had been involved in the legal case of El Dorado

Investments v. The Imperial Gold and Diamond Mining Company. Ursula's relief was tinged with disappointment. Dobbs, it appeared, had no connections to any of Lord Wrotham's creditors. There was a small part of her (certainly not one of her finer parts) that had wished there had something tangible, evil even, that she could accuse Dobbs of publically. Now all she had were lingering private concerns that were insufficient to air.

The list of investors in El Dorado Investments was a tangled web of trusts and companies, individuals and partnerships, none of which sounded in the least bit familiar. Not surprisingly, a large number of investors came from both Germany and Ireland. After reading the list of companies with fanciful names such as *Tir Tairngire* and *Gründewelt*, Ursula felt even more frustrated—she began to despair of finding any leads at all in the case.

The following morning they were to due to take the ferry across the English Channel to Dover. James met Ursula outside the pension dressed once more in his chauffeur's uniform. As she and Lady Winterton boarded the first class deck, Ursula sensed the lingering mistrust between James and Lady Winterton. Ursula for her part had always known, if she admitted it to herself that Lady Winterton had hoped at one time to win Lord Wrotham from her. It was not something she now resented and only occasionally did her own jealousy surface. Since Lord Wrotham's arrest it seemed petty to fall back on such old uncertainties. Lady Winterton always appeared, in that cool unruffled way of hers, to have accepted the situation with good grace. Clearly she also felt a good deal of loyalty to her maid Grace (who had been, Ursula could only infer, jilted by James at one time). Ursula could well understand such fidelity—she would feel the same way towards her own maid, Julia. She was only thankful that Lady Wrotham's loyalties now extended to her for there were few among London society willing to help her after the humiliation of Lord Wrotham's arrest.

It was James' behavior that both surprised and irked her—his chivalric need to look out for her on Lord Wrotham's behalf seemed unduly paternalistic and she was not entirely sure how to respond as a result.

Having endured enough hardship for one trip, Lady Winterton left them soon after they disembarked from the channel ferry in Dover. She had decided to make her way to her family's summer home in Sussex to recuperate for a few days before returning to her Kensington home. She left Ursula with a vow to continue to help as best she could, promising to contact her late husband's family in Dublin to see what inquiries could be made as to McTiernay's current whereabouts. Ursula was only too grateful for her help—though James remained as taciturn as ever in Lady Winterton's presence.

"You could at least be polite to Lady Winterton," Ursula admonished James after Lady Winterton had left them at the station.

"Giving advice on etiquette and decorum are we now, Miss Marlow?" James responded. Ursula felt her indignation rise. James never failed to make her feel as though she was standing on shifting sand—unsure what to believe, unsure whom to trust, and unsure why he continued to treat her with such a strange combination of affection and resentment.

"The last thing I need is to alienate one of the few allies I have," Ursula replied. "Lady Winterton's connections in Ireland may prove very useful in our search for McTiernay."

"I know," James admitted reluctantly before lapsing into a pensive silence that continued even as they walked along the train platform.

As the train for London was not due for another twenty minutes, Ursula excused herself. She caught sight of her reflection in the mirror of the railway station's Ladies room and, even she had to admit, no one was likely to recognize her the way she looked at the moment. Ursula returned to the platform just as the train drew into the station. She hugged her coat in tight as she hurried to join James who stood on the platform, head bent, stomping a cigarette butt out beneath his boots. His blond hair dusty with coal and his coat worn thin at the elbow, he looked like a disgruntled laborer on his way home from work. But as he raised his head, she could see the military bearing—the rifleman he once was—and James seemed now, to her, to be a much sadder man than she had noticed before. He looked like a man tired of carrying the burdens of the past.

CHAPTER TWENTY-TWO

"YOU STILL HAVEN'T TOLD ME why Lord Wrotham got with McTiernay and the Count in December 1911," Ursula said, once she and James had seated themselves in the second class train carriage. The morning train was almost deserted and they had the carriage to themselves. It was, Ursula reflected, the first time since that day at the Hotel Pariz in Prague that they had been alone.

"No," James answered. "I haven't."

"Now Lady Winterton is no longer traveling with us, are you going to?" Ursula asked. She felt sure James had been holding back from answering her questions in Lady Winterton's presence. He had certainly insisted that she say nothing about the discovery of Lord Wrotham's field book or the nature of his missions to Germany and, until now, Ursula had complied with all his demands for secrecy and silence. Now she wanted answers.

James seemed to consider the question. The minutes passed before he stood up abruptly, locked the carriage door, and returned to sit beside Ursula. Only then did he begin to talk.

"My role," he said, "has always been to assist Lord Wrotham with whatever inquiries he needed to undertake abroad. We were charged with finding out as much as we could about German military capabilities using Lord Wrotham's business clients, particularly those in the shipping industry. I would also help undertake any necessary observations—on ship building, naval exercises and the like. All very gentlemanly on his account I must say, with me as the eyes and ears of 'downstairs' as well as his chauffeur. You'd be amazed at the things I was able to see and hear in other people's homes, all because I was considered well nigh invisible as a servant." James paused.

"Go on," Ursula said.

"Two years ago Admiral Smythe asked Lord Wrotham about re-establishing ties with Fergus McTiernay. I knew a bit about his past at Balliol and in Guyana from the Admiral's files but Smythe insisted he needed Lord Wrotham to put all that aside. He'd heard rumors that the Ulster Unionists had established a secret committee to buy arms and to plan a campaign of armed resistance should the Home Rule bill pass. They even had a man, Major Frederick Hugh Crawford, who was charged with importing arms and drilling volunteers."

Ursula blinked rapidly.

"I see his name is not unknown to you," James observed.

It was the name McTiernay had supplied to use against Christopher Dobbs.

Ursula nodded, her face tightening. "I have heard of him," was all she would admit.

"Admiral Smythe's concern was how the nationalists in Ireland were likely to react and what they were likely to do in response to this," James continued. "So he asked Lord Wrotham to use his old college ties. Naval Intelligence wanted to know about any possible armament shipments and the like. But as you can imagine it took a great deal of effort for Lord Wrotham to convince McTiernay that he was the same man he knew at Balliol—they needed to work together to get to the point where both of them trusted one another once more. In December 1911, McTiernay asked Wrotham to help secure arms for the Irish Republican Brotherhood. He wanted to try to broker a deal with Germany to support an Irish Free State in the event of war with Britain."

"By then McTiernay was convinced of Lord Wrotham's loyalty?"

"Yes, though, you know, I never suspected that was in question—I think what happened in Guyana tested Lord Wrotham's trust in McTiernay and the Count—not the other way round. At least that was my observation after having spent time with them all."

"Tell me more about the meeting," Ursula prompted further.

"The meeting at the Count's castle was served multiple purposes— to try and assess whether such a deal was likely to occur, to identify who the major parties were, and to secure Lord Wrotham's bona fides with McTiernay."

"So what went wrong?' Ursula asked.

"There was always a risk that someone would find out about Lord Wrotham's ties with Naval Intelligence and that he and I would be exposed as spies. The British Government had made it quite clear that they would disavow all knowledge of our mission if Lord Wrotham was compromised. No one wants to admit that British agents are sullying their hands in the sordid world of espionage or that there is a risk of German agitation in Ireland—the Home Rule issue is fraught enough without the public fearing German involvement in a possible civil war."

"Was there any indication at the meeting that the Count was going to betray them? Is that how Scotland Yard and the War Office found out? Clearly they believe Lord Wrotham was actually selling British military secrets and trying to stir up German involvement in Ireland— not to mention planning to assassinate members of the royal family."

"That was just the Serbians' idea of a joke," James said.

"The Serbians?" Ursula queried.

"Don't ask . . ." James replied. "Their presence was somewhat of a mystery—but it was certainly unrelated to anything McTiernay was hoping to plan with the Count."

"But I still don't understand why members of Naval Intelligence won't explain Lord Wrotham's real mission to Scotland Yard—"

"As I said they warned Admiral Smythe and Lord Wrotham that they would wash their hands of the whole affair . . ."

Ursula bit her lip—surely there must be more to it than that? Would the British government really disavow all knowledge of such a mission?

"You still haven't said how you think they found out about the meeting," she reminded him.

"I don't know how anyone found out—the other main witness in the case, Padraig O'Shaunessy, was with McTiernay at the meeting, but I don't know why he turned informer—he was little more than a paid minion."

"Do you think Lord Wrotham suspected the Count or this man O'Shaunessy even then—is that why he buried his field book?"

"Whatever the reason, he didn't want anyone to find it. That's why I retrieved it—I was worried there was the always the possibility of scavengers finding it after the fire and turning it over to the highest bidder."

Ursula bit her lip. "I assume McTiernay's next target will be this man O'Shaunessy."

"Probably," James conceded. "At the meeting McTiernay had no qualms about killing two of his own men suspected of Unionist involvements—he's certainly not going to hesitate now."

Ursula opened her mouth to speak—tempted to tell James about McTiernay's man and the information he had given her to use against Dobbs', but something held her back. She suspected that if she was to have any chance of speaking to McTiernay, of getting to the real truth behind all that had happened, she would have to maintain her silence.

"When I heard of Lord Wrotham's arrest," James said. "I initially thought that it was just someone at the meeting who had betrayed him—someone who had no idea what his real mission was. But with all that has happened since and Admiral Smythe's disappearance and murder . . . none of it makes any sense to me. I fear, as Lord Wrotham suspects, that there's another 'game' in play at the moment. One of which we know very little."

"Do you think it was McTiernay who discovered the truth about Lord Wrotham's association with Naval Intelligence?"

"That doesn't make sense to me. If he suspected Lord Wrotham he would have killed him immediately—he would have no interest in an arrest or a trial."

Ursula fell silent. She was trying to make sense of all the pieces of evidence she had uncovered thus far but none of created a complete picture, certainly not one consistent with what she knew of the men involved.

James tapped his fingers on the leather train seat. "Tell me," he asked slowly, as if considering things further. "Where does Chief Inspector Harrison stand on the investigation into Lord Wrotham?"

Ursula licked her lips before replying. "I'm not entirely sure. I think he's torn. He clearly has a deep regard for Lord Wrotham—and a sense of obligation to him—but at the same time he's rattled by the evidence. I think he might believe Lord Wrotham capable—"

"Of treason?" James interjected.

"Of almost anything," Ursula responded bleakly.

CHAPTER TWENTY-THREE

CHESTER SQUARE, BELGRAVIA

THE POUNDING ON THE FRONT DOOR woke Ursula in the early hours of the following morning. She rolled over in bed and looked at the clock beside her bed. It was not yet six o'clock and the house was still dark.

The hammering below continued and Ursula slipped on her silk dressing gown groggily. She encountered Biggs on the stairs.

"What on earth is happening?" she asked.

"I believe it is Chief Inspector Harrison," Biggs replied calmly. "Shall I open the door?"

Ursula tied the tasseled silk belt around her tightly. "I think you'd better, before he forces his way in," she said. "Oh, and go tell James after you've let them in—he'd better know that Harrison's here."

"Yes, Miss," Biggs replied as he turned to make his way down the stairs.

Ursula was halfway down when Biggs opened the door to admit Chief Inspector Harrison and three other police constables.

"Really sir," Biggs admonished Harrison, pulling his own tartan wool dressing gown in close around his elderly frame. "Ladies should never be disturbed before ten o'clock."

"Where is she?" Harrison demanded, before he caught sight of Ursula on the stairs.

Harrison thrust a piece of paper at Biggs, his eyes never leaving hers. "I have a warrant to search the premises," he said.

"A warrant?" Ursula said with surprising calm. "How very dramatic of you. I suggest we at least pretend to be civilized human beings and discuss this in the front parlor." She walked down to the foot of the stairs. "Could one of your constables kindly close the front door before *all* the neighbors are disturbed."

Ursula turned to Biggs. "Perhaps you should warn everyone," she said with deliberate emphasis, "that police constables may soon be searching their rooms."

"Of course, Miss. Should I offer our guests any refreshment?"

"No," Ursula replied. "After I've spoken with my solicitor, I doubt they'll be staying long." She reached the foot of the stairs and drifted past Harrison, her silk dressing gown floating behind her as she walked.

"I do have a warrant," Harrison said as he accompanied her into the front parlor. His expression was one of barely restrained fury. Ursula had never seen him so discomposed before.

"So you say—but to what purpose?" Ursula asked. She was surprised by her own self-control. She and James had arrived home the previous afternoon and she still felt groggy and irritable from lack of sleep.

"Late last night Lord Wrotham was supposed to be transferred from Brixton to Strangeways prison in Manchester. He never arrived." Harrison's eyes drilled into hers as he spoke.

"What do you mean?" Ursula asked slowly.

"I mean we were moving him because of fears for his safety—and now he has disappeared."

Ursula was still confused. "I don't understand . . ." she said.

"The two policemen escorting him are dead and the police motorcar was dumped about three miles down the road. Witnesses reported seeing armed men in the area but as it all occurred under the cover of darkness no one can be sure what happened." Harrison's eyes flashed angrily as he spoke—he was having difficulty restraining himself.

Ursula felt the blood drain from her head and her face as a cold, numbness spread throughout her body.

"Do they know if he's alive?" Ursula asked hoarsely. She could think of nothing but McTiernay's mocking smile in the foyer of the Hotel Pariz, and the deep, dark pool of blood she saw in the doorway to Count von Bernstorff-Hollweg's room.

She raised her hand to her throat.

"Damn it woman, what did you do?!" Harrison demanded.

Ursula took a step back, recoiling from his anger. "You don't seriously think?—"

"I want to know where the bloody hell he is!"

On Harrison's signal, the three police constables started making their way up the stairs to begin their search.

"What is it that you hope to find?" she asked, surfacing from the daze for a moment. "A pair of wings?"

"Don't act as if you don't know exactly what happened?!" Harrison said. "Who did you pay to do this?"

Ursula inhaled deeply, her head was still spinning and she felt dangerous close to collapse. Summoning all her powers of self-possession beneath his onslaught, she said: "You overestimate my sphere of influence if you think I could have had anything to do with his disappearance."

"Don't be a bloody fool, Harrison," James' voice called out from the doorway, "or did you lose all your brains when you joined Special Branch?!"

Harrison spun around.

"Archie, what the hell are you doing here?!"

"Good morning to you too, Chief Inspector," James replied. He glanced at the clock on the mantel as he entered the room. "Seems a little early, don't you think, for such histrionics?"

"I am merely surprised to see you Archie," Harrison said, using James' first name. "I was under the impression that you had gone to ground. Otherwise, I would have had you arrested by now."

"What, on conspiracy to abduct a Lord?" James responded. "That seems a little excessive don't you think? Even for you."

Harrison's jaw clenched.

"What are you doing here Archie?"

"While I've been away, you seem to have forgotten your manners as well as your common sense," he said, ignoring Harrison's question. "Miss Marlow is quite clearly in shock. What did you hope to achieve barging in here with a search warrant?!"

Harrison's face was still white with rage.

"What are you going to say if they discover his body?" James asked, approaching Harrison with maddening calmness. "How are you going to explain that to the District Commissioner when Miss Marlow files a complaint about your harassment? You're an ambitious man, Harrison, think like one!"

James turned his attention to Ursula. "Miss Marlow," he said gently. "Perhaps you should sit for a moment—"

Ursula lowered herself into the chair before her knees gave way.

"Do these men have any idea what they are even looking for?" asked James, gesturing to one of the constables who was opening the drawers of Ursula's desk, "or is this all just show to make your point?"

"And what point would that be?" Harrison asked, his mouth drawn to a thin line beneath his moustache.

"That you and the rest of Special Branch really have no idea what is at stake here."

"I know that one man is dead and another conspired to murder the King and use German arms to foment a war in Ireland," Harrison said bitterly. "I also know that two of *my* men, my bloody men Archie, were murdered last night."

"Is that so?" James replied coolly. "Well, you should have taken greater precautions."

Harrison's jaw twitched dangerously. "And you should stick to driving motorcars," he snarled.

"You always did underestimate me didn't you, Ian?" James replied. Ursula was startled out of her thoughts by the unexpected use of Harrison's first name.

Harrison turned to Ursula. "Miss Marlow," he said. "I need you to get dressed and accompany me to the police station for questioning in relation to the disappearance of your fiancé while in police custody."

It was pure defiance that brought Ursula to her senses. "Lord Wrotham is not my fiancé," Ursula said, trying to keep her voice level and calm. "As you would know that if you read the newspapers." With shaking hands Ursula pulled her robe in tight around her. It was a relief to feel it the fabric between her finger tips, especially as she faced Harrison's hostility.

"Whatever your relationship to Lord Wrotham is," Harrison said, "we need to question you further. When was the last time you saw him?"

"Two weeks ago—before I left for Germany with his mother."

"Did he tell you he might be moved to another prison?"

Ursula shook her head.

"Then what did you speak to him about?" Harrison demanded.

"Byron mainly," Ursula replied. "Though perhaps we progressed to Tennyson too—I can't say I really remember."

"Do you think this is some kind of joke?" Harrison demanded.

"On the contrary," Ursula replied and a spark of anger flared. "The only thing I regard as a joke is your behavior. Do you honestly think I had anything to do with his disappearance? That I am standing here sick with worry because I don't know whether he is alive or dead—enduring this farce of a search—all because you and your department failed to do their job properly? You know the man—Lord Wrotham is the last person to shirk his duty just as he's the last person to be a traitor. If you weren't so caught up in your own petty ambitions you would see that—and you would know that what happened last night was a dreadful, dangerous thing. Has it failed to occur to you that the same people who murdered Admiral Smythe, who shot Count von Bernstorff-Hollweg in Prague, now have Lord Wrotham?"

After two hours of questioning in an unventilated interview room at Scotland Yard, Ursula was finally released. James was waiting for her outside. He too had been subjected to an intensive bout of questioning. Samuels was nervously waiting for them on the corner in Ursula's Silver Rolls Royce, 'Bertie.'

"Did they find it?" Ursula murmured quickly as she joined James, bypassing all preliminaries in her anxiety to know the fate of Lord Wrotham's field book.

James shook his head. "Samuels and I managed to hide it before they searched our room. It's safe."

Ursula visibly relaxed. "Where is it?"

"Hidden behind the skirting board in Samuel's room." James opened the passenger door of the motorcar for her as Samuels cranked the engine.

"Do you think Harrison finally believes you had nothing to do with Lord Wrotham's disappearance?" James asked.

"God only knows," Ursula replied, scrubbing her weary eyes. "He's calmed down at least."

"They'll no doubt have you and me under detailed observation now—so we must be careful," James warned. He slipped into the rear seat beside Ursula as Samuels started to drive off from the curb

"I'm not unfamiliar with their tactics," Ursula responded. "They've used them on fellow members of the WSPU, besides I don't have anything to hide."

"Well, I for one would rather not have Harrison nipping at my heels," James said. "I plan to leave for Manchester this evening—and then, depending upon what I discover—on to Dublin."

Ursula bit her lip. "Do you think . . ." she could not bring herself to ask the question.

"You mustn't give up hope yet," James replied but his eyes belied any hope of finding Lord Wrotham alive. "You should stay in London for the moment—until I know more."

Ursula, usually one to chafe under such pronouncements, merely nodded. She stared pensively out of the car window as they drove through Piccadilly Circus. The crowds and the noise were deafening to her ears. Ursula closed her eyes.

"You must focus on deciphering the field book now," James said.

Ursula opened her eyes quickly.

"Lord Wrotham's disappearance has convinced me that we should find out what it contains—this 'game,' whatever it may, be is playing out in ways I don't understand. Since you may be the best chance of deciphering it—I'm leaving it with you."

Ursula nodded, buoyed by the prospect of tackling an issue she had some hope of actually resolving.

"We can only hope it offers us some information we can use," James said with an air of despondency that deflated Ursula's hopes. "I'll contact you from Dublin if and when I have any news. You can join me there when I have found out where McTiernay has taken Lord Wrotham." This glimmer of optimism seemed forced, as if he was trying too hard to convince himself that things were not so desperate after all.

After a pause, Ursula looked away. "I think we all have to accept that the only thing I am likely to find in Ireland," she said, "is Lord Wrotham's grave."

CHAPTER TWENTY-FOUR

URSULA SPENT THE NEXT THREE DAYS holed up in her study trying permutation after permutation of possibly cipher keys to no avail. She started on the assumption that each number used was a substitute for the initial letter of a word in a particular text—but after many hours of using (what she considered) the most obvious books, she was no closer to discerning the code used. Ursula resorted to trying a frequency analysis on the first three pages of the field book, but, again this revealed nothing intelligible. It only confirmed her belief that a complicated substitution cipher must have been used.

She felt sure that the men at Naval Intelligence would have already sifted through the most likely texts in Lord Wrotham's library, but even they would have been unable to comb through the sheer number of possibilities. No, she reasoned there must be something specific that she alone was likely to guess—why else would Lord Wrotham tell James that she was the person most likely to work out the code he had used?

A telegram arrived from James on the third day which only served to increase her frustration. It read: *Trail from Manchester gone cold. STOP Possible he was taken alive. STOP*

"Damn it all," Ursula sighed. The papers on her desk slid off and scattered on the floor as she tossed her fountain pen down in disgust. "Why can't I work out this damn code?!"

Later that night, Ursula sat at the same desk, her head between her hands. The mantel clock struck midnight but still she remained motionless. She did not want to admit defeat. Stacked around her were all of the books she owned which she knew Lord Wrotham had in his collection. She also included all the books he had given her as gifts—but where to start? The possibilities for the code were virtually endless. She had never felt as useless or as stupid as she did now.

Biggs entered, silent and stealthy. He placed the letter beside her before she even heard him enter. She looked up with a start.

"What is it, Biggs?" she asked groggily.

"I found this slipped under the front door, Miss," he replied.

Ursula took the letter and, recognizing the handwriting, drew a sharp breath before opening it.

Who knows how much time you have left, if any? My offer still stands.

"Biggs," Ursula said slowly.

"Yes, Miss," he replied, turning around.

"Throw this in the fire and burn it," she said bitterly. Christopher Dobbs may think what he like, but she would be damned if she would give him the satisfaction of asking for his help—not at the price he wanted her to pay.

Another telegram from James arrived the following day, just as Ursula returned from an appointment with Doctor Unger of Harley Street.

Have arrived in Dublin. STOP Conflicting reports from contacts here STOP Will advise further. STOP Prepare yourself for the worst. STOP

Ursula read the telegram in silence before dismissing both Biggs and Julia from her presence. She was still no closer to deciphering the text in Lord Wrotham's field book.

"Tell everyone that I do not wish to be disturbed," she instructed Biggs, before shutting herself up in her study. She spent the afternoon sitting in the armchair by the dying coal fire, insensitive to the failing light or the growing chill in the room.

At six o'clock, Julia brought in a dinner tray, the contents of which remained untouched.

Just before nine, Ursula emerged from the study and walked upstairs. Julia undressed her in anxious silence, but for once Ursula would not be drawn into any discussion. She remained uncharacteristically taciturn and reserved. Finally, as she eased herself between the cool cotton sheets of her four poster bed, Ursula lay very still, hoping for some relief from her many worries and a dreamless sleep. Instead, exhaustion dragged her down deep into a cavern of dark and ominous dreams.

She had a vision of her mother lying ill in a dimly room. She saw her father's eyes as he looked up at her as he died. Her memories were fragile and glassy. She could still see their faces, still feel the sensation of loss smooth and cold against her heart—yet the feeling that she might easily clasp too tight, shatter those memories with the mere pressure of her fingers alone, remained. Ursula woke up to find her pillow wet with tears.

Ask me no more, she heard Lord Wrotham's voice, *thy fate and mine are sealed.* Ursula squeezed her eyes shut, remembering him reading that poem to her aloud. His words had been like a stream that carried her gently along, but her sweet reminiscence now offered no comfort. She opened her eyes and gazed up and the ceiling. She thought of the rest of the stanza—

I strove against the stream and all in vain
Surely it was not as easy as that?
Let the river take me to the main:
No more, dear love, for at a touch I yield;
Ask me no more.
Ask me no more. How could she of all people been so blind?

Ursula jumped out of bed and, pulling on her silk robe and slippers, hastened out of the bedroom and down the stairs to her study.

The book code was not based on anything in Lord Wrotham's library. It was based on the first book of Tennyson's poems he had ever given her. That she should have failed to realize until now that she had never seen that particular edition on his bookshelf seemed dull-witted in the extreme. She grabbed the book from the shelf and opened up its soft burgundy leather cover. From the teal and gold leaf pattern front-piece to the pages edged with gold, the 1899 edition was a beautiful book that included plates from Gustave Dore's famous drawings. Ursula hunted for the poem *The Princess* and then, on page 210, she found the passage she was looking for. Sitting at the desk she then counted the words, and after a few minutes of trying different permutations—first line number then word number, the first lines of Lord Wrotham's field book were finally clear.

"My orders require the re-opening of old wounds. Possibly it is my own despair that allows such reckless disregard for the pain that will no doubt be inflicted as a result. Betrayal is never something to be taken lightly. McTiernay may believe himself to be the penitent thief but the Count will always play the true role of Judas. A man's conscience and his judgment is the same thing; and as the judgment, so also the conscience, may be erroneous."

Ursula turned to the second page but as soon as she tried to apply the rules she had used to decode the first, she realized the code had changed. The cipher key no longer worked. She turned back and stared at the paragraph she had deciphered. Surely if Lord Wrotham had thought she would decipher this, he would have given her another clue? She read and reread the paragraph, her dressing gown pulled in tight around her, for the study was cold and the fire in the grate as yet unset. Finally realization dawned and with a swift look at the mantel clock—it was now nearly five o'clock in the morning—she knew exactly where she must go that day.

Oxford.

CHAPTER TWENTY-FIVE

BALLIOL COLLEGE, OXFORD

"MISS MARLOW!" Professor Prendergast exclaimed. "This is a surprise."

"Is it?" Ursula asked with a smile. She folded her motoring 'duster' over the chair and unwound the scarf from her hat. "Surely you must have suspected I would work it out."

Professor Prendergast sat down and pulled his pipe from his jacket pocket. He slipped a box of matches out of his waistcoat and smiled as he tapped the box lightly on the desk top.

"Perhaps I merely hoped," he answered with the barest hint of acknowledgement.

Ursula laid Lord Wrotham's field book out in front of him. "I deciphered the first entry—that was easy once I realized it came from the copy of Tennyson's poems that Lord Wrotham had given me—one he did not possess anywhere in his library. I guess he chose that particular edition as he knew that if anything happened no one would ever find it in his library or chamber—that it would be in mine was a clever twist. But of course that wasn't all was it Professor?"

"No," Professor Prendergast conceded.

"Because although I could decipher the first entry, the rest no longer followed the pattern—initially extremely frustrating, I have to admit, at four o'clock this morning. But then I reread the passage I had managed to decode and it all became so very clear."

"Did it indeed," Prendergast replied, tilting back in his chair. Ursula's eyes narrowed—she was piqued by the amusement she detected in his tone.

Ursula opened the field book and began to read aloud the last two lines of the passage she had deciphered.

"*A man's conscience and his judgment is the same thing; and as the judgment, so also the conscience, may be erroneous.* I recognized the last part as a quotation from Thomas Hobbes' Leviathan—which meant, of course, that I immediately thought of you."

"Bravo, Miss Marlow." Prendergast's tone still suggested amusement but his eyes remained watchful. "And what, pray tell, do you intend to do with such knowledge?"

"Nothing at all," Ursula replied. "Except to ask you to produce the rest of the code I need to complete my decryption."

Professor Prendergast fell silent.

Ursula leaned forward. "I need your help, professor," she urged. "You must understand the gravity of the situation—no matter what you promised Admiral Smythe and Lord Wrotham, their notebooks may provide the only clues as to what is really going on. Surely the fact that Lord Wrotham intended for me to decipher the first part of this indicates he wanted me to know what his field book contained."

Prendergast lit his pipe with deliberate slowness.

Ursula sighed. "But of course, when this was written, Lord Wrotham was probably thinking I would be the one to discover it. When he started these entries—back I assume in mid-1911 he had not hidden it. Nor, of course, had he been charged with treason."

"If Lord Wrotham had wanted me to provide you with the rest of the information you need to decipher the rest of his field book, he would have sent word," Professor Prendergast said. "As it is, he had not . . ."

"So you won't help me then?!" Ursula cried, slumping back in the chair. Her body felt suddenly sluggish, weighed down with the combination of lack of sleep and frustration.

"Look," she said. "I know Lord Wrotham's mission in Germany was part of Admiral Smythe's plan to monitor the activities of the Irish Republican Brotherhood and to discover who in Germany was willing to supply armaments to them. Part of the Admiral's plan required Lord Wrotham to heal the rift that had occurred between himself and Fergus McTiernay after the death of Bernice Baldeo in Guyana. I know all about the Imperial Gold and Diamond Mining Company and the court case brought against it, alleging fraudulent activities by directors such as McTiernay and Count von Bernstorff-Hollweg. I also know that Lord Wrotham was part of the cover up of all that occurred . . . and that it was the Count who was willing to testify against Lord Wrotham and have him charged with treason."

Prendergast continued to watch her closely.

"But don't you see, what is happening now has moved beyond the mere question of Wrotham and Admiral Smythe's objectives regarding the Irish Republican Brotherhood? McTiernay has murdered the Count. He has abducted and, more likely than not, killed Lord Wrotham—but to what end?" Ursula drew breath. Prendergast remained motionless in his chair—his pipe idle on the desk.

"If McTiernay was responsible for Admiral Smythe's death, why would he have left files that implicated himself?" Ursula said. "Lord Wrotham believed there was another 'game' being played here—one behind the scenes—and I intend to discover exactly what this game is. I need to know what's in Lord Wrotham's field book if I'm to have any chance of figuring out what is really happening. Please . . . without your help we may never know who has been orchestrating these events all along."

Prendergast raised his hand lightly. "Sit my dear," he said. "Sit . . ." He relit his pipe and sat in quiet contemplation. Ursula opened her mouth to implore him further but he waved her aside, demanding silence. After what seemed an eternity, he got to his feet with surprising speed. "You will have to wait here for a minute, my dear," he said before he wrapped his academic cloak about him and hurried from the room.

Ursula placed her head in her hands. *Was the professor mad? Had he listened to anything she had said?*

When Professor Prendergast returned a few minutes later, he was carrying a pile of manila folders all stuffed full of papers.

"We can use the Professor Bingley's room—you'll need to root around and find us some paper, pencils, oh, and the charcoal biscuits are in the top drawer, I think. I'll ask one of the scouts to get us coffee. I warn you this is going to take us both many hours, I'm afraid."

"What do you have there?" Ursula asked, getting to her feet. Her heart had started beating furiously as soon as she realized that Professor Prendergast intended to help her.

"These are the final set of keys for the codes used," Prendergast said. "They changed each month to limit possible exposure should either notebook be discovered."

"So I was right—Admiral Smythe and Lord Wrotham did entrust the key to their codes to you," Ursula said.

"Let's just say some members of Naval Intelligence like to use me as a kind of secret keeper." Prendergast said. "Though don't think that means I'm divulging anything other more than what I must—and don't get too excited, for these notebooks are likely to contain, in the most excruciating detail, all the observations made by Admiral Smythe and Lord Wrotham. They'll be full of naval exercises and ship specifications—the sort of things likely to bore us witless without a doubt. But if you think they'll be something in there that will help your investigations then—in light of the circumstances—we'd better get cracking . . ."

Professor Prendergast was right. The task of deciphering the pages in Lord Wrotham's field book was painstaking slow and the information covered, by and large, boring in the extreme. The entries did however form a clear picture of a man acting on behalf of Naval Intelligence—a man whose very rationale for attending the December 1911 meeting with McTiernay and the Count was clearly not to foment treason or rebellion in Ireland. It was sufficient, Ursula felt sure, to clear Lord Wrotham's name . . . should she ever be able to get the evidence in court . . .

But it was the entries right at the start that shocked both her and Professor Prendergast. Lord Wrotham's mission was more important that she had ever suspected.

Admiral Smythe is convinced that we have a German spy in our midst—for evidence of the most sensitive of Naval Intelligence dealings is now known within the German admiralty. Who this person is remains a critical question, and so our mission in December is all the more important. It has been deliberately set up to try and rout out the enemy within. Not even James is immune from suspicion—only the Foreign Secretary, the First Lord of the Admiralty, Admiral Smythe and myself know the true nature of my mission.

Prendergast watched Ursula's reaction carefully.

"At least now I understand why Lord Wrotham believed that without Admiral Smythe he could not defend himself against the charges laid," Ursula said, remembering the day Harrison arrested Lord Wrotham. "Do you think anyone else in Naval Intelligence or the government knew there was a Germany spy in their midst?"

"Only probably the Prime Minister. If the concern was of a German spy within the very highest circles of government then Smythe would have kept his suspicions very close indeed."

Ursula chewed her lip, ruminating on the implications of all she had read.

"Well, this is certainly evidence that could possibly clear Lord Wrotham of all charges—though probably not without corroboration from Admiral Smythe's encrypted notebook. The difficulty is . . ." Ursula's voice trailed off.

"We don't know who is the spy," Professor Prendergast finished.

Ursula nodded. "It could be almost anyone—it could even be you . . ."

Professor Prendergast laughed. "I assure you, I may hold some secrets but never any of the important ones. Naval Intelligence would never allow it!"

"I can't say I ever seriously thought it was you—not for a moment—but all this does pose a thorny problem when it comes to Admiral Smythe's notebook."

"It does indeed, m'dear."

"Admiral Smythe may have been murdered because he discovered the identity of the spy. His notebook may therefore reveal all . . . and exonerate Lord Wrotham. But if we tell Sir Buckley or Chief inspector Harrison we also run a risk—firstly that the murderer finds out we have deciphered the book—he or she may kill again to keep it secret.

The second risk is even more troubling . . . what if the German spy is in fact . . ."

"Sir Reginald Buckley?" Prendergast inserted.

When Ursula returned home a telegram from James awaited her.

Am on McTiernay's trail. STOP Do not leave London on any account. STOP

The following morning Ursula finalized her plans to travel to Ireland. It was time to confront McTiernay.

PART THREE

IRELAND

CHAPTER TWENTY-SIX

FERRY TO KINGSTOWN, IRELAND

THE FERRY LEFT HOLYHEAD just as the sun broke through the clouds. Although the crossing was relatively smooth for the time of year, Ursula still felt every dip and rise of the swell in the pit of her stomach. She had to stay on deck for fear she might be sick.

"I used to be a much better sailor," Ursula told Lady Winterton as she joined her at the railing.

Lady Winterton eyed her curiously. "There is another possibility, you know." Though there was no note of censure in her voice, Ursula still avoided meeting her gaze. "Have you considered the possibility . . ." Lady Winterton let the implication drift on the breeze.

"Yes," Ursula conceded finally.

"And?" Lady Winterton asked.

Ursula gazed out across the Irish Sea, her hazel eyes mirroring the seas tossing green and blue depths. She did not want to face the inevitable next question.

"Are you?"

A flock of gannets returning from the warmer southern oceans, dived and spun over the waves, allowing Ursula to feign distraction for a little while longer.

Eventually Ursula said, "I saw my doctor in London last week and he confirmed it." She paused, waiting for the wave of nausea to subside.

"Do you know what you are going to do?" Lady Winterton asked.

Ursula braced herself against the railing and shook her head.

"You will have to decide soon," Lady Winterton said, and her voice dropped until it was little more that a low murmur beneath the wind. "Grace already suspects, as I'm sure your staff do too . . ."

"I know," Ursula exhaled heavily.

"You are showing very early, my dear. I suspected even in Germany."

"Did you?' Ursula asked bleakly. "I had no thought of it myself . . . not until we returned to England. I just thought it was the shock of everything."

Lady Winterton lay a smooth gloved hand on her arm. "Take care," she urged. "For your child's sake as well as your own. All this dashing about and the strain of the case—it may take its toll."

Ursula hung her head. "You think I haven't questioned what I'm doing?! Ever since I found out I've been worrying whether I should even continue with my investigations. But I can't not know what's happened to him," she looked up at Lady Winterton. "I have to face the truth."

"Even if it means risking your unborn child?" Lady Winterton asked, "for likely as not Lord Wrotham is already dead."

Ursula remained silent. The wind whipped her coat, sending the hem billowing up, hitting the back of her calves with a ferocious flap.

Lady Winterton turned and leaned against the rail. "Ursula," she said quietly. "I know all too well what it's like to lose a child." She pushed back a strand of golden hair that the wind had loosened from beneath her hat. "Believe me, you don't want that on your conscience."

"Oh, Catherine," Ursula said, her eyes brimming with tears. "I had no idea"—She couldn't even say the words.

"There are few who do. I miscarried a week after Nigel died."

"That must have been"—Ursula paused, her voice choking. "I cannot even begin to imagine how that must have been."

"I felt as though I had lost everything." Lady Winterton swallowed quickly, turning away to hide her tears.

Ursula laid a hand on her shoulder. "I'm so terribly sorry."

"Time heals some wounds," Lady Winterton said, her voice muffled as she wiped her tears with a white handkerchief. "But not those that run so deep . . ." She inhaled deeply before continuing: "If you'll excuse me. I think I'll go below decks for a while."

"Of course," Ursula murmured. She held onto the railing and found comfort in the feel of cold steel beneath her fingers. Even through her gloves the cold sinewy coils of the metal felt reassuringly durable—A reminder that the present still held hope. As Ursula pulled away to leave, her glove snagged on a rough piece of rail. A tear ripped and drew blood. She quickly pulled off the glove and sucked her injured finger. It felt like an admonishment for having the temerity to forget for even one moment the precariousness of the present.

Though the crossing to Ireland was expected to take just under five hours, Ursula had booked herself and Lady Winterton adjoining first class cabins. Ursula came below decks to find Julia sitting in the cabin lounge, doing her embroidery. The servants' quarters in Chester Square already had a multitude of samplers and seat cushions each bearing an apt bible or scripture quotation. Ursula was afraid Julia might be planning on expanding her collection to include the main house as well.

"I'm sorry, but it looks as if you'll need to mend my gloves," Ursula said. "I snagged them on the railing outside."

"Is your finger all right?" Julia asked, putting aside her embroidery and rising to her feet. "Shall I get a bandage from the ship's doctor?"

"No, it's fine," Ursula said, as she pulled out her handkerchief and wound it round her finger, "though I might sit down for a bit. The sea air has given me a terrible headache."

"I brought some aspirin powder," Julia said quickly. "I'll mix some for you now."

"Thank you," Ursula replied and she sat down, feeling her pregnant body ease into the soft upholstery.

Julia soon returned bearing a tall glass of water and a bottle of Aspirin salts. She mixed the two with a tall silver spoon before handing it to Ursula.

CLARE LANGLEY-HAWTHORNE

"Julia?" Ursula asked.

"Yes, Miss."

"What would you do, if you had all the choices in the world?"

"I'd like to be a missionary I think, Miss," Julia answered easily. "But why do you ask?" The color suddenly drained from Julia's face, betraying her anxiety.

"Don't worry Julia, you know you are welcome to stay with me for as long as you like," Ursula reassured her. "I only wondered whether you would prefer to be doing something else."

"A mistress doesn't usually pay much regard to that sort of thing," Julia stammered. "But you don't seem surprised by my answer."

"Hardly," Ursula admitted. "It seems to be that ever since we returned from Egypt you've been headed in that direction. I guess with all that has happened of late, I just realize the precariousness of our lives. Perhaps I've been selfish wanting to keep you, but I don't want to hold you back. Not now. You should have the opportunity to pursue your dreams and I want you to know that, should you decide that being a missionary is your true path, I'll help in any way I can."

"Oh Miss!" Julia cried. "That is very generous of you."

"It's the least I can do," Ursula replied. "You should start making enquiries so that when this is all over, we can make the necessary arrangements." There was a momentary pause, as the ferry suddenly rose and fell sharply with the swell.

"Do you think he's alive?" Julia asked in a low voice as she watched Ursula take the final gulps of the aspirin suspension.

Ursula gripped the glass tightly in her hands. "I can only hope . . ."

"I will pray for you," Julia whispered. Ursula glanced up to see tears splashing down Julia's cheeks. "Don't mind me, Miss," Julia said, scrubbing her eyes with the back of her sleeve. "I just can't believe . . . I mean, I thought . . . I thought the fairy tale had finally come true for you. After all that had happened with your mum and dad—now this. It just doesn't seem right."

"I'm sure that's what many women feel, when all that they hope for, all that they cherish, is taken away from them," Ursula stopped. She could not let despair gain a foothold—not yet. Not until she knew for sure. Instinctively, she placed her hand on her belly and closed her

204

eyes once more. Was this how Lady Winterton felt when she had been reminded of her own loss? Ursula wondered, as the pain of her own grief tightened its grip once more. She thought of Lady Winterton sitting alone in her cabin and realized she would never know, never truly understand what it meant to be bereft, until she held Lord Wrotham's body in her arms. Until then there would always be doubt. Although she had endured her father's murder, she suspected her desire for vengeance would be different this time. She would not want justice to be served—she would want to wield it, as a man might wield a sword. She wanted to know who the German spy was that Lord Wrotham and Admiral Smythe had sacrificed everything to find. The anger was already within her, she felt it stir, raw and bloody, and she knew, should she discover McTiernay had killed Lord Wrotham, should she discover Christopher Dobbs was in any way involved, that she would exact a fearsome and terrible revenge.

CHAPTER TWENTY-SEVEN

DUBLIN

BY THE TIME THE MOTORCAR Lady Winterton had arranged for them had transported them to Dublin, Ursula had already succumbed to exhausted sleep. Huddled in the back on the red-buttoned leather seat of the Clement-Bayard Tourer, beside Julia, the lurch and swing of the drive had lulled her to sleep in a way that had eluded her for many nights now. Lady Winterton's maid Grace also sat in the backseat alongside them, while Lady Winterton sat next to the chauffeur in the front issuing directions. Although Lady Winterton's family in London had tried to minimize any contact with her late husband's family, Lady Winterton had kept in touch with Nigel's sisters and it was his eldest sister, Mrs. Mary Dooley, who had offered her Dublin home for them to stay. It was fortuitous that Mary had married the son of a wealthy Dublin solicitor for Lady Winterton's family continued to refuse to provide any financial assistance to her dead husband's financially strapped, but proud Irish family.

They travelled on the main road to Dublin through villages which in recent years had become virtual suburbs: After Kingstown, there was Monkstown, Blackrock and Rathmines—all passing in a blur of houses, shop awnings and tramlines. Ursula fancied she could still smell the sea air, even after they stopped at a small thatched tavern on the Kingstown Road. After a heavy lunch, Ursula slept for the final leg of the journey so deeply that she had no recollection of tire changes or petrol refilling or their approach through the outskirts of south Dublin. She woke as they drew up alongside a Georgian terrace home in Merrion Square, just as day faded into a grim grey twilight.

Ursula and Julia were ushered quickly upstairs. Soon a bath was being drawn and Julia was unhooking Ursula's dress and removing hairpins from her now unruly dark auburn hair. Lady Winterton's sister-in-law Mary had organized a supper for them and, as propriety demanded that Ursula changed for dinner, poor Julia had to hunt for the one unwrinkled evening dress to be found at the bottom of the trunk.

Lady Winterton was already waiting in the front sitting room when Ursula emerged downstairs. She was immaculate in an emerald green draped gown. Her pale angular features bore no sign of the emotional distress earlier that day. She appeared serene sitting on an upholstered blue chair, the color of which only accentuated her eyes. She was like a model sitter for a portrait painter Ursula thought, as she hesitated in the doorway. Mary crossed the room to welcome her, her feet lighting tapping on the parquetry floor. She was wearing pale pink which seemed to offset the darkness of her hair and eyes.

Ursula glanced down at the slightly rumpled tunic of her turquoise silk dress. When she had supervised Julia's packing, dressing for dinner had been the last thing on her mind.

"I hear you had a tolerable ferry crossing," Mary said, "but that you may still be feeling a bit delicate. Would supper still be amenable to you?"

"But of course," Ursula replied. "I must thank you for agreeing to let me stay and for all your hospitality. I only hope my presence here does not inconvenience you too much."

"No, not at all," Mary replied, though there was a tightness around her mouth that suggested a measure of apprehension behind the words. "I am grateful for anyone who brings my sister-in-law back to visit us. It has been too long, has it not, dear Catherine?"

"Too long indeed," Lady Winterton acknowledged.

Mary rang the bell for the servants to serve dinner. As she led the way through to the dining room, she turned to Ursula. "Catherine wrote to us about your enquiries regarding Mr. Fergus McTiernay. My husband, as you know is a partner in a firm of solicitors here in town. He is slightly acquainted with Mr. McTiernay but I'm afraid no one has heard from him for some months now."

"What about his wife?" Ursula asked.

"Oh yes," Mary replied, her lip curling in distaste. "We have all heard far too much from her and her radical speeches."

"Mary does not subscribe to our views about female suffrage," Lady Winterton interposed.

"No," Mary conceded. She gestured for Ursula to take a seat at the long polished dining room table. "But even those of my acquaintance who are proponents of the vote for women feel outraged by some of her comments. Why if she had her way we would all be chaining ourselves in the street or firebombing the houses of parliament!"

Lady Winterton caught Ursula's eye and they both suppressed their smiles.

Mary was soon tucking into a plate of lamb stew with relish. "I can tell you this," she said between mouthfuls. "Niamh McTiernay won't meet with you—of that I am sure, not while the Garda are searching for her husband."

"Please thank you husband for asking on my behalf—will he not be joining us this evening?"

"No," Mary said, a little too quickly. "He has been called away, unfortunately, on business."

"Oh," Ursula could think of nothing else to say. As she toyed with the food on her plate, she caught Lady Winterton and Mary exchange glances. Ursula guessed that Mary's husband was unhappy with the prospect of having her stay. Obviously Lord Wrotham's case and all its attendant notoriety was an embarrassment even here in Dublin. Ursula felt even more grateful for Mary's hospitality—she was sure it was only due to Lady Winterton that she was allowed stay.

"Mary," Lady Winterton prompted. "Perhaps I could approach Margaret Cousins and ask her about Mrs. McTiernay."

"Wasn't she one of the ladies who joined us on the march in November 1910?" Ursula queried.

Lady Winterton nodded.

"Oh, didn't you hear?" Mary replied. "She was imprisoned in January for her suffragette activities. I'm not sure that my husband would allow any of us to approach her now—I'm not even sure she's out of Mountjoy prison yet."

"Ah," Lady Winterton replied as Ursula shifted in her chair, discomfited. Clearly this was going to be more delicate than she had anticipated given Mary and her husband Patrick's political views. Ursula also suspected, as she noticed a portrait of William of Orange hanging on the wall in the dining room, that Mary's family were unlikely to be supporters of Home Rule. Indeed Lady Winterton had hinted that Nigel had been the only one among his family to tolerate, although not overtly support, Irish nationalism.

"I almost forgot," Mary said abruptly, patting the corners of her mouth with her napkin. "A gentleman called for you this afternoon, but I told him you had not yet arrived from Kingstown. He left his card for you"—Mary signaled for the footman to bring it to her—"Here it is."

Ursula took the card and read it quickly. *Mr. Archibald James, Esq. Mayfair, London.* Clearly James was no longer content to play the part of chauffeur. "Thank you Mary," Ursula said. "Mr. James is one of my . . . er . . . business associates."

"I thought as much," Mary replied. Her tone was decidedly brittle now and Ursula gazed across the table at Lady Winterton with a silent plea for a new topic of conversation.

"I was admiring your new gramophone player in the sitting room, Mary," Lady Winterton said obligingly.

"Perhaps we can listen after dinner," Mary replied. "We have some new recordings of Dame Nellie Melba that I've been told are excellent."

When the time came, however, Ursula demurred, citing fatigue from the journey and went upstairs instead. Before long she was slipping between the sheets, thankful for Julia's forethought in placing a copper bed warmer inside. Despite the fire in the grate, the guest room had a damp chill in the air, but no sooner had Ursula cocooned herself among the blankets and sheets then her head lay down and she fell into a deep and weary sleep.

In the morning she was awoken by Lady Winterton.

"What's the matter?" Ursula asked groggily as she tried to sit up. "Where's Julia?"

"We must move, my dear," Lady Winterton said urgently. "And leave Julia here."

"Why?" Ursula asked with the befuddlement of one barely awake.

"Julia was sharing her room last night with one of my sister-in-law's young scullery maids who has apparently been poorly for the last few days. She awoke in the early hours of this morning running a raging fever. My aunt's physician has just left—and has diagnosed scarlet fever. For you and the baby's sake we must leave immediately. Grace, thankfully, slept in separate quarters so she is hopefully free of contamination—but we cannot risk the possibility of any further exposure."

Ursula sat upright in bed as she absorbed the news.

"I've been trying to think of where we may best go—where your secret is unlikely to be discovered," Lady Winterton said, with a thinly veiled reference to Ursula's pregnancy. "We dare not risk a hotel in Dublin as there's too much opportunity for speculation as well as observation. No doubt the reporters will descend as soon as they find out you are in Dublin. No, I fear we must try and make our way to Nigel's old estate. I've sent just now word to the house-keeper to expect us. I'm afraid the house is in disrepair but it is isolated—hopefully enough to keep you safe from both prying eyes as well as sickness."

"What about James?" Ursula asked.

"I will make sure we get word to him," Lady Winterton reassured her.

"When do we leave?" Ursula asked, as she struggled out of bed. She wrapped a woolen shawl around her shoulders.

"Grace is repacking the trunks now. I think you should dress quickly—I will arrange for breakfast somewhere en-route—but Julia must stay since she has already been exposed."

"Yes, of course," Ursula responded.

"Then I will see you downstairs in about fifteen minutes—we'll have the motorcar waiting for us. All the staff have currently been advised to remain in their rooms until we have left. Thank God we found out before either of us had spent any time here. Let us just pray, for your baby's sake, we have both avoided infection."

CHAPTER TWENTY-EIGHT

THE WINTERTON FAMILY ESTATE,
COUNTY MEATH, IRELAND

THE JOURNEY TO THE OLD WINTERTON ESTATE took nearly three hours, most of which Ursula spent huddled in the backseat of the motorcar watching the rain lash down. Ursula had her face pressed against the window but she saw neither the streaks of condensation nor the splatter of raindrops against the thin cold glass. She was lost in her thoughts for most of the journey—even when they crossed the river Liffey and drove through the Northern slums of Dublin and Lady Winterton pointed out the great houses of Henrietta Street that were now squalid tenements. As the car made its way along the busy streets, Ursula, normally sensitive to social issues, was so preoccupied she barely noticed the children racing alongside, barefoot despite the rain, hands outstretched as they begged for money.

Once they had left the city, the rain set in and the colors of the countryside ran down the window pane—streaming down the glass like watercolors on wet paper.

Ursula had a leather bag on her lap and at the bottom she could feel Lord Wrotham's field book and her own notebook containing all of its contents deciphered. Ursula had decided not to tell Lady Winterton about the field book or the fact that she and Prendergast had discovered the true nature of Lord Wrotham's mission in Germany. There was too much risk that Lady Winterton may inadvertently reveal the truth to James (more likely out of pique than anything else) and the possibility that James was a German spy could not be ignored. Nevertheless having Lord Wrotham's field book with her provided some measure of comfort—he was innocent of treason after all. That comfort, however, was not sufficient to dispel the dread that came whenever she thought of him—for she may have found the truth too late to save him.

"We're nearly there," Lady Winterton said and the bleakness of her tone matched Ursula's mood perfectly. Ursula's glanced across, but Lady Winterton seemed absorbed in her own thoughts. She was staring dead ahead, her eyes glassy and cold, as if the thought of returning to a place that would be forever associated with pain and loss was almost unimaginable.

"I'm sorry," Ursula said quietly. "I'm sorry to have made you come back. I can see how difficult it is for you."

"Difficult?" Lady Winterton said dazedly. "I'm nearly home, that's all . . ."

Lady Winterton laid her head against the window. "Nearly home," she echoed, as a small child might.

As they pulled into a gravel drive, Ursula wiped the condensation from the window and peered out through the rain.

At the entrance to the estate stood two ivy-choked stone pillars. As they drove past Ursula could see the cracks in the stone and the ivy, which was growing rampant along the footpath, climbing ever higher, seeding these cracks with tenacious tendrils. Dark heavy-hanging branches of oak trees framed her first view of the house. She could see an overgrown front garden with the ruins of an old fountain, before the house itself loomed up quickly. A grey brick monolith with little in the way of architectural grace, the house was testament to some functional neo-Georgian aesthetic that favored structure and form above any kind of ornamentation. The windows were symmetrical, the entrance steps squat and uninviting, and the dark slate roof in urgent need of repair. Without the ivy's determined encroachment, the house would be as uniformly grey as any Lancashire factory.

As the motorcar drew up, a small, cat-like woman emerged from the front door, clad in a black uniform and a white lace cap and apron that harkened back to Victorian times. She had a tiny round face and dark almond shaped eyes that may have once been considered exotic but which now seemed eerily feline beneath the folds of skin that now surrounded them. As the lady in the white lace cap ushered them inside, Ursula pinched the inner edge of her wrist to try and overcome the unreality of her surroundings. The strange dissonant appearance of both the house and its housekeeper made her feel as though she had stepped into a Beatrix Potter story book.

As she took off her coat in the hallway Ursula noticed that the grandfather clock at the foot of the stairs had stopped at ten past two. There were still sheets covering the furniture in the formal room to the right of the entrance way. In the small drawing room on her left there was a fire, but the whole house had been dormant and cold for so long that it provided little in the way of heat. Ursula and Lady Winterton quickly walked inside and huddled in front of the fireplace—rubbing their ice-cold hands in a futile attempt to get warm.

"I've made up your old room, my Lady," the housekeeper informed Lady Winterton in a voice that was dull and flat without any semblance of the usual beauty and lilt of the Irish accent. "And I lit fires in the rooms on the first floor. I'm afraid the second floor guest rooms are completely unusable. The ceiling subsided with damp some months ago."

"Thank you Miss Cadogan," Lady Winterton said. "I've no doubt you have done your best on such short notice."

Ursula stood shivering by the fire. It seemed an ill-wind had brought her here and she felt as though she was far more likely to die of pneumonia in this bleak and decaying house than she would of any feared infection in Dublin. She turned and saw the motorcar draw away through the window—Mary's chauffeur was already returning to Dublin and the thought of being stranded here depressed Ursula even further.

"I'm sorry, Ursula," Lady Winterton said. "It's hardly an auspicious welcome to my husband's estate. But, as you must realize, he died penniless and the estate has been left for ruin. I try and spare what I can from the income my family gives me, but there is always so much that needs doing."

"Please," Ursula said, summoning all her good manners despite the fact that her teeth were chattering. "Do not concern yourself on my account . . ."

"Would you care for some tea?" Miss Cadogan, the housekeeper, inquired—her eyes were dark and shrewd as they looked Ursula over. Ursula knew by now that in her day dress any keen observer would soon recognize her current condition.

Ursula nodded gratefully. "Tea would be lovely."

"Grace has gone upstairs to unpack the trunks and will be down shortly," Lady Winterton instructed Miss Cadogan. "Perhaps after tea, you could show Miss Marlow to her room and make arrangements for us to have a light dinner. Grace knows her way around and can help you with anything else you may need before you leave for the night."

Lady Winterton turned to Ursula as the Miss Cadogan left the room. "I'm afraid I cannot afford to have her on full time—she usually comes by three times a week to check on the house. I'm afraid we'll only have Grace to look after us until Miss Cadogan returns on Wednesday."

"Please don't worry on my account," Ursula assured her. Her face was pink with embarrassment, for she hated seeing Lady Winterton's discomfiture regarding the state of her husband's estate.

"You know that my family controls all my money and that they refuse to let me spend what I would like on restoring this house to its former glory," Lady Winterton said, keeping her voice low as if she feared Miss Cadogan could hear. "Nigel left me with a considerable number of debts as well as the upkeep of this place—it's all I can do to stop it from decaying completely. If my father had his way it would have been sold by now."

"I can imagine you feel the need to hold onto the place," Ursula responded quietly.

"I always thought I'd return and live here someday . . . though I confess there are also days when I wish I could just be done with it," Lady Winterton admitted.

"Well I for one, am grateful that you brought me here . . . and for your compassion for both me and my baby. There aren't many who would . . ."

"Nonsense," Lady Winterton's response was swift. "I only wish you could have seen this place when Nigel was alive—it was glorious."

Ursula looked about her dubiously. She doubted such a place could have ever, in anyone's imagination been considered glorious. Yet she understood, all too well, Lady Winterton's need to revere the place that would forever be associated with her husband. In the current circumstances, how could she not? Ursula only hoped that word had gotten back to James about the reason for her abrupt departure from Dublin, and that he would contact her soon regarding McTiernay. Empathy she may have for Lady Winterton, but it was not enough to dispel the unease she felt being in this house. In her current state of anxiety she could well imagine the spirits of the dead haunting her here—in this place of decay and ruin—in this place that seemed as cold as a tomb. Ursula shivered, for her nightmares were desolate enough; she needed no further darkness to embrace.

CHAPTER TWENTY-NINE

AFTER TEA, MISS CADOGAN SHOWED URSULA up to her room. As they progressed up the stairs and walked along the draughty corridor, Ursula noticed the bare walls bore the blanched outlines of where paintings had once hung. All of the rooms they passed still had cover sheets over what little furniture remained. There was a pervasive smell of damp in the air; a sense of decay and age that sent Ursula's spirits lower than they had been for months. Instinctively she placed her hand on her belly as if protecting the unborn child within.

"Here you are then," Miss Cadogan said as she led Ursula to the last open doorway. "I've tried to make it as comfortable as I can, though truth be told, it was one of the few rooms in any fit state to be used. I only sorry I haven't had a chance to remove all the old things that were stored in here."

"I'm sure it will be more than adequate, thank you, Miss Cadogan," Ursula replied as she followed her into the small narrow room. The windows, though they had been cleaned, were still opaque with age and disuse, and let in little in the way of sunlight (which, on this day there was precious little anyway). The iron four poster bed had been dusted and reset with fresh linens, yet the thick Victorian bed spread folded on top looked as though years of filth and despair had irredeemably altered and darkened the fabric so that whatever pattern it once held could no longer be distinguished. The walls of the room must have once been painted a pale yellow, but they too had darkened over time, till they had become the color of dried birch leaves.

In the corner of the room was a large wooden trunk covered with a dust sheet. Once Miss Cadogan had left, Ursula lifted the lid cautiously only to find, to her horror that inside the trunk lovingly packed in straw were the obvious reminders of childhood: a button-eyed Teddy bear; a wooden train set, a book of Mother Goose tales; baby clothes in tissue paper, and a lace christening cap wrapped in a silk handkerchief.

Ursula stepped back quickly, letting the lid bang close and the dust sheet crumple to the floor. Surely this was not the proposed nursery, she thought in horror, as she sat down heavily on the bed. Her eye caught the faint outline of a frieze along the top of the walls—the barest outline of what had been planned—shepherds and trees, sheep and roosters. Ursula could not hide her dismay.

"Will that be all?" Miss Cadogan's voice from the doorway jolted Ursula from her thoughts. "Yes," she stammered. "Yes, of course . . . You should go see to Lady Winterton," Ursula said. "I am sure I am quite capable of splashing some water on my face before supper." She looked around searchingly.

"Water jug's over there, Miss, on the cabinet."

"Thank you."

"I can remove the trunk if you'd prefer," Miss Cadogan said, in her funny abrupt tone. "This was the Master's room when he was a boy and we had hoped . . ."

Ursula's face paled even further with the reference to Lady Winterton's lost baby and Miss Cadogan nodded sagely. "I can see why it might distress you . . . but I was not to know you were with child."

"No . . . No . . . Of course . . ." Ursula wasn't sure what else to say.

"It'll all be put to rights one day of course. Her Ladyship will see to that. One day the house will restored to its rightful place."

Ursula's face must have revealed her skepticism.

"You just see!" Miss Cadogan insisted. "I know she has grand plans!"

Ursula bit her lip. Lady Winterton could hardly have 'grand plans' when her family refused to let her use any money to restore the place. Ursula found herself staring helplessly into space, trying to think of a suitable response while Miss Cadogan made a great show of fluffing the pillows on Ursula's bed and straightening the bed linen.

"It was such a pity," Miss Cadogan continued. "For her Ladyship I mean. It should have never have ended the way it did."

"No," Ursula said awkwardly.

"He was still so young, but then the doctor always warned that it would be the drink that would take him in the end."

Ursula frowned, she had assumed Miss Cadogan had been referring to Lady Winterton's unborn child. Now she looked at the floor, embarrassed at the thought of that her few careless words could now discredit Lady Winterton's husband's name.

"I'm sorry," Miss Cadogan said hastily, perceiving Ursula's discomfiture. "I thought you knew."

"Just that he died," Ursula said shaking her head. "That's all Lady Winterton told me."

"So she didn't—" Miss Cadogan stopped herself.

"Didn't?" Ursula prompted.

"She didn't tell you that he committed suicide?"

Ursula awoke in the middle of the night with a raging thirst. The room felt stuffy and yet still cold. The fire in the grate seemed to have sucked all the oxygen from the room but its heat dissipated so quickly that it failed to make its way across the room to where the bed was situated. Ursula huddled beneath the sheets until her thirst finally drove her from her bed. She shrugged on a cardigan over her nightgown, grabbed a shawl and pulled on a pair of woolen socks to keep herself warm as she ventured out. The hallway outside was positively glacial— a damp, icy darkness now seemed to consume the house.

With a shiver Ursula drew the shawl and cardigan in around her as she groped her way down the corridor, cursing herself for not having the foresight to ask for a flashlight or candle by which to guide her way. Her thirst however compelled her to find the kitchen. There was, of course, no staff to speak of—only Lady Winterton's lady's maid,

Grace, and she was no doubt at the very top of the house asleep in the servant's quarters. Lady Winterton's room was on the other side of the landing but Ursula hardly liked to disturb her for something as trivial as a drink. Ursula's eyes eventually adjusted to the darkness as she made her way down the staircase.

At the foot of the stairs Ursula found a gas lamp and a box of matches on the hall table. She lit the lamp and, holding it by its brass handle, made her way toward the back of the house where, she assumed, she would find the kitchen. She soon found it and, after a few desultory pumps at the old-fashioned sink, she managed to get the water to flow. Unable to find a glass she used a teacup instead, gulping three cupfuls down in quick succession. She then refilled the cup for a final time and started making her way back along the hallway. Past the kitchen and dining room, Ursula found a narrow room lined with bookshelves—the moonlight picking out the gold lettering on some of the spines nearest the window. The room was sparsely furnished but, as Ursula thrust the gas lamp inside, she immediately recognized the place as a library or study of some sort—most probably Lord Winterton's given the heavy wooden shelving and dark masculine brown wallpaper.

"What are you doing?" Lady Winterton's voice made her jump.

Ursula turned quickly to find Lady Winterton standing behind her with a small portable flashlight in hand.

"Just needed a drink of water," Ursula explained, holding up her cup. "Sorry I didn't mean to wake you."

"I was afraid you may have taken ill," Lady Winterton said. She stepped forward and touched Ursula on the forehead and cheek. "You do feel a little feverish."

"Do I?" Ursula responded blankly.

"Yes, you should get back to bed as quickly as you can," Lady Winterton advised. Her tone betrayed her concern. "I will call for a doctor in the morning—just in case." Ursula had to admit she did feel a little clammy and disorientated and now fear gripped her like a vise. She squeezed her eyes closed for the anxiety of illness was so great—the threat to her unborn child so disquieting—that it made her head throb.

"Come with me," Lady Winterton said firmly as she took Ursula's arm and steered her back towards the staircase.

By morning Ursula had barely slept and Lady Winterton insisted she stay in bed while Grace went to fetch the local doctor. When the esteemed physician finally arrived he pronounced her fever to be little more than a 'nervous reaction to the country' which failed to inspire much in the way of confidence. Ursula finally fell asleep around eleven and when she awoke the house was silent and still. Even the clock on the bedside table had ceased its ticking. Ursula had no idea of the time but as she got out of bed and walked over to the window she could see the sun was now low in the sky and she guessed it was close to four. From this vantage point she could see across the fields to a small copse of trees. The low grey clouds had lifted and the sky had emerged blue and clear. Ursula felt her forehead with the back of her hand and hoped the fever had broken, for she no longer felt clammy or racked by thirst. Indeed she felt restless, longing to be free of the oppressiveness that this room—this house—seemed to produce.

Ursula quickly dressed and headed downstairs, her footsteps echoing along the empty corridors and near deserted rooms.

"Lady Winterton wasn't expecting to see you up and about," Grace's voice called out from the hallway. Ursula spun round. "You startled me!" she exclaimed. "The house felt so quiet I thought I'd been abandoned."

"Lady Winterton's out visiting some of the tenants on the estate," Grace explained. "Would you care to wait in the front parlor? I can get you some tea or a late luncheon if you would like."

"Actually," Ursula said, "I feel like trying to get some fresh air."

Grace looked at her dubiously. "It's alright," Ursula reassured her. "I am feeling much better—I just need to stretch my legs a bit—especially as it looks as though it may have finally stopped raining."

"Very good Miss," Grace answered noncommittally. "I'll be heading off to the village soon to pick up further provisions."

"Tell me," Ursula prodded gently. "How is Lady Winterton doing?—I'm worried it must be very hard for her being back here."

"She's always a little sad when we come back, Miss . . . I think the reminders are too much for her sometimes."

"Yes," Ursula murmured. "You were her maid when Lord Winterton died, were you not?"

"I was . . ."

"Had he been ill for a long time before it happened?" Ursula asked.

"He'd been bad for while . . ." Grace acknowledge. "But I think it was the court case that finally did it"—she pulled a handkerchief from her apron pocket with a sniff—"Robbed him of all hope it did and then it was only a matter of months . . ."

Grace hesitated, as if she concerned she may have betrayed her mistress' confidence.

"Please don't feel embarrassed," Ursula said hastily, although she dearly wanted to question Grace further. "I never liked to ask Lady Winterton—and I certainly didn't mean to upset you—it's just my curiosity." Ursula gave an apologetic smile. "Forgive me."

Grace nodded and blew her nose loudly. Ursula told Grace she would bundle up warmly and take a brief walk around the estate.

"When is Lady Winterton likely to be back?" Ursula inquired, as she bundled on her jacket and overcoat.

"She said not until supper—she was planning on dropping in on a few of the neighbors as well."

"Thank you," Ursula responded. "I'll probably be back well before her, but if not, can you please tell her where I've gone and that I am feeling much better. I don't want to worry her any more than I already have."

Grace bobbed a curtsey and said, "Right you are, Miss."

In her thick brown woolen coat, sensible boots and her hat pulled down warmly over her dark auburn hair, Ursula made her way out of the rear door of the house and set off across the thick green meadow that lay at the back. Tangled with brambles and weeds, it was hard to tell whether this had ever been a cultivated garden or if wild fields had always backed onto the estate. About half a mile through the thick grass, Ursula came upon the ruined remains of a small stone building. It looked as though it had once been a cottage. Inside there were rusting farm implements and what appeared to be a pair of wrought iron gates propped up against the remains of one the walls. The gates caught Ursula's eye for they had the remains of elaborate iron-scrollwork still visible. Ursula gingerly stepped through the doorway, careful not to step on the rusty pitchfork that lay on the ground submerged by weeds. Using her sleeve she pushed aside the cobwebs to read the scrollwork. *Tir Tairngire.*

Though Ursula had no idea what it meant, the name itself was not unfamiliar. She tried to recall where she had seen the name before but could bring nothing to mind. With one final glance at the broken gates, she retreated from the cottage. By now the enthusiasm and energy with which she began her walk had died and she began to feel tired.

She was still ruminating on the name—irritated that she could not remember where she had seen it before—when she returned to the house. The smoldering remains of a small bonfire greeted her near the back door.

"That was a short walk, Miss," Grace called out. "I still haven't had a chance to head off to the village." She pointed to the fire. "Her ladyship wanted me to try and clear some of the old rubbish about the place. Hope the smoke won't bother you."

"Grace," Ursula said. "Do you know what Tir Tairngire means?"

"But of course Miss, it's this place isn't it . . ."

"Ah, of course . . ." Ursula said softly to herself before she turned back to Grace and asked. "Do you know what it means?"

"The Land of Promise, Miss . . . It's what Lord Winterton named this place after he took my mistress to be his bride. He had grand plans, he did—wanted this to be one of the finest estates in all of County Meath."

But that was not how it turned out, Ursula thought, remembering where she had seen the words *Tir Tairngire* before. She gazed at the smoldering fire. The edge of a pamphlet was still visible and the scorch marks reminded her of dark green foliage; the white paper, the edge of a waterfall . . . A flame flared, and the red-orange flash was like the burst of sunlight through a forest canopy.

No, Ursula thought, *that was not the way it turned out at all.*

CHAPTER THIRTY

LADY WINTERTON DID NOT RETURN from visiting tenants on the estate until late in the afternoon and by then Ursula had retired once more to her room. She needed time to be alone with her thoughts and feigning sleep was as good an excuse as any. Below she could hear Lady Winterton's voice as she closed the front door and called out for Grace to take her coat. Ursula heard a motorcar draw up in the driveway and she sat up on the bed. She heard Lady Winterton's voice once more from below and waited.

Before too long, there was a cursory knock at her bedroom door. Ursula got up and took a step back, as the door opened abruptly. James stood in the doorway.

"I thought I told you not to come to Ireland?!"

"James," she said, feeling relief and apprehension in equal measure. "You had me worried . . . why did you not leave a message with Lady Winterton's sister-in-law, Mrs. Dooley? A calling card was hardly sufficient."

"Why did you leave Dublin?" James demanded. "I visited you the morning after you arrived but you'd already left. Mrs. Dooley said she thought you had gone to a hotel. I wasted two days trying to find you until I thought to try the old Winterton estate. God only knows what possessed you to come here!"

"When you visited Mrs. Dooley did she not say anything about Julia's condition?" Ursula said.

"Condition?" James responded. "I spoke with Julia and she seemed fine—just put out that you had apparently insisted on leaving her there."

Ursula sat down on the bed heavily.

"Are you all right?" James asked. "Lady Winterton said you had been feeling ill," His gaze flickered to her belly. "I just assumed you had left because . . ." he paused awkwardly.

"My condition?" Ursula supplanted.

James nodded.

Ursula bit her lip and replied. "It was scarlet fever we were concerned about—but I'm guessing by the look on your face that no one in the Dooley household was sick . . ."

"No," James answered with a frown. He took two steps towards her but stopped as Ursula held up her hand. "What is it?" he asked.

"Nothing," Ursula shook her head and murmured. She was not ready to voice her suspicions until she had a better idea of what this 'game' was really all about and just who exactly was involved. She had not forgotten Lord Wrotham's field book or the possibility that James was a German spy.

"I have bad news I'm afraid," she finally said. "I wasn't able to decode the field book." Ursula hoped her face did not betray the fact that she was lying.

James continued to regard her with confusion. "That's a pity," he admitted. "But it doesn't explain why you're acting the way you are—what has happened?"

"Nothing," Ursula said firmly. Her tone broached no further inquiries.

"I came upstairs to tell you that I didn't come alone," James said but as Ursula's face filled with hope, he quickly added: "Chief Inspector Harrison is with me."

"Oh," Ursula responded dully.

"He's waiting for you in the front parlor," James said. "Though I suspect he has little in the way of news for you."

Ursula rose to her feet, feeling a still, cold numbness within.

With a complete lack of propriety, James caught her arm as she passed.

"I've found McTiernay," he said.

"Do you know? . . ." Ursula could not continue.

"There's no word on whether Lord Wrotham is alive or not. I haven't told Harrison of my enquiries yet, and would prefer that he remain in ignorance—for now at least. I think we should consider our next move before involving the Chief Inspector or that idiot Sir Buckley."

Ursula nodded. "Harrison will certainly not hear of it from me. Tell me though, when do you plan on confronting McTiernay?"

"We must move quickly. He never stays in one location for long— but in the meantime you'll have to deal with Harrison. I'm afraid he discovered me in Dublin and insisted on seeing you the moment I found you. He said he needed to speak with you."

"And I with him," Ursula replied enigmatically and James frowned once more.

Ursula paused, her hand on the doorknob. "Where is Lady Winterton?" she asked. James shrugged. "Somewhere in the house—but Harrison insisted on seeing you in the parlor alone."

"Promise me one thing," she said, her hand reaching to where James' remained clasped to her arm. "Promise me that you'll see this thing through to the end."

In a gesture that seemed both deeply tender as well as protective, James touched her left cheek with the back of his other hand. "How can you doubt it?" he whispered.

"Because I doubt everything now," Ursula replied as she opened the door.

"You're going to have to trust someone," James reminded her.

"Really?" Ursula answered as she passed him in the doorway. "What makes you so sure I trust you?"

"Miss Marlow," Harrison said. As her rose to his feet to greet her, she saw the shock hit him with full force.

Ursula steadied herself as she entered the room. Harrison's expression had a greater impact than she could have ever imagined. She saw his disbelief turn to dismay as he stammered, "I should have come sooner . . ."

"Why?" Ursula replied. "If you had known would it have made you any less likely to have suspected me responsible for Lord Wrotham's disappearance? Would the fact that I am carrying Lord Wrotham's child have compelled you to solve this case any quicker?"

"You must know I have been doing all that I can . . ." Harrison replied, his face flushed. "I'm only sorry that I accused you of being complicit in Lord Wrotham's abduction but I . . . I had no idea of your current condition . . ."

Ursula had never seen him so stripped of all pretense, of all the trappings of manners or protocol that had kept him at a distance until now.

She lowered herself into a chair opposite him and bade him to sit.

"It's all right," Ursula continued and it seemed surreal to be reassuring him of all people. "I appreciate how shocking this must seem to you, but I thank you for your compassion. I wouldn't have expected it."

"What did you expect—my condemnation?" Harrison said hoarsely.

"Of course—what else would I expect from any man?"

Harrison flinched. "I've certainly given you little reason to think of me as any better," he admitted.

"Well, perhaps we can now work together," Ursula said. "James tells me you wanted to see me but that you have no news regarding Lord Wrotham." Ursula could hear the cold blank timbre of her voice.

"It is true I have nothing further regarding his fate . . . I do, however, have information regarding Count von Bernstorff-Hollweg's death. The German authorities have confirmed they are investigating the fire at his castle as arson and have identified a man matching McTiernay's description as one of the key suspects in the incident. The police in Prague have also confirmed that they have evidence linking McTiernay to the murder of the Count at the Hotel Pariz."

"Do the German authorities have any idea why the castle was burned?" Ursula asked.

"Their cooperation does not extend that far I'm afraid, but our theory is that he hoped the Count would perish in the blaze—but there may have been additional reasons. We may never know what incriminating evidence was destroyed by the fire."

Ursula remained tight lipped.

"Christopher Dobbs has also supplied us with information revealing the extent to which McTiernay tried to sell him both information as well as procure armaments."

"Has he now," Ursula answered skeptically.

Harrison frowned.

"Don't you think, given all that you know about Dobbs, that it's just a little too convenient that he is helping the Crown case against Lord Wrotham?"

"I am as wary as you—believe me," Harrison said. "But Sir Buckley trusts Dobbs implicitly."

"Wonderful . . ." Ursula muttered.

"Dobbs is now a man with powerful connections," Harrison reminded her.

"As if I could ever forget," Ursula responded. She then struggled to her feet. "No"—she gestured to Harrison as he rose to his feet—"I am quite capable of walking across the room. I'm pregnant, not incapacitated . . . and besides, I have something for you."

Harrison eyed her curiously as Ursula got up and walked over to the bureau where she had hidden Lord Wrotham's field book as well as her notes. "I deciphered this while we were still in England, but have been waiting to put it to good use. Now seems as good a time as any to do just that."

She pulled out the package she had wedged at the back of the bureau drawer, and turned back to Harrison.

"This contains," she said, opening up the brown paper wrapper and pointing to the cover of Lord Wrotham's field book, "all of Lord Wrotham's observations from his time in Germany in 1911. It fully details his mission with respect to McTiernay and how Admiral Smythe and he hoped to discover the identity of a German spy they were convinced was operating at the very highest government levels. There are entries relating to naval exercises, ship building and conversations Lord Wrotham had with various German officials regarding a possible war with England. There are also details regarding

Lord Wrotham's mission to deceive McTiernay into thinking he was a fellow Irish patriot. I am prepared to give you the notebook and all my decryptions on one condition."

"Which is?" Harrison asked slowly. From his face it was clear he was stunned.

"That no matter whether Lord Wrotham be discovered alive or dead, that he be publicly cleared of all charges. Nothing less than a complete exoneration will suffice. Tell Sir Buckley that if this does not occur, I will release details of Lord Wrotham's field-book to the press. I doubt anyone in the War Office wants another wave of fear-mongering and invasion hysteria—and believe me, the *Daily Mail* will use all of Lord Wrotham's observations to demonstrate that Germany is mobilizing for war. I also doubt that Sir Buckley will want the public to know that Admiral Smythe believed there was a German spy in his midst . . ."

Harrison tugged on his mustache. "Does the field book confirm that Lord Wrotham was acting on Admiral Smythe's orders when he met with McTiernay and the Count?"

"Yes," Ursula said. "It does and I am sure Admiral Smythe's notebook will confirm this—you can tell Sir Buckley I know how to decipher that for him too—though not until Lord Wrotham's good name and reputation have been restored." *And I've learned whether Sir Buckley is the spy Lord Wrotham and Admiral Smythe were looking for,* Ursula thought grimly.

"If Lord Wrotham is truly innocent of all the charges laid against him then I have no problem agreeing—I cannot, however speak for Sir Buckley."

"But you must—without his assurance, believe me I will contact Hackett at the *Daily Mail.*"

Harrison's eyebrows raised. "You are certainly very decided in this matter . . . but why did you not give me this in London when you first deciphered it and learned the truth?"

"Because there are bigger things at stake here . . ." Ursula replied enigmatically. "I must ask you," she continued, "to wait at least a week before you act on this."

"Again, I find myself wondering why you are telling this to me now?"

"Because I may not be alive later to do so," Ursula replied. "I need to make sure the field book is in good hands."

"Ursula," Harrison warned. "I know James and Lady Winterton are trying to help you but you must know that no good can come from confronting McTiernay. I urge you to tell me where McTiernay is and return to England."

Ursula remained silent.

"Think about your condition!" Harrison protested.

"In my condition," Ursula responded. "I need to know what has happened to the father of my child. I could not stand living with the uncertainty—the not knowing whether he lies in some ditch or shallow grave . . ." Ursula's voice quivered.

"Oh, Ursula," Harrison said quietly, and his informality seemed strangely poignant. "You don't want to do this."

"I need to see him," Ursula insisted. "For one last time. Even if it be at his grave. I have to know what happened."

Harrison's rubbed his moustache. "I will wait a week before I show Sir Buckley the field book," he finally agreed, "and you have my personal assurance that if it contains what you say it does then Lord Wrotham's name and reputation will be restored."

"As insurance I sent a copy of some of the more inflammatory extracts regarding Germany's preparations for war to my good friend Miss Stanford-Jones in America. She has instructions that, should anything untoward happen to me and a full retraction of all charges against Lord Wrotham fail to be made public, then she is to send these to the *Daily Mail*."

"I never doubted your resolve in this matter," Harrison reminded her. "And I continue to owe Lord Wrotham a debt of honor which I intend to repay"—he gestured for her to remain silent—"despite what you may think about my ambition . . . It has not clouded my loyalty."

Ursula nodded. She was satisfied, though the numbness within continued. It felt as though all joy, all happiness, had abandoned her.

Harrison leaned forward in his chair and regarded her sadly. "You must realize, Ursula, that the resolution you truly seek is not in my hands."

"I know," Ursula answered and her voice was hollow. She gazed out across the room, to the window and the fields beyond, her thoughts turning over the uncertainties in this case, uncertainties that meant that all her assumptions regarding the case could be wrong. She had to tread carefully now, lest all that she was about to set in motion come to naught.

CHAPTER THIRTY-ONE

THAT EVENING JAMES, URSULA AND LADY WINTERTON sat in uncomfortable silence across the chipped-veneered dinner table. Ursula toyed with the food on her fork, her appetite diminished. James, finishing his plate of roast beef, placed the silver cutlery down with a clang. It seemed to awaken them all from their thoughts.

"Ursula, you really need to eat," Lady Winterton admonished. "You've hardly touched anything."

Ursula looked up from her plate and murmured. "Just not hungry I'm afraid."

The thought of cyanide poisoning was, however, never far from her mind.

"Let us hope you're not going to relapse," Lady Winterton said. "Does James know of yesterday's fever?"

James frowned and regarded Ursula with concern. She shook her head and muttered, "I'm fine . . ." But this did little to assuage him—or to lift the oppressive air of gloom.

Ursula chastised herself—she needed to use every opportunity to try and work out this case—not wallow in her own pity or fall prey to little more than suspicion and fear. As Grace served a meager dessert of fruit and cream, Ursula rallied her spirits.

"Catherine," she said. "James thinks he has found McTiernay."

She waited and watched for Lady Winterton's reaction.

"Really?" Lady Winterton's eyebrows rose. She cast a quizzical glance at James across. "You said nothing of it earlier."

"Chief Inspector Harrison doesn't know," Ursula interjected, averting her gaze from the angry flash in James' eyes.

"What are you planning on doing?" Lady Winterton's question was addressed to James, but her eyes kept flickering to Ursula's face.

"I haven't decided," James responded coolly. Ursula watched them both carefully but there was no evidence of collusion or of Lady Winterton's true motives either. There was nothing but antipathy and with that Ursula had to be satisfied, for James refused to be drawn on any further aspects of the case or McTiernay. By the time coffee was being offered the room had once more descended into sullen silence.

"Is there anywhere that I can send a telegram from nearby?" Ursula asked, taking a final sip of coffee from her chipped china cup.

"Yes, there's a post office in the village," Lady Winterton replied. "Grace can go in the morning if you'd like."

"James will go for me, won't you James?" Ursula asked.

James nodded, still watchful.

"Who are you sending a telegram to?" Lady Winterton inquired, raising her cup to her lips. She paused for a moment before taking a sip.

"Why Pemberton, of course," Ursula answered. "Chief Inspector Harrison said that Christopher Dobbs has been helping with the case and I'd like to know a little more about the evidence he's providing them."

"I had no idea Dobbs had become so involved in the case," Lady Winterton's tone was light and Ursula suspected it would take more than casual questioning to get Lady Winterton to divulge the true nature of the game she was playing. Ursula strongly believed, however, that Lady Winterton was the person who had blackmailed the Count into testifying against Lord Wrotham. Somehow Dobbs also knew this yet Ursula still had no evidence of anything more than a social acquaintanceship between Dobbs and Lady Winterton.

Ursula knew she had to tread carefully lest Lady Winterton sense Ursula's suspicions.

"Dobbs is nothing but a charlatan," James interjected and Ursula was surprised by the bitterness in his voice. Clearly James knew all about Dobbs' past sins.

"At least he's a gentleman," Lady Winterton replied acidly. "Which is more than can be said for you."

For the first time that evening, James cracked open a smile and laughed. "Coming from you," he said. "I'll take that as a compliment."

Lady Winterton flushed and for a moment Ursula detected once more the frisson of mistrust and wariness between them. It was like watching a cat and a dog circle one another, teeth bared, each silently waiting to see what move the other will make.

The next morning, after a fitful and hunger-panged sleep, Ursula stood in the library, watching from the library window as Lady Winterton approached across the meadow. The sun was low on the horizon behind her and framed with heavy massing clouds.

"You want me to cycle to the village to send this telegram to Anderson rather than Pemberton?" James asked.

Ursula nodded but did not turn—her attention was still focused on Lady Winterton.

James read the text of the message aloud. *Investigate Tir Tairngire on the investor list STOP Check who else knows STOP Dobbs?*

"I don't understand . . ." James said with obvious confusion.

"No," Ursula replied enigmatically. "You aren't meant to."

James followed her gaze. By now Lady Winterton was crossing the rear courtyard as she made her way to the front door. She was holding a basket of bread in one hand and a wire milk bottle holder in the other.

"Ursula," he said. "Is there something more you need to tell me?"

"No," she replied as she continued to stare out of the window bleakly. The front door closed and they could hear Lady Winterton and Grace talking in the hall. "Not yet."

James excused himself as soon as Grace and Lady Winterton entered the library. Ursula saw Grace's cheeks grow pink as he passed her in the doorway, before Lady Winterton hastily instructed her to go and make tea. Lady Winterton turned to Ursula with a sigh. "That girl is hopeless—you'd think she'd have learned from last time!"

"I guess some of us are just perpetual romantics," Ursula said with a wan smile.

"It could be worse I suppose," replied Lady Winterton lightly. "She could be madly in love with a Bolshevik!" Ursula knew Lady Winterton's levity was for her benefit but she could summon no more false good humor.

"Where's James off to anyhow?" Lady Winterton asked.

"Just to send the telegram I mentioned last night," Ursula replied.

"Ah," Lady Winterton answered. "You didn't want Grace to go . . ."

"It's not that so much as I wanted James out of the house for a while," Ursula answered. During the night she had wondered whether playing into Lady Winterton's mistrust of James could have its advantages.

It took all of Ursula's self-control not to ask Lady Winterton the questions she knew she would one day ask. Until Lord Wrotham's fate was known she could risk no such disclosure. Until then, until Ursula could confront McTiernay, Ursula knew she had to play a dangerous game with Lady Winterton. A game of deception and disingenuous smiles. Of feigned friendships perhaps and, almost certainly, the bitterness of betrayal.

"Can you do me a favor?" Ursula asked.

"But of course, my dear."

"Can you keep an eye out for James—I want to take a few moments to check his belongings. Grace put him in one of the old servants' rooms I believe."

"Yes, she did . . . It was a trifle indiscreet I thought, but no doubt it was wishful thinking on Grace's part."

"I won't take long—but this may be my only chance."

"I take it you still don't entirely trust James?" Lady Winterton asked. Her eyes followed Ursula closely.

"You warned me, did you not?" Ursula replied. "How else am I to be sure?"

"Certainly prudent of you," Lady Winterton replied. She licked her lips. "I wish we could all be so cautious in giving our trust."

"Yes," Ursula agreed. "Sometimes it is those closest to us who inflict the most pain." She worried she may have tipped her hand for she detected a flash of something in Lady Winterton's eyes. Suspicion perhaps? Acknowledgement? It flared so quickly, however, that it was soon gone and Ursula, as she made her way out of the room and up the stairs, was not sure she had not imagined it after all.

James had brought only a small canvas knapsack with him and Ursula felt decidedly self conscious rummaging through it even though she knew his undergarments, at least, were hanging up outside on the clothes line. If she had been hoping to find a secret stash of letters or perhaps James' own notebook then she was sorely disappointed. The only item of interest was a round of ammunition in the rear pocket, and an old photograph of whom she could only assume were his mother and father.

"Damn," Ursula muttered under her breath. She sat down heavily on the bed. Even though she calculated she could be no more than five months pregnant, her body felt as though it was stretched and aching already. By now she felt unsettling stirrings within her and the bond of attachment to her unborn child felt so strong Ursula wondered how she was going to able to cope with all that was too come. Her love was so raw and so primal she knew she would do anything to protect it.

Ursula gazed about the room and her eyes caught sight of James' Norfolk jacket hanging on the hook behind the door. Given the current weather James had gone out with his heavy woolen greatcoat over his shirt and boiled wool jumper. Ursula walked over and checked the outside pockets of the jacket but they were empty save for a tin of cigarettes. She opened the jacket and felt for an inside pocket—which to her chagrin was also empty. While ferreting around inside, however, Ursula felt the outline of something in the jacket lining. She took the jacket off the hook and laid it out on the bed to investigate further. It required considerable attention to the details of the seam and the stitches, but Ursula managed to locate and extract the thin piece of paper. It turned out to be a telegram with a German Imperial stamp on it—sent, it appeared, from the main London post office. It contained just two sentences.

Hotel Pariz STOP Prague STOP Continue to keep Marlow close STOP Any further communications should be addressed to Dismas c/Drogheda Post Office STOP

The sender identified was Mr. Fergus McTiernay.

CHAPTER THIRTY-TWO

"**WHAT THE HELL IS SHE DOING HERE?!**" James demanded as he tied a petrol can on to the rear of the motorcar. He pointed to Lady Winterton who was adjusting the scarf on her hat as if preparing for a day's vacation motoring around Ireland.

"I asked her to come with us," Ursula replied. "She once knew McTiernay—perhaps it will help."

Ursula sincerely hoped she sounded calmer than she felt. Ever since learning that James was really McTiernay's man, she had been unable to reign in her anger. For some reason his betrayal galled her deeper than Lady Winterton's. Although Ursula was still far from understanding the truth, she felt sure that Lady Winterton's actions, no matter how despicable, were motivated by a desire to avenge her husband and seek redress for the losses occasioned in Guyana. James' motives were, she suspected, far less noble. It took all of Ursula's self-restraint not to confront them both—but she would do nothing until she knew of Lord Wrotham's fate. At least Harrison had the field book, Ursula rationalized. She could only hope she had done enough already to exonerate Lord Wrotham should today's encounter with McTiernay end badly.

James wiped his oil smeared hands on his handkerchief and kicked one of the rear tires to check it was secure. James had driven the car into the driveway earlier that morning but Ursula did not like to inquire too closely as to its origins—she was convinced it had probably been stolen.

James pulled Ursula aside. "This is madness—you are risking more than just one life now."

Ursula prized his hand from her arm. "I know," she replied. "But she is coming with us all the same."

As if sensing there was a hidden meaning to her words James frowned, but as Lady Winterton was now climbing into the rear of the motorcar, he said no more.

"Are you ready?" Lady Winterton asked Ursula.

Ursula looked at Lady Winterton and felt a strange sense of calm. "Yes," she said, meeting Lady Winterton's shrewd blue eyes.

As James navigated down the narrow lane, Ursula stared bleakly ahead, fearful, yet determined to face the truth, whatever it may mean for her and her child.

The address James had for McTiernay was for a small farmhouse located in-between the villages of Dunmore and Drogheda. James informed them loudly, above the noise of the engine, that he estimated it would take them nearly five hours to reach the farm. He had packed petrol cans, spare tires and an assortment of provisions designed to deal with the perils of traveling along the roads in Ireland that were best suited to horse and carriage than motorcar.

Five hours. Ursula felt deadened by the prospect. Five hours of waiting with the knowledge that, although she did not know the full extent of the betrayals involved, she was sure of one thing: A reckoning of the dark days of the past was close at hand.

It was nearly three o'clock in the afternoon, some six and a half hours since they had set out that morning, when they finally reached the muddy road that led to the farmhouse where McTiernay and his men were believed to be holed up. The drive had been fraught with mechanical problems and by now James' shirtsleeves were covered in grease and his impatience and anxiety had increased tenfold.

James pulled the brake lever, bringing the motorcar to a grinding halt. "Perhaps we should wait until morning," he cautioned, looking anxiously at the sky, but Ursula refused to be deterred.

"No," she said. "You would have told him to expect us today—Just as you've been telling him everything, all along."

Lady Winterton's knuckles whitened as she gripped the passenger door. Ursula, however, remained surprisingly composed. James turned in his seat but before he could speak, a shot rang out across the green meadows and hedgerows. They all ducked for cover.

Ursula caught sight of a man standing in plain view on the rise of the hill in front of them, his rifle trained on the car.

"Raise your hands," James instructed quickly. "There's sure to be more of them."

Both Ursula and Lady Winterton remained seated in the back of the motor car, hands above their heads. The rifleman strode down the hill before being joined by two more men. They approached quickly.

"Keep your hands where we can see them," one man shouted. "Slowly now—then, all of you, out of the motorcar."

Ursula cautiously alighted, followed by Lady Winterton. James was the last to get out of the motorcar and he did so with slow, carefully measured movements. None of McTiernay's men acknowledged him as one of their own.

Ursula, Lady Winterton and James stood, ankle deep in red-brown mud, as the men searched each of them.

"You can tell McTiernay that we're here," Ursula said. "No doubt he's expecting us."

"It's not what you think," James hissed as the men led them towards the fields.

Ursula ignored him.

"I have not betrayed him," James whispered, his voice low but insistent.

"Spare your breath," Ursula replied. "I found the telegram in the lining of your jacket. You've lied to me all along. You knew what McTiernay was planning—what he was going to do in Prague, just as you knew what he'd do with Lord Wrotham."

"No—that's not true. I was as shocked as you. I would have told you if I had known what had happened to his Lordship. Believe me. Trust me. Things are not what they seem."

Ursula looked away.

Lady Winterton, who up until then had been trudging along in silence, tripped over a rock and fell to her knees. Ursula helped her up. The soft pink of Lady Winterton's skirt was now black with mud and soil.

They walked for nearly a mile across the broad green meadows. As the sun dipped behind the hills, they came to a ridge. Below them spread the valley—green upon green, with a grey stone farmhouse nestled amongst the trees. Approaching them was the man Ursula recognized as McTiernay.

"Lady Winterton," McTiernay called out. "I had not expected to see an old friend such as yourself here today."

"I came to make sure Miss Marlow was treated well and unmolested by your men—should we find you here. I remember many of the brutes from parties at my husband's estate years ago—and I'm sure they have not changed."

"Indeed they have not," McTiernay said. "And you have not either. Nigel always said your beauty would be timeless."

"As is your silver tongue . . . Nigel always said you could sweet talk your way out of most things," Lady Winterton replied, though her tone was neutral her eyes betrayed her resentment.

McTiernay raised one eyebrow before turning to Ursula. He gave her a mock bow, his dark curly hair as unruly as ever and his blue eyes, as they met hers, showed he had not forgotten their last encounter at the Hotel Pariz.

"Miss Marlow," McTiernay said. "You seem in remarkably good health for a woman in your condition," he looked at her belly with a mixture of curiosity and surprise. Clearly James had failed to tell him of this particular development.

"You know why I am here," Ursula said hoarsely. "Tell me is it the man or the grave that I can expect." Nothing could mask the anguish behind her words.

McTiernay merely pointed across the flagged stone path that led across to a series of stone buildings. One of McTiernay's men was scrubbing down the doorsill to one such building, a bucket of water beside him. Ursula looked on in horror as he tipped the water, for it turned pink as blood washed away from the stone. Her hand leaped to her throat. Her knees felt as though they would collapse beneath her and she bent over, breathing hard, to try and stop the world from spinning.

"Where is his body?" Lady Winterton demanded.

As she spoke the door to the farthest building opened and a tall man emerged. Although dressed in laborers' clothes, there was no mistaking him. From the dark hair that fell over one eye, to the way he flicked open his cigarette case and took one out, lighting it with an icy arrogance that seemed ingrained in every movement and gesture.

McTiernay turned to Ursula. "This is a working farm," he said pointing to the bloody pool of water on the doorsill. "And we need to eat."

"Wrotham!" McTiernay shouted. Ursula sucked in her breath as the man across the courtyard raised his head and looked over at them. There was no disguising the shock that registered in his eyes.

"Told you to expect a surprise," McTiernay called out with a cavalier lack of compassion that was all the more chilling. "Well," he amended with a meaningful look at Ursula's belly. "Two surprises actually."

As Lord Wrotham approached Ursula noticed that, despite her first impressions, there was a stiffness in his gait, a gauntness in his face that suggested he was in pain. Yet she no longer cared. Fury had taken hold.

"How dare you!" she cried. "How dare you let me think . . ." she choked on her words, hot tears pouring down her face.

He reached out to her but she refused his embrace—striking out with her fists, beating against him with angry sobs that rose like a banshee wail. "I didn't know if you were dead or alive! How could you leave me to face that alone?! Not one word?! Nothing!" Her words dissolved into incomprehensible cries.

"Ursula?" Lord Wrotham's voice was little more than a rasp.

She pushed him away as her boots struck the stones and dirt.

"Ursula?" Lord Wrotham repeated before collapsing to his knees. Head bent, he coughed so violently that blood smashed in a fierce splatter upon the ground.

"My love," Ursula whispered in horror, her fury spent. "What have they done to you?" She crouched awkwardly beside him, lifting his face in her hands. She drew him close till he could rest against her. He placed both his hands upon her belly and closed his eyes.

It was McTiernay's voice that broke through the suspension of time and space. Ursula, drained now of all emotion struggled to her feet, helping Lord Wrotham who with great effort pulled himself up off his knees, wracked by violent coughs once more.

"It's pleurisy—or so we think," McTiernay said. "But we can't exactly bring a doctor out here, now can we."

"Ignore him," Lord Wrotham said wiping his mouth and brow with a handkerchief. "It's nothing more than bronchitis—hardly surprising given the weather in this God forsaken country."

"Ah, you were always one for exaggeration," McTiernay answered with a smile. He gestured to the fields and sky. "You English have no stomach for real Irish weather!"

Ursula's eyes narrowed, her anger rising once more. She did not want to accept that McTiernay and Wrotham were bantering like old friends. Not when she knew all that McTiernay was capable of. Not when the truth of this game had yet to be revealed.

"How can he still be alive?" Lady Winterton's voice startled them all. Her face was ashen.

"Lady Winterton," Lord Wrotham said slowly. He blinked as if adjusting to the light. "I find it surprising that you, of all people, should be here . . ." His face was impassive but Ursula saw his eyes flicker to James for just a moment. Up till now James had remained a silent bystander. He now stepped further back into the shadows beneath the farmhouse eaves.

"Didn't you know, she's been helping with Miss Marlow's investigations," McTiernay said. Though he smiled, Ursula saw the muscles in his jaw tighten.

"You should have killed him!" Lady Winterton spat. "He's a British spy!"

"Why on earth would you think that, my dear." McTiernay's tone remained casual, light even, but Ursula was not deceived. The mood and tensions between them all were shifting fast.

"Because I was Admiral Smythe's lover," Lady Winterton said coldly. "I found out all I needed to about him, about Lord Wrotham, about their plans for you . . . You're a fool Fergus if you think he's the man he once was."

"Admiral Smythe's lover?" Lord Wrotham asked. "And, no doubt, his murderer too . . ."

Lady Winterton regarded both McTiernay and Wrotham with undisguised loathing.

"Did you really think I could forget the wrongs done to my husband? I have waited years setting this in motion and Smythe was as easy to manipulate as you both were. To think he was actually worried about a German spy in Naval Intelligence but never thought to worry about the woman with whom he was having an *Affaire de Coeur* . . ." Lady Winterton's top lip curled as she pronounced the French with derision.

"So who did you pass the information on to?" Lord Wrotham asked. The coldness in his grey-blue eyes was more terrifying than any outburst. Ursula held her breath.

"Was it Dobbs?" Wrotham asked.

"How else do you think I could get the information to Germany," Lady Winterton replied scornfully. "And who better to use than Dobbs? His contacts were more than willing to pay."

"And I suppose you thought you could use the money to help restore your husband's estate?" Ursula said, remembering what Miss Cadogan had told her about Lady Winterton's 'grand plans'.

"If you think that is all I want," Lady Winterton said, "then you are as much of a fool as them."

"Oh, I know your pain runs much deeper than that," Ursula answered quietly. "Doesn't it Catherine? There's the child you lost. The husband who committed suicide rather than face financial ruin . . . and all because of what? A failed investment in Guyana? No, it was much more than that—it was the betrayal of friends. It was the fact that two of them, the Count and McTiernay, placed their own greed above friendship. They swindled everyone involved in the Imperial Gold and Diamond Mining Company—and then, Lord Wrotham made sure justice would never be served when he defended them in the law case brought by the investors. You must hate them all so very much . . ." Ursula voice was almost gentle but it incensed Lady Winterton. Her face white, her hands shaking, Ursula recoiled for fear of what Lady Winterton might do.

"I knew Nigel invested and lost heavily," McTiernay said, running his fingers through his black curls. His face was etched with guilt. "But suicide? No . . . That cannot be. We were never told that."

"No," Lady Winterton replied, struggling to keep her voice calm. "My family ensured that there would be no such taint upon my good name. An impecunious husband was bad enough but one who lost everything on a speculative venture in Guyana/ One who then drank himself into oblivion and eventually hanged himself? No, they made sure no one in London society would ever learn the truth."

"In the end you knew how each man would behave," Ursula said. "You knew the Count would buckle under blackmail, you knew McTiernay would avenge himself for any betrayal and you knew Lord Wrotham would play the honorable part you had planned for him. All you had to do was set your plan in motion and let them die at each others' hands."

"I should have killed you long ago . . ." Ursula was startled by Lady Winterton's malevolence.

"You certainly tried at least once . . ." Ursula said.

"The cyanide was for Lady Wrotham, not you," Lady Winterton spat. "Though I was worried when you started asking questions about Admiral Smythe's possible affairs that you might discover the truth. I thought Lady Wrotham's death would divert your attention and bring new pain to her son. But in Germany . . . When James appeared, I knew, I should have never let you live. Why else do you think I dragged you from Dublin? I was just waiting for the right time to administer the poison . . ."

Lord Wrotham stepped forward, placing himself between Lady Winterton and Ursula.

"Your grudge," he said. "Is against me, not her."

"Without her you would be dead by now!" Lady Winterton spun round to confront McTiernay. "What kind of fool are you—to believe this man to be a patriot. To have risked all to get him out of England when he is nothing but a traitor to you. Admiral Smythe all but admitted the truth to me. How else would I have been able to access his files and leave the evidence for the police to find? Think, Fergus . . . Think! This man is not an Irish patriot. He has used you all along."

Ursula saw the doubt in McTiernay's eyes. Saw the pieces fall into place. Saw his confusion turn to rage.

Ursula felt James' hand on her arm. He gave an almost imperceptible shake of his head.

McTiernay drew his revolver from its holster and pointed it at Lord Wrotham. On his signal, each of the men with rifles trained their guns on Lady Winterton, Ursula as well as James.

"Did you?" McTiernay asked. "Did *you* betray *me*?"

His face bore an expression Ursula had not expected—Anguish. Gone was the cold impassivity she had seen. Gone was the cavalier disregard for life she had witnessed in Germany. No, this wound cut more deeply that she could ever have imagined. McTiernay's face revealed the young man he had once been—the friendship that he had held onto despite the years—and the loyalty that, should it have been broken, threatened to undermine everything he knew about himself.

Lord Wrotham regarded McTiernay with steady blue-grey eyes.

Lie. Ursula silently prayed. *Think of me. Think of your unborn child. Lie to him.*

"Yes," Lord Wrotham said.

Ursula squeezed her eyes closed and waited for the inevitable sound of gunfire and death.

The world remained silent.

McTiernay's hand shook as he held the revolver.

"The old loyalties died long ago," Lord Wrotham said and though his voice was calm, his face mirrored McTiernay's anguish. "In Guyana."

"I did not murder her," McTiernay whispered hoarsely. "No matter how much you believe that I did. I am innocent of Bernice Baldeo's death. I tried for years to repent for my part in the whole sorry business . . . but murder of an innocent woman . . . How could you think that of me?"

Ursula thought of St. Dismas. *The Penitent Thief.* It must

have been McTiernay's way of atoning for the fraud he and the Count committed.

"No," Ursula said suddenly, for it was now so very clear. "It was Admiral Smythe who killed that woman. She knew what was happening with Imperial Gold and Diamond Company—knew the British were buying up the small mine holdings and protecting colonial interests. She threatened to divulge the fraud as well as the hidden objectives of the company and Smythe had to kill her. That's why he covered the case up—that's why he insisted on Lord Wrotham ensuring no further investigations were made."

"Your false loyalties blinded you even then," Lady Winterton said to Lord Wrotham. "Admiral Smythe has been running from the shadow of that woman's death ever since. He would cry out at night—haunted by her in his dreams. He was so lonely, so dedicated to his country that you never even thought to consider his guilt. It made him all the more malleable and when the time came, I thought cyanide poisoning would be the most appropriate death."

"Don't you think there's been enough blood spilled to avenge the past?" Lord Wrotham said quietly. McTiernay's gun was still trained on him.

"Whatever I did, whatever fraud I committed, I did it to secure Irish freedom. We needed the money. Everything I did, I did for my country," McTiernay whispered.

"As," Lord Wrotham said, raising his hand to grasp McTiernay's gun. "Did I. Don't you think by now we should both bow out gracefully and admit defeat? My mission was clear and yet I was prepared to let you carry out yours. Smythe and I were willing to pay that price if it meant we discovered the identity of the German spy within our ranks."

"So that was why . . ." James murmured to himself.

McTiernay's face continued to betray the conflict of loyalties he felt.

Finally, he lowered his gun.

"No!" Lady Winterton screamed. "No!" she repeated. "You have to kill him." In a frenzy she pulled something from the inside of her blouse, something that must have been concealed in the bodice of her corset. She lunged at Ursula, taking even James by surprise as she yanked Ursula's head back, holding a thin silver blade of a knife against her throat.

"Shoot him!" she instructed McTiernay, "or Ursula will die."

"You don't want to do this," McTiernay said softly. "This is not the way you want to end this."

A shot rang out in the distance, echoing across the green fields. Ursula felt Lady Winterton's body stiffen against hers and the blade nicked her skin, drawing blood.

McTiernay stepped forward. "It's a warning shot from one of my men. It can only mean one thing. The Garda are here." He shielded his eyes and Ursula followed his line of sight. A man on the hill behind the farmhouse was signaling frantically. "They're coming from the Drogheda road," he looked at Lady Winterton. "You and I might have to accept the inevitable."

"Pick up the gun and shoot him," Lady Winterton said. "Or I will draw the knife across her throat."

Lord Wrotham raised his hands. "If it's me you want," he said. "Then I would willingly exchange my life for hers. Let her go and I will gladly take her place."

"You must think me a weak-minded woman indeed," Lady Winterton said. "I know I am physically no match for either of you—but Ursula? Ursula I can kill and in so doing I will leave you with the same legacy I have endured these past four years. You will lose the one you love as well as your unborn child. That may even be revenge enough for me. Why should she not suffer? Why should you not suffer, as I have suffered?!"

One shot was all it took. It happened so fast Ursula was not sure she herself had not been hit, there was blood splatters and fragments of bone and the very air around her seemed to go red. But then she felt Lady Winterton's body slump behind her, the knife against her throat fell away. Ursula reached up and gasped. But the blood now covering her was not her own. James had managed to reach for a gun and had killed Lady Winterton with a single rifle shot to the head.

CHAPTER THIRTY-THREE

"THERE'S NO TIME FOR TEARS," Lord Wrotham's voice was gentle but insistent. He lifted her by her arms. Ursula was still dazed and disorientated. *So much blood.* The back of her dress felt wet and sticky and Ursula could not bear to think of it. Lady Winterton's body lay crumpled on the ground. One side of her skull was shattered. *So much blood.* Ursula could not get the words from repeating in her mind.

"It was what I was trained to do, remember," James said before turning to McTiernay. "Our motorcar is on the other side of those fields," he told him. "We might make it—unless you want to prepare yourself for a siege. Do your men have any other means of transport?"

"There's an old lorry in the barn." McTiernay signaled to his men.

Ursula stared at James in confusion.

"You'll never survive," Lord Wrotham said to McTiernay. "You have to go."

"And you?"

"Get your men to bind Ursula and me and leave us as if we had been your prisoners. It should be sufficient. It may at least buy you a little more time."

"What about her?" McTiernay pointed to Lady Winterton's body.

"An unfortunate accident. I will not lay her death at your door. As it is, Harrison may hunt you down just for thwarting his ambitions."

McTiernay looked intently at Lord Wrotham. There was a silent exchange of looks, that seemed to Ursula to have a deeper significance. Perhaps it was an unspoken truce or pact—whatever it was, it seemed to satisfy.

James acknowledged Wrotham with a tip of his head and again Ursula was confused. "What?! You can't tell me you're actually going with that madman?" She struggled against him as the rope was tied tightly against her wrists.

"It's what I was trained to do," James replied.

McTiernay handed him another rifle. "Are you ready? I can't spare any more ammunition I'm afraid. We'll just have to make do with what we have."

"Ah James," Lord Wrotham said bleakly, as one of McTiernay's men bound his ankles and feet with thick rope. "Smythe always suspected you were McTiernay's man all along."

"You know how it goes, my Lord," James replied with an enigmatic smile. Ursula thought she caught a glimmer of understanding in James' face as McTiernay turned to leave.

Once James, McTiernay and his men had fled, Ursula and Lord Wrotham remained propped up against the farmhouse wall. Lady Winterton's body lay a few feet away.

"Ursula," Lord Wrotham finally spoke. They could see Chief Inspector Harrison and his men approaching in a line above the ridge.

"Yes," she answered wearily.

"Did James find my field book?"

"Yes."

"Did you manage to decode it?"

"Yes."

A ghost of a smile.

"I thought you might."

"Professor Prendergast sends his regards." Ursula's face was deadpan. "But next time he asks that you remember the old Hobbesian adage: *Vengeance thy name is woman.*"

"Hobbes never wrote that."

"No," Ursula replied looking at Lady Winterton's body. "But maybe he should have."

The headline in *The Times* the following Monday read:

DARING IRISH RESCUE. ENGLISH LORD SURVIVES MALICIOUS PLOT TO BESMIRCH HIS NAME. ALL CHARGES OF TREASON DROPPED.

EPILOGUE

THE TIMES' OBITUARY, LONDON, MARCH 27ᵗʰ 1913

Lady Catherine Natasha Winterton died of injuries sustained from a fall from her horse in Co. Louth, Ireland. Daughter of Lord and Lady Perceval Winterton of Kensington, London and Winterton Lodge, Sussex. Lady Winterton was vacationing with friends when the accident occurred. A memorial will be held this Saturday at St. Stephen's Church Gloucester Road at 1:00pm. Mr. Christopher Dobbs, the well known industrial magnate and philanthropist has established a charity in her honor. The family asks that all donations be addressed to the Lady Catherine's Charitable Trust.

LONDON SOCIETY COLUMN of *THE DAILY TATTLER*
APRIL 15ᵗʰ 1913

News of the elopement of Lord and Lady Oliver Wrotham has taken London society by surprise. Rumors surfaced just last week after Lord Wrotham was released from a Swiss sanitarium after a dose of pleurisy, no doubt compounded by his Irish ordeal. It is believed that the couple are honeymooning abroad, though exactly where no one is telling—though witnesses report to the Daily Tattler that the couple were seen last week boarding a private yacht owned by Hugh Carmichael in Trieste.

Ursula joined Lord Wrotham on deck to watch the sun set over the Mediterranean. Although pale and thin from his illness, Lord Wrotham had lost none of his urbane Englishness. He wore his cream suit, striped necktie and fob watch with all the formality of an evening top hat and tails. Her days of even relative sophistication were, however, long gone, Ursula reflected ruefully, as she gazed down at her long cotton day dress ballooning out over her ever increasing frame.

"James sent word that he and McTiernay are now in America," Lord Wrotham said, putting his arm around her.

"Pity Freddie is back in London," Ursula replied. "They would have all got on famously." Ursula's tone may have appeared blithe, but she had not failed to notice the shadow that passed over Lord Wrotham's face as he reflected on the past few months.

"Tell me," Ursula asked after a pause. "Was James really working for McTiernay all along?"

Lord Wrotham smiled. "James' loyalties have never been in question. Besides, he provided a useful insider into McTiernay's operation."

Ursula frowned, that was by no means a definitive answer.

"Why was McTiernay convinced that James was still loyal to him—even after Lady Winterton told him you were an English spy?"

"Because of James' past," Lord Wrotham replied. "It's the reason why James and Harrison both feel they owe me a debt—a debt I keep telling them that has been well and truly paid. It arises from a case they handled involving Irish bombers in London. They were called to a warehouse on the East End docks and discovered a cache of Irish arms and explosives. Both James and Harrison were young and inexperienced policemen at the time. They had no idea what they were getting into and were unarmed. As luck would have it, I was in the area, visiting your father's warehouse as it turned out. I stumbled into the situation. Things got unpleasant but Harrison and James always credited me with saving their lives—Nonsense really, but it did provide us with an ideal opportunity to gain a foothold in the Irish Republican Brotherhood. One of the men arrested that day eventually turned informer. We used him to introduce James and McTiernay—and our plans fell into place. James has continued to walk the fine line between British and Irish spy ever since—his orders were to stay with McTiernay and that's what he has done."

Ursula suspected Lord Wrotham was down-playing the role he had in saving Harrison and James but she was willing, this time, to wait until he was ready to tell her everything.

"Did Harrison ever let you read Admiral Smythe's notebook?" Ursula asked.

"Yes," Lord Wrotham said. "It confirmed all that Lady Winterton said—Although Smythe never suspected that it was she who was his so called German spy. There's no hard evidence that she actually sold any information to Christopher Dobbs so I'm afraid the man still walks free. With the threat of war, men like him will only grow even more powerful."

"Enough!" Ursula protested, laying her head on his shoulder. "I don't want to hear that name for a very, very long time—besides," she said. "I have some news of my own."

Lord Wrotham looked down. He raised one eyebrow inquiringly.

"I saw a doctor just before we left Switzerland," Ursula said as Lord Wrotham absent-mindedly stroked her hair. "He's pretty sure—"

"That you are expecting a boy," Lord Wrotham interrupted.

"How very aristocratic of you to presume as much," Ursula answered "It's not that at all."

Lord Wrotham looked down at her with sudden concern. "Then what?" he asked.

"Well, he's pretty sure . . ." Ursula dragged it out with a secret smile.

"What?!" Lord Wrotham demanded impatiently.

"That we're expecting twins."

CPSIA information can be obtained at www.ICGtesting.com
Printed in the USA
LVOW07s1702160715

446498LV00002B/262/P